DEATH

Climbs a Tree

Also by Sara Hoskinson Frommer

Witness in Bishop Hill
The Vanishing Violinist
Murder & Sullivan
Buried in Quilts
Murder in C Major

DEATH

Climbs a Tree

Sara Hoskinson Frommer

St. Martin's Minotaur
New York

www.minotaurbooks.com

Library of Congress Cataloging-in-Publication Data

Frommer, Sara Hoskinson.
    Death climbs a tree / Sara Hoskinson Frommer.— 1st ed.
        p. cm.
    ISBN 0-312-32921-0
    EAN 978-0-312-32921-1
    1. Spencer, Joan (Fictitious character)—Fiction.   2. Women
environmentalists—Crimes against—Fiction.   3. Symphony
orchestras—Management—Fiction.   4. Women musicians—Crimes
against—Fiction.   5. Women detectives—Indiana—Fiction.
6. Mothers and sons—Fiction.   7. Indiana—Fiction.   I. Title.

PS3556.R5944D43 2005
813'.6—dc22

                                                           2004066443

First Edition: August 2005

10 9 8 7 6 5 4 3 2 1

This one's for Marcia.

Special thanks to

Jon Bourne
Charles Brown
Laura Bybee
Karen Foli
Charles Frommer
Isabel Goldberg
Dick Hamlin
Kim Harris
Laura Kao
Jeff Kirby, Indiana Geological Services
Joyce Kostelecky
Susan Kroupa
Gary Lane, Professor Emeritus of Paleontology,
Geological Services
Eileen Morey
Jeanne Myers
Jack Parker
Rhonda Rieseberg
Abby Samulak, 911 dispatcher
Anne Steigerwald
Paula Sunderman
Barbara Wild
and to my agents, Stuart Krichevsky and Shana Cohen,
and my editor, Ben Sevier

DEATH
Climbs a Tree

1

I can't play the concert," Sylvia Purcell said. "I have to sit in a tree."

Joan Spencer's jaw dropped. "What are you talking about?" Sylvia was one of her best first violins. And she'd had the nerve to smile when she dropped her bomb.

Joan didn't have time to throttle her. The Oliver Civic Symphony rehearsal was already starting. Nicholas Zeller, their young concertmaster, was on the podium, signaling to the oboe for an A. "We'll talk at the break," she told Sylvia.

Joan had scrounged up enough violinists by early April to eke out a spring children's concert. As long as no one came down sick, she had figured they'd probably make it, but it was too late in the season to line them all up against the wall and give them flu shots. Managing a community orchestra in a town as little as Oliver, Indiana, was never easy, and Joan could pay players only in a dire emergency. Mostly she made do with the dedicated volunteers of the Oliver Civic Symphony and an occasional Oliver College student, though students could be iffy when exams threatened. In a real pinch, a trombone or cello might cover the notes of a missing second bassoon, but no one could cover for a first violin. If the firsts sounded thin, so would the whole orchestra.

Attendance tonight was decent—not perfect, but good enough not to set off Alex Campbell, their pudgy, volatile conductor. When Alex let loose, she could shrivel amateur musicians.

Having dug music folders out of the box for three people who had stuck theirs in the wrong place instead of taking them home to practice or absorb by osmosis, Joan finally sat down, unzipped her case, and pulled out her viola. Just resting her feet felt good. She'd barely had time to walk home from her day job, change clothes, deal with supper, and haul the music to rehearsal. She was stretching the shoulder rest across the back of her viola when the oboe sounded the official A.

"You all right?" John Hocking asked her. Nicholas frowned at him, and a cellist went, "Shhh!"

Joan shrugged and mouthed "fine" while they waited for the woodwinds and brasses to tune before the strings got their chance. She'd enjoyed sitting at the back of the viola section with John, a cheerful engineer, since she first arrived in Oliver a few years ago.

An hour later, when Alex put down her baton and announced the break, Joan laid her bow on the stand and her viola in its case. She had a horror of sitting on it.

Sylvia parked her own instrument on her seat and met Joan in front of the conductor's podium. She wore several earrings in each ear and one in her right nostril, and her unkempt hair overpowered her slight frame. Her calloused, bare feet looked chilly in Birkenstock sandals under a long cotton skirt on this March evening. She came across as flighty, but she was a solid player Joan usually could count on. Much too good to lose to a stunt like tree sitting.

"So what's this all about?" Joan gentled her tone.

"I told you," Sylvia said. "I can't play the concert." Her sparkling eyes destroyed any sympathy Joan might have felt about her problem.

The trombones, working over a hard spot during the break, drowned out Sylvia's next words. Joan led her beyond the violin section to the table where women of the orchestra guild had set out coffee, juice, and homemade cookies. The trombones were still loud, but she and Sylvia would be able to hear each other.

"Why not?"

Sylvia tucked a handful of chocolate chip cookies into her skirt pocket and bit into another one. "We're sitting in a tree in Yocum's Woods, out by the edge of town, where they want to put up low-income housing. It's my turn."

"What's wrong with low-income housing?"

"Nothing. But not there!" Her eyebrows peaked, and her voice rose. "That land doesn't need high-density construction. It's fragile karst topography—that means it's full of sinkholes and underground streams. Do you have any idea of the trees they'd destroy? And the birds and other wildlife they'd drive away? Already last week I saw a black-and-white warbler and a spectacular red summer tanager. Those birds need wooded habitat. We've gone to all the meetings and tried to fight in every way we know, but nobody will listen. Now we're protesting with our bodies, like Julia Butterfly."

"Who?"

"Julia Butterfly Hill spent two whole years in a tree out in California, in a protest against clear-cutting. An inspiration to us all. I'm going to read her book while I'm in the tree."

Joan tried to imagine two years in a tree. "So you're in it for the long haul." And I've lost a good first violin.

"That's right. We are!"

"Couldn't someone else take the next couple of weeks? Just to get us through this concert?"

"No. I told you, it's my turn. This is a lot more important than a concert."

"Why did you even come tonight?" She could have told me over the phone, Joan thought.

"I need to speak to the players at the end of the break," Sylvia said through a mouthful of chocolate. "Enlist their support."

"You want more? We won't have enough to play the concert. It's bad enough to lose one first. If you talk any more violins into it . . ."

"Don't worry. One person is enough in the tree. But I'll need help from people down on the ground."

"Keep it under two minutes—we're pushed for time. We're playing through Britten's *Young Person's Guide to the Orchestra* with the narrator for the first time tonight."

"Who's narrating?"

"Jim Chandler."

Sylvia wrinkled her nose.

"What's the matter?" Joan hadn't met the man. Had they picked someone who couldn't read music well enough to know when to come in? "His business supports the orchestra financially, and I'm told he's done amateur dramatics."

"I know. I work with him. Thinks he's God's gift to women. You'll see. But it's all right." The sparkle returned to Sylvia's eyes. "I won't be here after tonight. I won't even be at work."

"Right," Joan said. You'll be freezing your whatsis off up in a tree. I hope you swap that cotton skirt for something warmer. And how will you climb a tree in sandals? "You'll

4

have to tell Nicholas yourself. He may want to move you to the back of the firsts for the rest of this rehearsal."

Sylvia looked alarmed. "I haven't even told Birdie yet." Birdie Eads, another young working woman in the first violin section, often rode to rehearsals with Sylvia, and during the breaks they talked more with each other than with anyone else. "Only one I told was my boss. She didn't take it too well, but I've saved up enough vacation that she can't say no."

"Better tell Birdie now. Then Nicholas." Nicholas Zeller, their young and ambitious concertmaster, chewed out the strings if they bowed up when he'd chosen a down-bow or talked while he was tuning the orchestra. Not to mention latecomers like Sylvia. As second chair first violin, Sylvia sat next to the concertmaster, who was, of course, first chair and always knew when she was late. Sylvia could tell him herself. Joan didn't want it dumped on her. She had enough trouble dealing with the conductor.

Time to drag the players back to work.

At the podium she found a good-looking man of about forty charming the conductor, pudgy, graying Alex Campbell. Alex was tilting her head and smiling up at him in a way Joan had never seen her smile at anyone.

Alex tore her eyes away from the hunk long enough for introductions. "Joan, this is our narrator, Jim Chandler. Jim, this is Joan Spencer, our manager."

"Alex has been telling me about you." He turned warm brown eyes on her. "She says you've been wonderful for the orchestra."

"Thanks, Alex." Joan smiled. If he could have such an effect on their conductor, of all people, maybe he really was God's gift to women.

Alex waved off her thanks. "Time to get started."

Joan climbed up on the podium and tapped Alex's baton. "Break's over, everyone. A couple of announcements. First, I want to introduce Jim Chandler, who will be narrating the Britten. Jim's with Fulford Electronics. They've supported the orchestra for years."

The players applauded. Apparently considering that an invitation, Chandler stepped forward. "I'm glad to be here. This is as close as I'll ever come to playing with an orchestra. As for supporting you, you're our community orchestra. After all, three Fulford employees are players—Sylvia Purcell, Birdie Eads, and John Hocking." He gestured to them to stand up, but they only waved their bows. "And I'm telling all the Scouts in my Boy Scout troop they have to come to the concert." Out of his line of vision, Birdie Eads rolled her eyes.

"Thanks, Jim," Joan said, and turned to the orchestra. "And now Sylvia wants to ask for your help."

Sylvia stood where she was and kept it short, not preaching, but stressing the urgency of her cause. She didn't mention not playing the concert but promised to stick around after rehearsal to answer questions.

Looking like thunder, Nicholas stepped up on the podium then, nodded for the oboe's A, and turned to the winds. Sylvia must have told him what she planned to do.

Joan made it back to her seat in plenty of time to check her tuning.

Alex began with the Britten. Joan was relieved when Jim Chandler's voice poured out like melted chocolate. The words themselves were boring, though, and she wondered how well they would hold the attention of the kids in the audience. Nothing like the gripping story of *Peter and the Wolf*, though she was glad the poor kids were getting something different this year. But she couldn't help wishing for the rhymes Ogden

6

Nash wrote for *Carnival of the Animals*. Oh, well, she thought. Another concert. At least Jim is coming in more or less on time with the music.

Even so, the many narrative introductions to the variations involving individual instruments, from the flutes and piccolos to the xylophone and whip, ate up much more rehearsal time than fighting through the music alone would have done. The commonsense thing to do would be to dismiss the narrator for the next rehearsal or two and bring him back closer to the performance. But common sense was not in charge. After they struggled through the fugue, Jim smiled down at Alex and said, "I think that went well, don't you? When do you want me here next week?"

She all but batted her eyelashes at him. "First thing, if you can make it. It adds so much to have you here."

He murmured something that made her blush. Alex blushing? Joan could hardly believe her eyes. Then he waved at them all and left the stage.

Alex tapped her baton. "Sousa, please." It would be their first run-through this season of "Stars and Stripes Forever." Joan hoped their young piccolo player had it under her belt—the girl had struggled with some of the hard bits in the Britten. But she whipped flawlessly through the rapid variations on the tune to which Joan remembered singing "Be kind to your web-footed friends," and the orchestra stamped the floor in approval.

Afterward, the tuba player, a boy Joan knew was still in high school, raised his hand and asked to try it.

"That solo?" Alex said, her eyebrows high.

"Sure. I learned it in marching band. I mean, there wasn't much to the tuba part, so I borrowed the piccolo part, just for the fun of it."

7

Joan held her breath. If he could pull it off, the kids in the audience would love it. But she knew better than to try to pressure Alex into anything.

Alex looked at her watch. "We still have a couple of minutes. All right, take it from the piccolo solo, this time with tuba instead of piccolo."

The boy was amazing, and the orchestra roared its delight. Even Alex was beaming.

"You win," she said. "We'll use you both. I'll want you in front of me, where the children can see you. If you don't want to stand, we can put a chair over there for the tuba." She pointed to the spot usually reserved for the soloist in a concerto.

When the boy went back to zip his tuba into its case, the trombone player next to him pounded him on the back, and his smile threatened to split his face.

Tory, Joan remembered. His name is Tory Isom. And the piccolo is Heather Mott. I'll have to list them both on the program as soloists. Gives me something better to use in the publicity for the children's concert than Britten and a businessman. We'll have to get the paper to shoot a photo of them. Play up the contrast between the tuba and piccolo.

She'd almost forgotten what being short a first violin would do to that section, but when people were packing up, Birdie Eads came over to her.

"Where does this leave me?" she asked, worry all over her round face. If Sylvia was a lark, Birdie was a hen. Not a bird you could imagine very far off the ground. "Will I move up to Sylvia's chair?" Birdie sat third, behind Nicholas and Sylvia.

"I imagine so. We'll have to ask Nicholas, but I don't know why not." Unless I miraculously find some terrific violinist who ought to sit up there with him. Fat chance. I'll be lucky to find anyone at all.

"So everyone will move up one?"

"Probably, until Sylvia comes back. She's going to be hard to replace. Any suggestions?"

"No." Birdie avoided Joan's eyes. She looked nervous about moving up to sit with Nicholas.

Joan could understand that, but she wasn't about to ask. With luck, she'd be home before Alex realized one of her best violinists was deserting her for a tree.

2

hen Joan opened the paper at breakfast a week later, Sylvia Purcell stared at her from the front page. She'd turned in the sandals for sneakers and was well wrapped in sweats and what looked like a warm winter jacket. The flyaway hair had disappeared under a knitted hat. Maybe she could survive a few chilly nights. If she had a sleeping bag, anyhow. The picture showed her on some kind of platform up in the tree, with a tarp fixed overhead and folded into walls she could let down from the roof. At least she wasn't straddling a branch, and the tarp should keep her from drowning if it rained. The caption said she was seventy feet from the ground. Like sitting on top of a seven-story building.

"Swap you sections?" Joan's son, Andrew, asked, holding out the Lifestyle section. Now a junior at Oliver College, Andrew kept his expenses down by living at home. Since Joan's marriage to Detective Lieutenant Fred Lundquist of the Oliver Police Department, money hadn't been so impossibly tight, but she was still grateful for Andrew's college scholarship and his good sense.

"In a minute. I just want to read about Sylvia."

Andrew's dark, curly head peered over the paper from the other side of the table. Even sitting down, he was tall. "You know her?"

"She's one of my first violins. Was, anyhow. She's missing our next concert to sit up in that tree. Last week she told me she wouldn't play, but she had no qualms about asking the orchestra to support her. She needs people down on the ground, she said. I'm not sure what for."

"All kinds of things, Mom." He drowned another stack of pancakes in syrup.

Joan couldn't understand how he stayed skinny with all those pancakes. Just looking at them, she could feel herself expand to a size 14.

"I promised to take food out there." He lit into the pancakes.

"You did what?" Fred came into the kitchen in a trim sport coat, his thinning blond hair damp and smelling like Joan's shampoo. He dropped a kiss somewhere in the vicinity of her mouth, sat down beside Andrew, and reached for the pancakes. They stuck to Fred better than they did to Andrew, but his large Swedish frame could support the pounds.

"I volunteered to help the tree sit."

"It's illegal trespass. You know that, I assume."

"Oh, come on, Fred." Andrew had a dripping forkful of pancakes halfway to his mouth. "How big a deal is trespassing? You planning to arrest her?"

"Not if I can help it. But I may not have any choice. The property owners would be within their rights to bring charges. And that could include anyone down on the ground."

"Good thing it's so near the city line." Andrew turned to Joan. "It's only a hundred yards or so, Mom. I could run that far and not work up a sweat."

"Your friend up in the tree couldn't," Fred said. "And city cops could pursue you into the county. Believe me, if I could move those trees across the line and dump them in the sheriff's lap, I'd do it. I'm afraid someone's going to get hurt."

"Get hurt?" Andrew's voice rose. "You wouldn't *hurt* anyone over this."

Fred raised his eyebrows. "We try," he said with a little too much patience, "not to hurt anyone if we can help it. But if we have to force her down, it could get ugly. And who knows who's going to come out of the woodwork to protest the protesters."

"So she needs protection, not persecution." Andrew gripped his fork. Joan couldn't remember when he and Fred had been at loggerheads like this. She hated it.

"Just keep your distance from her. I don't want to see her hurt any more than you do. And I don't want to see you tangled in something more than you can handle." Fred put his hand on Andrew's shoulder. Joan was sure Fred didn't want a fight with Andrew any more than she wanted to see it.

Andrew released his grip on the fork. "You mind if I take her some of your bread? Maybe some ham and cheese? Feeding someone isn't getting tangled."

Fred's dad, a baker, had brought his sons up knowing how to bake bread, and Fred kept them supplied whenever the pressure of his job allowed.

"Ask your mother." Fred stood. "I don't want to have anything to do with it. See you tonight." He gave Andrew's shoulder one more pat, swallowed the last of his coffee, and left.

Could have been worse, Joan thought. She let out the breath she'd been holding.

"You go right ahead and take it," she told Andrew. "And anything else you think she'll eat. Something hot to drink, too.

Does she have a thermos?" It seemed the least she could do for a good violinist.

"Yeah, Mom. They know how to do it." He finished the last bite of pancake and put his dishes in the sink. Then he spread out the sandwich makings on the kitchen counter and set to work.

"You planning to bike out there?" Joan asked him.

"Sure, why?"

"I could give you a ride."

"I can manage."

"I know, but I'm kind of curious."

"Deal. I'm a little tight for time."

Joan brushed through her straight brown hair, twisted it and pinned it up on her head, and grabbed her shoulder bag. Her spring jacket would be enough, now that the sun was up. "Let's go."

Nothing in Oliver was very far away. They reached the woods in ten minutes.

"Turn here," Andrew told her.

Joan turned onto a winding gravel road with trees on both sides. It threatened to shake her gizzard out, if it didn't do in her old Honda Civic wagon first. She slowed to a crawl.

"We're almost there," Andrew said.

They rounded a curve and reached a small clearing edged with what looked like surveyors' stakes.

"Stop here. We walk the rest of the way." He slid out of the car almost before it stopped.

Joan picked her way over the uneven ground, glad it wasn't muddy. Andrew's hiking boots were better suited to the terrain than the citified walking shoes she wore to and from work.

There wasn't any construction equipment in the clearing, but she could see what looked like bulldozer tracks, and some of the tree stumps looked fresh. Ahead, Andrew was calling up into a huge oak a little way inside the woods. Far above, the leaves were still only tight buds. Joan wasn't good at identifying trees by their bark, but the old leaves on the ground left no doubt. Rounded, knobby oak leaves, not pointy ones, meant a white oak, she thought. Anyone, though, could spot Sylvia's oak tree by the wooden platform high off the ground. Rather than being nailed into the branches, the platform seemed to swing from ropes, and what looked like a hammock was slung even higher.

A familiar face peered down at them.

"Joan! What are you doing out here?" The voice was faint.

"I came with my son!" Joan yelled back.

"Wait." Andrew punched numbers on his cell phone. "You'll wear your voice out." Looking up into the tree, he talked into the phone. "Sylvia, I brought you some food. My mom came along." He handed Joan his phone.

"Joan?" Sylvia's voice was easier to hear now that it was in her ear. "I didn't know Andrew was your son."

There's a lot we don't know about each other, Joan thought. "I'm glad you have a cell phone. I was worried how you could let anyone know if you needed help."

"I'm lucky the signal is so good out here."

"What happens when the battery runs down?"

"I have spares, and whoever brings me food and stuff takes them off to recharge."

Now Joan could see a basket coming down to them on a rope. Andrew reached up for it and swapped the garbage bags in it for the sandwiches and drinks he'd brought in clean bags. The way he held one black plastic bag he'd picked out of the basket suggested that it held worse than mere garbage. At his signal, Sylvia began hauling the basket back up.

"How do you two know each other?" Joan asked when the two-handed operation was complete and Sylvia was sitting down again, with the phone to her ear.

When Andrew and Sylvia answered at the same time, she couldn't understand either of them. She erased the air with her hand. Andrew nodded and hushed.

". . . in the park," Sylvia finished whatever she'd been saying. "Later, he came to a meeting on campus. Anyone can volunteer. We sign up volunteers wherever we can, like orchestra rehearsal. Can't you just picture old Alex carting off my toilet bag?"

Joan could hear the laughter in Sylvia's voice.

"Did you get any takers at the orchestra?"

"Birdie Eads, of course. We're good friends. And John Hocking, probably 'cause he knows me from work. And one of the French horns, and a trombone. Not Mr. High-and-Mighty Nicholas, of course, even if I do sit with him. He's holding it against me that I'll miss the concert. I'm a little surprised to see you, Joan. Thank you for coming." It was the most gracious speech she had ever heard from Sylvia.

"Sure. Not Jim Chandler?"

"He hasn't offered, but he could. He lives over there, across the creek." Sylvia stood up as easily as if she weren't floating in a tree and pointed, but Joan couldn't see anything but trees. "From up here I can see that far. I'm glad the leaves aren't out yet. It's still cold at night, but a lot more interesting than it's going to be when the trees leaf out and block my view of everything more than a few yards away. And I've got a good sleeping bag."

"Good luck to you, then. I'll give you back to Andrew." Joan handed him the phone and walked into the woods, the bare branches moving overhead and the thick layers of dead leaves a rustling cushion under her feet. Even bare, the trees cast enough shade to make the woods feel cool, and she could smell the rich, damp soil the rotting leaves produced. It was still early for morels, though, and she wasn't surprised not to see any. She would come out mushroom hunting in a few weeks. She had learned to love morels as a child living in Michigan, where her family had hunted for them.

The sound of an engine startled her. Who else would be here so early in the morning? Was Fred right about the people coming out of the woodwork? She turned to hurry back. Her foot caught in a greenbrier, and she grabbed a sapling to keep from falling.

I'm being silly, she thought. It's just someone else Sylvia signed up.

But now she could see Andrew and another man in the clearing, facing off. The stocky man wore jeans, boots, and a stripe of blaze orange on his jacket. An orange cap with a bill hid his hair, but nothing could obscure his freckles or his sunburned nose. At the moment, only his short legs kept him from being nose to nose with Andrew.

"She'll be up there exactly as long as we let her be." The man reached up to punctuate his words with stiff finger jabs to Andrew's chest.

Andrew stood his ground, but his words were mild. "Not up to me."

"You better believe it. We have a schedule to keep, and when she's in the way, I call in the cops and out she goes." Two more jabs with the last three words.

Andrew looked down at him. "Keep your hands to yourself," he said softly.

"Or what?"

"Or *I* may be the one to call the cops," Joan said.

The man whirled. "What the . . . who are you?"

"My name is Spencer. The man you're poking is my son. My husband is Lieutenant Fred Lundquist of the Oliver Police Department." She didn't ordinarily throw Fred at people like that. Still, it seemed the thing to do at the moment. She expected Andrew would tell her to butt out, but he looked amused.

The man actually pulled off his cap, uncovering a shock of hair even redder than his nose. If he'd ditch the hat, he wouldn't need that vest, even in hunting season. "Tom Walcher. Walcher Construction." He stuck out the hand that had been jabbing Andrew.

Startled, she gave him hers and wished she hadn't when he crunched her fingers.

"Look, lady," he said. "You gotta understand, that woman's sitting on top of our job site. She's a liability to us, and we can't be responsible for what might happen to her way up there. Besides, we've got a schedule to meet. If that woman up there and your son down here get in our way, we'll stop them."

"Legally, I hope."

"They're not legal! There's a law against trespassers, and that's what you all are: trespassers."

Joan turned to her son. "Are we done here, Andrew?"

"I think so." He put the phone to his ear. "Sylvia, I'll talk to you later." He stuck it back in his pocket. "And you, I'm sure, Mr. Walcher." He slung Sylvia's garbage over his back far more casually than he'd picked it up. "Come on, Mom."

Joan turned her back on Tom Walcher and walked carefully past the bulldozer tracks and stumps to the car. Not a good time to fall on her face. Andrew, with his surefooted boots and long legs, reached the Honda ahead of her, but her dignity was intact. She watched him open the hatch and stick the bags in the back. Don't break, she begged the bags. Please don't break!

$\mathscr{3}$

On the way back to town, she asked him, "Where are you going to dump that stuff?"

"Don't worry, Mom. I'll take care of it." He reconsidered. "You mind if I throw her laundry in with mine? She won't have much."

Her Andrew, volunteering to do laundry? Had he fallen for Sylvia? Or only her environmental cause?

"Go right ahead."

He flipped his cell phone open. "Sylvia? You okay?" He listened. "Nah, I think he's all bark. But if you have any trouble with Walcher or anybody else, you call. . . . Sure, me or Skirv or any of the others. We'll be there in a flash. . . . Uh-huh. See you." And he tucked the phone away.

Didn't sound like a guy calling a woman who interested him. She supposed Skirv could be the percussion player she knew from the orchestra, but as unreliable as he was, she'd hate to need him for anything important. And she couldn't imagine him standing up to Tom Walcher.

"Andrew, do you think you could get out there in time to stop any trouble?"

"If you could lend me the car, maybe. It's not as if you used it during the day."

Joan felt herself being sucked deeper and deeper.

"Don't get into something you can't handle."

He laughed. "Walcher? You saw him. You called his bluff with Fred, and he folded."

She wished she could be so sure. She pulled up at the Oliver Senior Citizens' Center and left the motor running. "I'll walk home—you leave the car there. If you need it for a real emergency, call the center and let me know. Leave a message if I don't answer."

"Thanks, Mom." He unfolded himself from the passenger seat and came around to take her place behind the wheel. "That reminds me. Rebecca called earlier. Nothing special, she said. She's fine. Just kind of checking in."

"Does she want me to call back?"

"Nope. Just said to tell you she loved you."

That was something. For years her daughter wouldn't have made such a call. Nowadays, she even made noises about coming home to Oliver to be married, whenever she and the concert violinist to whom she was engaged got around to it. Joan would call her, but not now. She was already tight for time.

She stood at the door to the center and watched Andrew drive off. It felt strange to arrive at work in a car. At least she wouldn't miss out on walking home.

"Trouble at home?" Annie Jordan asked when Joan went in. Annie was a stalwart at the center who answered the phone and did whatever else was needed without thought of payment for her services. This morning she was sitting at Joan's desk, an Aran pullover taking shape under her ever-present knitting needles and crooked, arthritic fingers. She reached up to stick a cable needle into the white bun on her head.

Joan checked her watch. Late enough that she probably should have called ahead. Well, there had to be some perks to being the center's director. "No, we're fine. I went out to see the tree sitter who was in the paper this morning. She's one of my violinists."

"I saw that article. Can you imagine doing that?" Annie hardly looked at the complicated pattern she was creating in yarn.

"I can now. I drove out there with Andrew. He took her some food."

"He sweet on her?"

"Hard to tell these days." Joan kept her voice casual, but she knew it wouldn't fool Annie. "I don't think so." I hope not, she thought. She's much too old for him. At least thirty. Though who am I to say? Fred's that much older than I am.

Her attempt to be rational wasn't working. The difference between her early forties and Fred's early fifties hardly seemed to matter, but at twenty-one, Andrew was still a college student and her baby. She was fighting an uphill battle to try to remember that he was an adult.

"I knew her mother," Annie said. "She looks just like her."

"Knew?"

"She died young. Hit by a truck. Those girls had to finish growing up by themselves. Their father was never much use. Then he died, too."

How much difference had that made in how Sylvia turned out? Joan had been a grown woman by the time her own parents died. Young, but grown. "And she has a sister?"

"Two or three. They've scattered. Sylvia's pretty much on her own now. I wonder if she'll lose her job over this business."

"She said she had vacation time coming."

"If they honor it," Annie said.

"She works at Fulford. Why wouldn't they honor it?"

"You never know. People can always find an excuse to let you go."

"If she loses her job, the orchestra might lose her for good." A new worry, but she banished it. The orchestra was her other job. It wasn't fair to the center to let it intrude here. "Anything happening here, Annie?"

Annie tucked her knitting into its bag and yielded Joan's desk chair. She waved at the mail. "A few phone messages, but nothing to worry about. You want me to put your name in the pot for lunch?" The center was a senior nutrition site, which served low-cost hot meals at noon. Annie called them "eats for old folks," but anyone was welcome to eat there, and Joan did from time to time, especially during the cold winter months.

"Yes, please." She hadn't asked Andrew to fix her a sandwich while he was raiding the kitchen for Sylvia, and the elderly Fuji apple in her desk drawer wouldn't see her through the day. Odds were good she wouldn't manage supper before rehearsal in the evening, either.

Routine as it was, the rest of the morning flew by. Long before lunchtime, the meat loaf and apple pie were calling to Joan's nose. She made herself take part in the center's late-morning exercise class to make up for the morning walk she'd missed, but also to keep herself from drooling over the papers on her desk.

When the time finally came, Sylvia Purcell was the topic of those gathered at the long folding tables.

"I remember how we loved those woods when we were children," one man said. "We tramped through them and thought we were great outdoorsmen."

"And what are we going to breathe when they cut down

all the trees, I'd like to know," said his wife. "Someone ought to give that girl in the tree a medal."

"Her father would split a gut if he knew she was pulling such a dumb stunt," a second man said.

"I think her mother would get a kick out of it," said the woman next to him. "She was big on environmental causes. That woman had more causes than anyone else I know."

"She cared about poor people," Annie said. "And this project they're fighting is for poor people."

"Yes," said Mabel Dunn. "Like Cindy Thickstun. You know Cindy, and her daughter. The daughter has four little kids and barely makes ends meet. Since her husband took off, she's been living with her mom. That makes six people in Cindy's little two-bedroom house. Cindy's sleeping on the sofa, and her grandchildren are really getting on her nerves, day after day, all cramped like that. She can't pay their rent, and she's desperate to move them into decent housing her daughter can afford. I know they're on the list for those apartments. That's who Miss Save-the-Trees is hurting."

"And Diane Barnhart, who cleans for me," said Annie. "Diane has the contract to clean all those apartments when the construction is finished. It comes to way more than she makes in a year. She's married, but Bert's unemployment ran out months ago, so now he helps her. I don't think they have enough to eat."

The moist, flavorful meat loaf turned to dust in Joan's mouth. Did Sylvia have any idea? Did she care?

Did Andrew?

Later, at home, she still hadn't seen him by the time she had to leave for rehearsal, but she left him a note offering to drive the next time he went. Not that he and Sylvia would be likely to change their minds because of Cindy Thickstun's

23

daughter or Diane Barnhart's need for work. She already knew what Sylvia would say: low-income housing would be fine, but not there.

Still, they should hear about it from someone other than Mr. Walcher.

The tension in the orchestra put a mere tree sitter out of her head. Alex Campbell, pointing her baton like a dagger, descended on Joan the minute she lugged the box of music onto the stage.

"You knew she wouldn't be here and you didn't tell me! How could you do that to me? How can I play this concert with so few firsts? Where do you expect me to find another violin at this late date? The board won't let me hire one!"

Trying to stop Alex in mid-rant would only prolong it. Joan waited her out.

"I have a couple of leads, Alex. Haven't heard back yet."

"And you're just sitting on your backside waiting for them to call you?" She was off again.

"I'll let you know the minute I know more."

Birdie Eads, now sitting in Sylvia's chair, next to Nicholas Zeller, looked as if she'd lost her best friend, as indeed she had. For the near future, anyhow.

While they were rehearsing the Britten, Nicholas pounced on her more than once, increasing Birdie's obvious misery. Once, Joan could see, it was because Birdie didn't turn a page quickly enough for him. Usually on the outside chair of the second stand, she was used to having the player next to her do that job. To make matters worse, Alex drilled the violins mercilessly in the segment of the piece that illustrated what their instruments could do. Birdie was near tears when Alex exploded at all of them for less than absolute clarity in the rapid, very high runs at the end. Joan thought the flutes and piccolo passage had sounded much more jumbled, but they had escaped. Not that she wanted to hear them raked over the coals in the same way.

Jim Chandler's smiles in Birdie's direction as he introduced the violins again and again when Alex made them go back over their bit didn't seem to help at all. Nor did the rest Birdie got while the violas worked to maintain a full tone on the long legato lines in their part. Finally, the whole orchestra struggled to hang together in the fugue at the end. It would be easier, Joan suspected, if they all practiced the theme at home until they could play it up to tempo. But she knew the odds were against that. Too many players, herself among them, lived busy lives and trusted the notes to sink into their brains and fingers in just two hours a week.

During the break, Birdie was still sitting in her seat, shrunk into herself. Joan made a point of speaking to her.

"You holding up all right without Sylvia?"

"I hate him!" Birdie burst out, and then covered her mouth with her hand and looked around as if to check whether Nicholas had noticed.

"He didn't hear you. He's back there eating cookies. Look, Birdie, if it's that bad, I can arrange with Alex to move someone else up here and let you go back to your old seat."

"It doesn't matter." But her face screamed the opposite of her quiet words.

"You sure?"

Birdie nodded.

"All right. But if you change your mind, you tell me, and I'll do it. He doesn't scare me a bit. I have children his age."

A little smile. "Thanks."

"Good. Bad enough we have to do without Sylvia. You're just as important."

At the end of the rehearsal, the substitute oboe player snagged Joan to beg a ride home, and for the moment she forgot about the violins' woes.

Finally, having dropped off the oboist, she pulled up in front of her own little house.

Fred came out in his old jeans to meet her and carry in the box of unneeded music folders. At one time, the manager and librarian jobs had been separate, but Joan had already been orchestra librarian when she'd stepped in to fill the manager's shoes, and she'd needed the extra income, small as it was. She still was glad to have it. Besides, finding and training a new librarian was one more job she didn't want to face. Hauling the music folders back and forth and returning all the rented parts seemed a small price to pay in comparison. But she welcomed Fred's help.

Arms full, he bent to kiss her. "How was rehearsal?"

"Pretty good. No major explosions, but some small ones. And I still don't have a replacement for Sylvia."

"People making these noble gestures don't think of the folks they discombobulate."

"You sound like my old ladies." She held the door for him.

"Those old ladies are pretty smart." He parked the box of folders between the end of the sofa and the wall, and Joan laid her viola case on top of it. The box was an eyesore. From time to time she flirted with the idea of coming up with some kind of lid and using the box as an end table, but she never quite got around to it.

"Andrew home yet?" she asked. She curled up on the sofa.

"Haven't seen him." Fred's voice was mild. He and Andrew must have reached something like a truce. "Move over, woman." He sat down beside her, tucked her into his arms, and began nuzzling her ear.

Andrew picked that moment to arrive home, banging the back door and coming through the kitchen into the living room as usual. Joan stifled the impulse to jump away like a guilty teenager. Fred's muscles didn't even tense.

"Hi, Mom, Fred." Cool, that was Andrew. Even with what looked like a box of tampons in his hand. Whether to Sylvia or the cause, that was devotion. "I saw your note, Mom. She needs some stuff tomorrow morning. Want to go along?"

"Sure."

Fred didn't say anything. A few minutes later, though, he took himself off to bed.

Joan sighed. She supposed it could be worse.

Early the next morning, the second trip to the woods seemed shorter than the first. Joan was still getting up the gumption to say something to Andrew about what she'd heard at the center when he pointed to the turnoff. But she really wanted to tell those stories to Sylvia. It's not as if Andrew were up there delaying the construction himself, she thought. He's only bringing her food—and tampons.

Andrew touched the keys of his phone as he walked across the clearing ahead of her, bags over his back. "Got your stuff, Sylvia," he said into it.

Joan stared up into the oak. Bright sunshine blinded her, but she could see the basket easing its slow way down. She soaked in the sunshine, grateful for an excuse to enjoy it out in these beautiful woods. Loudmouth cardinals filled the air with song.

Andrew was chatting with Sylvia and reaching up for the basket when it crashed at his feet.

And Sylvia crashed down on top of it.

4

At first, Joan didn't know it was Sylvia. At first she didn't know what had happened.

One moment, she was looking up into a tree, worrying about nothing more urgent than trying to persuade Sylvia to consider the people who needed the low-cost apartments. The next, she was staring stupidly at the body crumpled on the ground. Soft as the layers of leaves had felt when she'd walked on them, they hadn't been able to cushion Sylvia against such a terrible fall.

Andrew was already on his knees beside her. "Sylvia? Sylvia? Mom, call 911! I think she's alive!"

Jerked into action, Joan remembered seeing the phone fly out of his hand when Sylvia hit the ground. Dropping to her own knees and scrabbling where she thought it had landed, she was hugely relieved to spot the little screen still glowing green through the brown leaves. She ended Andrew's call and dialed 911. "Send an ambulance to Yocum's Woods! A woman just fell out of a tall tree." She listened to the dispatcher. "Yes, the tree sitter. Please, send help right away. She's badly hurt. . . . Joan Spencer. . . . No, I don't live here. Nobody lives here!"

The dispatcher was insistent that she needed Joan's address and phone number. What possible difference could that make? Joan wanted to scream at her. But she gave them.

"Yes, I'll stay on the line, but that won't help you find us—I'm on a cell phone. . . . Right, those woods. From the turnoff it's a few hundred yards to the clearing. . . . Thank you. And would you tell Lieutenant Fred Lundquist, please? Tell him his wife called it in."

"Mom! What did they say?"

"They're on the way. They know where we are." Still on her knees, Joan held the phone to her ear.

"Don't hang up," the dispatcher was saying.

"I won't. What should we do for her?"

"Don't move her. Check that she's breathing."

"Is she breathing?" Joan asked Andrew. Through the heavy jacket, she couldn't tell.

He put his cheek to Sylvia's face. "Yes."

"Is she conscious?" the dispatcher asked.

"I don't think so."

"Can you get a pulse?"

"I'll check," Joan said. "Just send the ambulance!"

"It's on the way. I need more information from you."

"Tell them to hurry—she isn't moving." Without breaking the connection, Joan stuck the phone in her jacket pocket, scrambled to her feet, and walked back to Andrew. "How is she?"

"Still breathing."

Eyes closed, Sylvia moaned.

"Sylvia?" he tried. When she didn't answer, he reached out but then pulled his hand back. "I'm afraid to touch her. She's all broken up."

Joan could see impossible bends of Sylvia's arms and legs

through her coat sleeves and sweatpants. She hated even to think about internal injuries.

Sylvia looked pale. Shocky. "Run back to the car, Andrew. Get Fred's old blanket." Too bad we don't have her sleeping bag. But we have her clean laundry!

Joan pulled sweaters, shirts, and underwear out of the bag at her feet to spread over the still body on the ground. Sylvia had landed belly-down, but Joan could see the left side of her face. A red spot on her temple was already beginning to swell. A thin line of bright blood ran down from the corner of her ear to join another from her mouth and stain the clean long johns draped around her neck and shoulders.

Andrew stood over them now, unfolding the worn blanket. "It's dirty."

"Better than nothing."

Together, careful not to disturb her injured limbs, they cocooned Sylvia in it. Then Joan heard the siren.

"Hang on, Sylvia," she said. "Help's coming." Could she hear?

"I'll go." Andrew ran toward the sound.

Joan fished the phone out of her pocket. "We can hear the siren. My son has gone to meet them."

"I've been calling you." The dispatcher sounded testy.

"I was covering her. She's very pale. Bleeding from the ear and mouth now, too."

"They can see your son. And your husband's on his way. He says to wait for him. That's all. You can hang up now."

Joan did and pocketed the phone. Was Sylvia still breathing? Even leaning close, she couldn't tell through the blanket.

The siren wailed through the trees and cut off suddenly, but it was a fire engine, not an ambulance, that rounded the last curve into the clearing. Two uniformed EMTs ran over with a backboard. Andrew was close behind them.

"Okay, lady, we'll take it from here." The man didn't shove Joan out of the way, but he might as well have.

Fighting the urge to tell him to be careful, she backed off and stood by Andrew, whose eyes were fixed on Sylvia.

The men worked quickly and professionally, monitoring Sylvia's vital signs as they flung aside the blanket and laundry, collared her neck, splinted her poor arms and legs, rolled her onto the board, and strapped her to it.

Another siren, and the ambulance pulled into the clearing. Two more EMTs ran to the tree, pulling a collapsible gurney. They conferred briefly with the first pair. When they picked Sylvia up and loaded her onto the gurney, she cried out. Then, after covering her with a spotless white blanket, they slid her silently into the ambulance.

Fred pulled off the narrow road to let the ambulance pass. It was running with lights and siren, a good sign that they hadn't given up on her yet.

When he rolled up to the clearing, Joan and Andrew were sitting under the tree. Andrew, hunched over his own long legs, looked forlorn. His relationship with Sylvia mystified Fred. Andrew had said very little about her, but his actions spoke devotion. Or was he suddenly concerned about the environment? Just because he didn't talk about it at home . . . But if pushed, Fred would put his money on the woman.

His own woman looked up at him. She started to get to her feet but then patted the leaves beside her. He dropped down on the damp ground.

"You all right?"

She shook her head.

He raised her chin and kissed her before she could answer. Were those tears on her eyelashes? He tasted the salt.

"Oh, Fred!"

He held her to him. "Bad?"

She nodded against his chest. "I'm sorry. It's beginning to sink in." He felt her shivering, in spite of the warm sun shining down into the clearing, and wrapped his arms around her.

"What happened?" He looked over her to include Andrew.

"She fell," Joan said.

"Just like that?"

"It doesn't make sense," Andrew said suddenly. "She knew we were here. She was standing there letting her basket down, and then it was as if someone shot her, you know? She kind of flew out of the tree. All of a sudden."

"You hear a shot?"

"No," they both said.

"No sense at all." Andrew shook his head.

"You ever know her to faint?"

They shook their heads.

"Was she depressed?"

"No!"

Where was that anger coming from? Fred wondered. "There's no shame in it, son."

"She wasn't trying to kill herself." Andrew said it flatly.

"What makes you so sure?"

"She's devoted to this protest. If she wanted to commit suicide, she'd arrange for someone to take her place. She wouldn't give anyone an excuse to stop it."

Fred thought of suicides he had worked. Some had been concerned enough about someone else to try to minimize the pain they caused. Others hadn't looked beyond their own pain.

He looked at the clothes littered on the ground. "All this stuff fall out of the tree?"

"No," Joan said. "It's the clean laundry Andrew was bringing back to her. We covered her with it. And your grungy blanket. For once I was glad it was there." She pointed at the plaid thing his ex-wife had kept threatening to throw away. Maybe that's why he'd hung on to it. Joan wasn't fond of it, he knew, but she'd never said anything resembling a threat.

"So what did fall?"

They looked at each other and then around them.

"Sylvia and the basket she was sending down. She landed on it." Andrew pointed. The wicker splinters had poked holes in the plastic bags protruding through the basket's remains, which smelled like only one thing.

Fred wondered whether the splinters had poked holes in Sylvia, too. The EMTs must have noticed, but just in case, he pulled his cell phone out and called the dispatcher. "Warn the ER there may be human feces in her wounds."

"I'd better bury it." Andrew got to his feet. "There's a shovel in the car."

Fred saw what looked like a piece of old clothesline. "She used that rope?"

"Yeah. To let the basket down."

"You been digging holes around here?" They'd hear from the property owners about that.

Andrew shot him a look. "No. But I can't put this in Mom's car."

"You better believe it!" Joan sat bolt upright, her shivers gone.

Andrew laughed, but it didn't reach his eyes. "If you could see your face . . ." He started toward the car.

Fred stood. "Hold off."

"Why? You're not protecting a crime scene."

Why indeed? Why would a woman who had been holding her own up on that platform for a week suddenly fly off it?

"She ever complain of dizzy spells?"

"No," Andrew said. "She walked around up there like a steelworker on a skyscraper."

Joan nodded.

"And she didn't roll off in her sleep," Fred said. "Not when she was letting the basket down to you."

"And talking to me. She slept up in that hammock, so she wouldn't fall." Andrew pointed to where it swung above the platform.

"So why now?"

They had no answer. But Andrew was right. There was no obvious crime. A woman had simply fallen out of a tree. Her bad luck to be seventy feet up when she did it.

"What did she say before she fell?" Fred asked. Maybe when she came to, she'd be able to tell them what happened. He wasn't counting on it, though. Odds were good the injury that left her unconscious would have erased her memory of the fall.

Andrew thought a moment. "Something about a bird she was worried about."

"That's one of the reasons she was up there," Joan said. "She didn't want the birds to be driven away by the construction. She mentioned hawks and one I can't remember. A red one."

"And the land," Andrew said. "This is the wrong kind of land for what they want to do."

"I'll report it as an accidental fall," Fred said. "Anyone can trip. The whole business is just plain dangerous. Go ahead and clean up."

"She didn't trip." Andrew shook his head. "Do I need permission to dig a hole?"

"I suspect Mr. Walcher would prefer it to the alternative." Joan stood and brushed the worst of the leaves and dirt off her slacks. Her knees were smeared, as was her face.

"Walcher?" Fred asked.

"The construction boss. He was giving Andrew a hard time yesterday. Threatened us with the cops. I told him we had one in the family." For the first time since he'd arrived, her smile lit up her face.

"Good thing he didn't call us," Fred told her. "If we got a complaint, we'd have to act on it." Of course, then she might not have fallen. But if she had, it would have been our fault. "Go ahead, Andrew. Dig your hole."

Andrew loped off toward the car.

Joan was already picking up the laundry she'd used to cover Sylvia and stuffing it into the plastic bag she'd taken it out of. "Nobody's going to complain now. Her tree-sitting days are over, anyhow, this spring. I only hope she'll be able to play the violin by next fall." Wrinkling her nose, she dug into the smashed basket and began transferring clothes from the torn laundry bag to the whole one.

Then she spotted the other cell phone. It had to have fallen with Sylvia, who had been talking to Andrew.

Andrew came back with their long-handled shovel. "Mom, what are you doing?"

"Collecting her dirty laundry for you to wash."

"Not me!" Andrew said.

"No worse than diapers. You'll see." She smiled at Fred.

"Gross!" Andrew sounded about twelve.

Joan continued what she was doing. "Unless you want to

explain to Sylvia why you buried her clothes. And here's her cell phone. It landed a few feet away."

Andrew nodded and took it. He put his shovel into the dirt at the edge of the clearing. "I don't want to dig near the trees," he said as he dug. "Walcher's already chewed up too much of this area."

Ought to make your digging easier, Fred thought. "Okay if I leave?" he asked Joan.

"I'm all right now, thanks. But I'd better call work. I'm already late, and I have to clean up—I can't go in like this."

"I'll see you two at supper then." He leaned down and kissed her, keeping his distance from her filthy hands.

Andrew threw another shovelful of dirt out of the hole. "Not me. I won't be there. I'm going to take Sylvia's place."

5

*J*oan wanted to curl up into herself or scream. Fred, his back rigid, had left them without a word, but she felt stuck as long as Andrew was digging. He was making quick work of it. Clenching her jaw, she bit back the objections that threatened to escape her lips and jammed the last of Sylvia's laundry into the bag.

Andrew measured the depth of the hole with the shovel. Joan eyeballed it at about three feet.

"You done?" he said.

She nodded, still not trusting herself to speak.

He tossed the basket into the hole, filled it in, and tamped it down with the shovel. "Okay, then, let's go."

"Home?" Had he changed his mind?

"I need to take care of a few things." He grinned at her. "I won't stick you with the laundry, Mom."

As if she cared. "I'm not worried about laundry!"

"I'll be fine."

"Like Sylvia?" She hadn't meant to say it.

"I won't take the kind of chances she took." He wiped the

shovel off on the leaves, picked up the bag of laundry, and started toward the car.

She wished she could believe it. Just being up that high was taking chances. He had to know it. And for what? A few trees that would end up being cut down anyway?

Andrew tossed the reeking laundry bag into the wagon's wayback and belted himself into the passenger seat. "Remember the first time I climbed a tree?" he said. "Dad got all bent out of shape, but you stood up for me."

Joan started the car. "That was easier. I could face a broken arm, but this . . ." She shuddered. Considering the bleeding from Sylvia's ear, she had to wonder about a head injury and brain damage. How much of Sylvia would be intact once she woke up?

"I'll be fine," he said again. "You'll see."

On their way out of the clearing, they met Walcher, in a pickup. Too late to see the ambulance, Joan thought. It gave her some satisfaction to think he'd missed the whole thing.

Back at the house she called the senior center, saying only that she'd had an emergency and would get there as soon as she could. Then she shucked her filthy clothes and let the hot water sluice down her skin. She'd have to wash the steering wheel, too, she thought while she scrubbed her hands with a brush and hot soapsuds. Maybe with bleach.

Dressed in fresh clothes and feeling clean from the skin out, she pulled her damp hair into a French braid down the back of her head. She heard the washing machine begin to fill. Thoughtful of Andrew to wait until she'd finished her shower. She would have hated for that lovely hot water to turn cold on her. He'd want to take a shower himself—the last one for some time, she realized, if he stuck to his guns.

He was waiting for her in the living room.

"I have to do it, Mom."

She took a deep breath. "How can I help you?" He reached out to hug her, but she backed away. "Oh, no, you don't. I'm finally clean."

"Sorry."

He had washed his hands, she saw, though there was still grime under his nails, and his clothes were as muddy as the ones she'd thrown in the hamper. On the sofa, he'd stacked his own sleeping bag and winter jacket, a flashlight, his toothbrush, even textbooks. How much course work was he planning to miss? And how much did he think he could study, up in a tree?

He followed her gaze. "I've talked to my professors. They're okay with it."

Already? She was impressed. Maybe he'd been planning to take a turn after Sylvia all along. At least he wasn't risking his scholarship.

"They'll give me makeup tests."

"How long do you plan to stay up there?"

"A couple of weeks at most. Not as long as Sylvia would have. Some of the others will take over from me. And they'll keep up their shifts as ground support. The guy I talked to volunteered to set it up."

"That's good. How are you going to get all this stuff out there?" I really need to go to work, she thought, but she knew she'd take him if he needed her.

"I've got a ride. The guy driving me out will help me get up to the platform, too."

That problem hadn't occurred to her, but now she pictured the tree, with its long straight trunk, unbroken by many branches. Sylvia could have used a few more branches to slow her fall. Or would that have made her injuries even worse?

39

"How did Sylvia do it?" Climb the tree like a telephone lineman? It seemed unlikely.

"With a rope ladder, but it's still up in the tree. We've figured a way."

She saw a coil of thin cord beside his textbooks and tried to erase the picture of him dangling in midair from something so flimsy. "You have your cell phone."

"And Sylvia's. It still works. They just paid the bill, I know—it's for whoever is up there to use—so I can give you the number and you can use mine."

It was small comfort. Sylvia's phone hadn't saved her.

The Oliver Police Station was quiet for the moment, but Fred's stomach was still churning. Bad enough to have Andrew involved with the woman, but up there himself? Even though today's fall proved how dangerous it was to be there at all, Andrew had no idea what he would be up against if the police had to bring him down. Or if the construction people simply ran a bulldozer into the oak tree. Even cutting down all the trees around it would leave him vulnerable to wind and would weaken the roots of his tree.

Fred dreaded most of all being called to haul Andrew down. Joan would never forgive him if he did anything to hurt her son. He'd have a hard time forgiving himself. He was genuinely fond of Andrew. More than fond, he realized. Nothing he could do to help him right now, though. He made himself turn to the task at hand.

Sylvia was in critical condition, the nurse had told him when he called. Still unconscious, but holding her own. Could he locate her next of kin? They hadn't found a phone in her name or an address or medical information in her pockets.

He'd promised, but a quick check of DMV records showed

only a post office box as her address. Nothing that would lead to helpful neighbors. As a last resort, he supposed he could ask Andrew to look through her things in the tree, but he didn't want to have anything to do with sending Andrew up there. Still, Andrew might know her well enough to have heard about her family, or he might know friends who would know.

No answer at home, and Joan would be at work by now.

Then he remembered. Sylvia had played in the Oliver Civic Symphony.

He picked up the phone.

"Senior center." Joan sounded pleasant, professional, and calm. Not the woman he'd found trembling under the oak tree.

"Joan, it's me."

"You still mad?"

"I'm not mad at you." He smiled and hoped she could hear it over the wires. "We can't let this business come between us."

"No."

"I'll do everything I can to keep him safe."

"I know."

He thought he could hear her smiling back.

"Have you heard anything more about Sylvia?" she asked.

"That's what I called you about. She's alive, but they need to locate her family. I can't even find her address. What can you tell me?"

"My orchestra address list is at home, in my desk. But you could ask at Fulford—that's where she works. She probably has medical insurance through them, too. She's pretty tight with Birdie Eads, who works there. Birdie's another of my violinists. She's as likely to know about Sylvia's family as anyone." She paused. "Go gently with her, Fred. This is going to hit her hard."

"I promise."

"Annie Jordan told me the other day that Sylvia grew up in Oliver, but her parents were dead. She has a couple of sisters, if I remember right. Long gone from here. Want me to ask more?"

"Please. Call me if you hear anything specific."

"I will. And Fred, you tell me if you hear anything about Sylvia."

If she dies, you mean. "I will." He felt better when he hung up, even though as far as he knew, nothing had changed about Andrew. He hadn't even asked her about Andrew. But it hadn't seemed to matter.

So Sylvia was local. For some reason, he had assumed she'd come as a student. Sergeant Johnny Ketcham was his best source of information about anyone with a local history. And he was at his desk, Fred saw through his open office door. He reached for his jacket.

"Got a minute, Ketcham?"

Ketcham looked up over his wire rims. "Sure, what's up?"

"Grab your coat and come with me to Fulford Electronics. I want to pick your brain."

Ketcham drove while Fred filled him in. "Sure, I know her. Well, her family. Father a drunk, mother killed in a head-on with a semi. Left three little girls. The older two left Oliver a long time ago, before Rick Purcell finished drinking himself to death. Sylvia was the baby, about ten when her mother died. Her sisters pretty much brought her up. Ought to be past thirty by now. But I haven't kept up on her sisters."

"Then let's hope she told someone here."

Ketcham parked in a spot marked "Visitors." Fulford Electronics was a medium-sized low cinder-block building, painted white, with its name in understated blue lettering above the door.

Fulford had not wasted a lot of money on appearances inside, either. Or maybe efficiency and prudent use of customer funds was the image it wanted to project. Three plain black chairs with minimal upholstery on their seats and backs were less welcoming than those in most dental offices.

A gray-haired receptionist with a sweet, grandmotherly face looked up from her flat-screen computer when they approached her desk. "Can I help you?"

Fred showed his badge. "Lieutenant Lundquist and Sergeant Ketcham," he said. "We have some questions about Sylvia Purcell."

"She's in trouble with the police, isn't she?" the woman said. She sounded worried. "For sitting in the tree?"

"No." Could this be Sylvia's friend Birdie? "She's not in trouble, but I'm afraid she's been hurt. We want to find her family."

"Oh my God! I knew it!" The woman's eyes filled with sudden tears. "We tried to tell her, but she wouldn't listen. And now she's dead."

"No, ma'am," Ketcham said. "She's alive."

"The hospital asked us to find her family," Fred said. "She ought to have someone there."

The receptionist wiped her eyes. "Sorry. I don't usually get so emotional, but we've all been worried about her. I'll ring Birdie Eads from Personnel for you. If anyone knows about Sylvia's family, Birdie will." She tapped buttons on the phone in front of her and spoke softly into her all but invisible headset.

Fred paced in the small lobby. Ketcham stood quietly.

"You can go back, Lieutenant," the woman said. "Straight

down this hall and take a left at the double doors. Personnel is the second door on the left. And I hope she'll be all right!"

"Thanks."

They didn't need her directions. A short, well-endowed blonde who had to be Birdie ran to meet them halfway down the hall. "Jenny said she's hurt! What happened? Did she fall out of that tree? Is she going to be all right?"

"Yes, she fell," Fred said. "But she was alive when she reached the hospital. That's all we can tell you at this point, except that they want to find her next of kin."

"They think she'll die," Birdie said, and now her eyes teared up, too. "They probably want her organs, the ghouls." Her voice cracked, and a tear ran down the side of her nose.

"Don't jump to conclusions," Fred said, immediately wishing he hadn't put it that way. "They may need consent for surgery."

Ketcham handed her a clean white handkerchief—trust Ketcham to have one ready.

She took it and blew hard. "Come on. Let's see what we have in our records. I know she has a sister in Iowa. That's the one she's closest to."

Birdie was leading them to the office when a good-looking man in a gray suit and tie came down the hall toward them. His face was so unlined that the hints of silver over his ears might have been painted there for good effect. He smiled down at Birdie. "Visitors on company time?"

She glared up at him. "No, Jim. Police."

"What's the trouble, officers?" A full, rich baritone now. Sounded like a man gunning for an Indianapolis TV news anchor's job.

Fred stopped himself before his imagination got him into trouble. "One of your employees was injured, sir."

The smile broadened. "Not my employees. I'm just one of the peons." He stuck out his hand. "Jim Chandler, sales and service."

Fred thought Chandler's strong, warm grasp ought to serve him well in sales. "Lieutenant Lundquist. This is Sergeant Ketcham."

Ketcham and Chandler exchanged nods.

"So who's hurt?"

Birdie answered. "Sylvia. She fell."

The smile disappeared. "That's terrible. She was taking an awful risk, we knew. How bad is it?"

"Bad enough that the hospital wants to reach her family," Birdie told him. "So if you'll let us past, I'm going to check our records."

"Of course." He raised his hands and stepped back. "And if there's anything I can do, anything at all, please let me know."

"Thanks," Fred said, and followed Birdie Eads into Personnel to a desk by a window. A simple brass nameplate identified it as hers. Whatever her job, she wasn't in the secretarial pool.

Sitting at her computer, she quickly pulled up Sylvia's record. By now a little circle of women had gathered behind them and were conversing in shocked whispers.

"There. Her emergency contact is Linda Smith, Waterloo, Iowa. That's the sister I remember. She's closer to Sylvia's age, and I think they really understand each other the best, too. I'll copy her street address and phone number for you." She whipped out an index card and wrote in a clear, round hand.

"You have her medical insurance, too?" Fred asked.

"Of course. It's through the company. I'll call the hospital and give them all that. I'm only sorry I don't have Linda's e-mail

45

address. Sylvia probably does, though. Trouble is, we're careful about passwords around here. I couldn't get to her address book, and the person who could is out sick today."

"We could check her home computer, if she has one," Ketcham said. "But we don't even know where she lives."

"Of course," Birdie said. She took back the card and added a local address and phone number.

"Does she live alone?" Fred asked.

"Yes. But I have her spare key. We swapped, in case we got locked out. We've rescued each other more than once." She bent to pull a leather shoulder bag from a bottom drawer. After rummaging only briefly, she held up a key triumphantly. "Here it is!"

They thanked her and made their way back to the parking lot.

"Let's check her apartment, see what we can find there," Fred said. "Be good to put the hospital in touch with her doctor, anyhow."

Ketcham drove while Fred tried the Iowa number on his cell phone, but after four rings, a cheerful child's voice told him no one could come to the phone right now and invited him to leave a message after the beep. He disconnected and punched the numbers in again, in case the first message machine had been a wrong number. But the same recorded child answered. "This is Lieutenant Fred Lundquist, calling from Oliver, Indiana," he said then. "We urgently need to reach Linda Smith. It's about her sister Sylvia Purcell." He left his cell phone number but didn't mention the police. "I don't want to panic some kid," he told Ketcham. "I'll keep calling."

6

oan couldn't concentrate. Fortunately, none of today's activities at the center required her active participation. The bridge and craft groups could take care of themselves. The exercise group had its own leader, a lissome young thing in spandex whom the men enjoyed from the moment they saw her. The women were won over by her friendliness and her ability to adjust her routines to their stiffening limbs.

After laying out the monthly newsletter on the computer, Joan spent some time phoning her emergency orchestra personnel list in search of a replacement for Sylvia, but students with exams looming the week after the concert were harder to enlist than in the fall. By now she was offering them cash, and still she had no takers.

"I don't doubt that you could play it with only one rehearsal," she told one, though she was stretching the truth, "but it's not just the performance. We need you to support the others during rehearsal as well." That part was absolutely true. The other violinists were already demoralized by Sylvia's absence, even before she fell. They didn't need a last-minute sub showing them up at the concert without bothering to turn up for the work sessions. Crossing off one more name, she broke the point of the pencil.

Finally she got a tentative yes from a woman who had played with the orchestra in the past and so didn't expect to be paid. "Trouble is, I can't be sure I'll make the concert," the woman said. "My baby is due a week later. And I'll need a babysitter during rehearsals for my two-year-old. Can you get me one?"

How hard would it be to find a sitter compared to a first violin? Joan promised without blinking, even though the woman hadn't been entirely clear about who would pay the sitter. Hugely relieved even to have a possibility, she relaxed.

Now she couldn't keep the vivid memory of Sylvia's fall in the back of her mind or block out the unreasonable certainty that Andrew would be horribly injured in the same way.

She could no longer suppress the urge to check on him. She called his cell phone number, and he answered immediately.

"You all right? I didn't startle you up there?"

"I'm not going to fall, Mom. I'm not in the tree yet, anyway." He sounded breathless.

Joan breathed more easily, at least for the moment. "Have you been running? You sound like it."

"We're still working on the rope."

"What do you mean?"

"We borrowed one, that's not the problem, but getting it up there is. We thought we could throw a cord over the lowest branch to haul it up, but it's way too high. So now we're shooting the cord up there with my Wrist-Rocket. Remember my Wrist-Rocket?"

"That slingshot you broke windows with?" She remembered all too well. At about twelve, he'd bought one with his own money and done serious damage to two neighbors' windows before she'd confiscated it. According to him, he'd been aiming at tin cans on a fence post.

"Yeah." She could almost hear him blush.

"But I hid it!" She didn't remember where, much less packing it when they moved to Oliver.

"You couldn't hide stuff from me for long, Mom. I found it right away and hid it in my room, but I didn't dare practice with the thing. I think it's going to do the job if I ever get my aim back."

What else had he found? Did any parent have true privacy with kids in the house? She wasn't going to think about it. Not now, anyway.

As if he could read her mind, he said, "I never poked in your stuff. Only my own."

"Uh-huh." A dim memory was returning of that Wrist-Rocket buried in her underwear drawer.

"Gotta go, Mom."

She supposed she ought to wish him good luck, but of course he'd hear it as meaning that she wanted him to be able to climb onto Sylvia's platform. Actually she wanted him safe on the ground.

"Good-bye, Andrew." Hot tears threatened. She would *not* cry.

"Bye, Mom." And he disconnected.

The day dragged after that. She ate lunch at the center, and when someone asked her about Sylvia, she didn't know how much she could say. It's not like a murder, she decided, where the next of kin has to know first. And she didn't have access to protected medical information.

"Sylvia's had a bad accident," she told them, and after that, they hung on to every word. "She fell out of the tree this morning."

"Is she alive?"

"She was when the ambulance came."

"You were there?" they chorused.

"Yes."

"Poor thing," Annie said. "I can't imagine surviving a fall like that."

"It would smash every bone in your body," said a retired nurse. "She's in for a long haul."

"Fool kids," said a man named Ed something. "They go out there with stars in their eyes, and then they see what happens. That'll be the end of that!"

"Cindy will be relieved if it is," Mabel Dunn said. "Now maybe they'll build the place, and her daughter can move all those grandbabies out of her house."

"And Diane Barnhart will get the work," said Annie. "Only she wouldn't want to get it that way."

"Bert might," Vernon Pusey said. "He's a hot-tempered son of a gun." Bert was Diane Barnhart's unemployed husband, Joan remembered. "But you're dead wrong, Ed, and so'd Bert be if he tried a stunt like that. This ain't gonna be the end of it. Some other fool kid is bound to take her place."

Joan pushed back her chair. "Excuse me," she managed before escaping to the restroom.

"Let her go," she heard Annie say behind her. "I think her son cares about Sylvia. He's probably pretty torn up over this."

Remembering Sylvia's broken body, Joan shuddered. She splashed cold water on her eyes and avoided looking at her face.

Pull yourself together, she told herself firmly. This could be a long haul. You don't worry like this when Andrew goes out in traffic on a bike or when he borrows the car, for that matter. They're probably both more dangerous than what he's doing now.

In a few minutes she returned to the table.

"We weren't sure you were coming back," Mabel said.

"You all right, honey?" Annie asked.

"I'm fine, thanks." But the remains of her meal had no appeal. "Anybody want my apple pie?"

"Don't mind if I do," said the man who thought Bert Barnhart had a hot temper, and for a moment she couldn't remember his name. Vernon Pusey, that was it. Some days Joan wished for name tags. Did Vernon think Bert Barnhart would actually do something to make Sylvia fall? *But she just fell. I was there. I know. Or do I?*

Fred and Ketcham had no trouble finding Sylvia's place. She lived in an old house that had seen better days, on one of the tree-lined streets near the campus. In its glory, the peeling frame house had probably belonged to a professor or maybe a doctor. Its generous front porch still featured an old-fashioned porch swing. Now, though, its five or six bedrooms had been broken up into apartments, each with its own entrance and mailbox on the porch.

Running his finger down the row of doorbells, Ketcham said, "Purcell, number three. Must be over here." He led the way around the wraparound porch to a side entrance.

Sylvia's apartment turned out to be three rooms on the first floor. Windows on the east, south, and west sides of the house drenched it in sunshine, though a huge maple tree about to leaf out soon would shade her kitchen and living room.

Her violin case stood in one corner of the living room near a music stand and a stack of music in a brick and board bookshelf. A shabby sofa and old carved oak rocking chair faced each other. Bright rag rugs warmed the floor. No desk, and no sign of anything likely to hold the information they needed to find.

In the kitchen, clean dishes stood in the drainer, and a dishrag had been draped over the faucet to dry. Limp macramé plant hangers hung empty in the windows. "She must have someone else looking after her plants," Ketcham said. There was no phone or notes, not so much as a refrigerator magnet.

"Let's try the bedroom," Fred said. Somehow he hadn't expected this woman to be so tidy. He could only hope it meant she was methodical about her record keeping.

"Here we go," Ketcham said. Beside the water bed, which took up most of the floor space in the bedroom, stood a huge oak rolltop desk. He rolled it up to expose a laptop plugged in through a hole in the back of the desk. "Ought to be fully charged, if she left the electricity on. Maybe if we get lucky we can figure out her password."

"Give it a try, but maybe we won't need it."

While Ketcham sat down and waited for the laptop to boot up, Fred opened the file drawer of the desk. He pulled out a fat manila folder marked simply "Linda" and flipped it open. It was filled with letters, photos of Linda and her family, and drawings her children had made, with notes on the back in their mother's handwriting from the children to Aunt Sylvia. Linda's name and phone number, both of which they already had, were printed neatly inside the folder itself, along with her e-mail address, which Ketcham copied onto a piece of scrap paper from one of the rolltop's cubbyholes. Nothing else new, except that now they'd recognize Linda when they saw her. She resembled her sister slightly but wore her hair short and tended toward blue jeans rather than the flowing skirts Joan said Sylvia wore. They both studied Linda's laughing face but didn't remove any pictures.

Another folder was labeled "Medical Insurance." Good. Linda would be able to take that to the hospital when she finally arrived, but Birdie Eads had promised to call with the information before then. But no doctor bills or record of a personal physician.

Nothing about the tree sit. He wasn't surprised. If it was in writing at all, Sylvia would be more likely to keep that information in her computer, protected by her password. Ketcham was typing in several sets of letters and numbers, with no luck so far.

"I don't know enough about her to make good guesses," he said.

Fred almost missed a slender "Family" folder. Tucked out of alphabetical order at the back of the drawer, it hid behind "Rent" and "Utilities."

Inside, he found a single sheet of paper. It listed Sylvia's parents, with their birth and death dates, and three daughters: Linda, Martha, and Sylvia. Martha was now Martha Rutledge, in Sydney, Australia. There was an address, but no phone or e-mail. And no family pictures.

No sign of a love life, either. No letters or pictures, old or new. And Ketcham hadn't mentioned anyone.

Fred shoved the paper over to Ketcham. "This is it," he said. "We're not going to find anything more here. Nothing we have any business finding, anyway." It wasn't as if she were a victim, whose whole life would be fair game.

Ketcham shut down the computer, and they locked up behind them and left. After making one more attempt to reach Linda, Fred phoned the hospital. The nurse he'd spoken to before was still on duty.

"She's hanging on by a hair, Lieutenant. Did you reach her family?"

"No. I've left my cell phone number, but you might want to call yourself." He gave her the number and Linda's name. "One of us will get through eventually. I'll send her an e-mail, too, soon as I get back to my desk."

"I always hate it when the family doesn't arrive in time. I'm not sure how much difference it will make to this patient, though. She's comatose."

7

hey should have been going back to the station, but Fred couldn't resist checking on Andrew. "Take us out to Yocum's Woods, would you? I want to look at the scene one more time," he told Ketcham.

"You worried about him?" Ketcham was nobody's fool.

"Yeah." Fatherhood had come late to Fred, when he'd married Joan. With her two children already technically adults, he seldom felt fatherly toward either of them. But he and Andrew had connected. Irked as Fred was at Andrew for doing it, this tree-sit business was eating at him more than just as a cop. The thought of Andrew lying comatose in the hospital hurt.

As if going out to see him could make any difference.

They bounced along the washboard gravel road. When they could see the clearing, it was empty. Only the ruts made by the EMTs and ambulance showed that anything had happened there at all. Fred didn't know what he'd expected to see. Maybe the kid hadn't made it back, after all.

Leaving Ketcham in the car, he walked over the rutted ground into the woods and squinted up the oak's tall, straight trunk, unbroken by branches. "Andrew? You up there?"

A dark, curly head popped up from the platform. "Fred?" It was faint, but he heard it.

Then his cell phone rang. With luck, it would be Linda Smith, answering his call. He put it to his ear.

"Fred, it's me, Andrew." The head poked over the edge again, and Andrew waved at him.

"How did you know my number?"

"I don't know. Guess you gave it to me for something."

"You all right?"

"Sure. You ought to try it. I've got all kinds of conveniences."

"Anything out of place? Anything that looks wrong?"

Andrew paused. "Kind of hard to tell, since I was never here before, but it's pretty much what I expected."

"Be my eyes. What do you see?"

"It's beautiful up here. I can see so much farther than when I'm on the ground, especially with my binoculars. Way into the woods, and across the creek over there." He pointed, but he didn't stand up to do it.

Kid had some sense. Good. "And on the platform?"

"It smells from all the rain we've had. Her tarp didn't keep her dry, but we got a better one. And there are wooden walls about a foot high on three sides. That helps. If it blows in or if I want privacy, I can let the tarp down outside the walls. Anyhow, Sylvia's sleeping bag was really gross. I sent that and the rest of her clothes down with Skirv, the guy who was helping me."

Skirv? Fred didn't push it, but he filed the name away in his mind. "What's up there now?"

"My bag of extra clothes is hanging by the hammock. Here on the platform I have room to take a few steps, and there are enough ropes to hang on to. But mostly I sit or lie down. Trust me, Fred, I'm the cautious type."

"I hope so. What else?"

"There's a propane stove and one cooking pot with a lid, if I want to fix something hot, but someone's bringing me supper tonight. I've got a box of all kinds of food, trail mix and beef jerky, ramen noodles and stuff, and a knife, fork, and spoon. A plastic plate and cup. A bucket lined with a plastic garbage bag I can close with twist ties and cover with a lid, to keep the stink down. I won't need to use it as much as she did."

"Right." A built-in advantage to being male. It wasn't as if he needed to hide his scent from deer or other game, as he would if he were hunting.

"Toilet paper rolls on a stick. Soap and gallon jugs of water. A rope to hang up wet towels or whatever. A new basket to replace the one I buried. My books. A notebook and pens. I kept Sylvia's books, too, in case I get bored. She only had a few. Her bookmark was in *Legacy of Luna*. That's the one by Julia Butterfly Hill, about sitting in a tree for two whole years. A battery radio. And she had candles and matches."

"You be careful with those, and the stove." A forest fire— that's all they'd need.

"I will. I don't expect to use it or the candles. People bring food and water, and I brought my flashlight and extra batteries for it and the radio and phone. That's about it, except for a new basket and plenty of rope."

"How smooth is the surface of the platform?"

"You mean could she have stubbed her toe on something? I don't see anything. It's pretty smooth. And all the stuff is hanging up, not on the platform."

"Thanks, Andrew." Fred's neck was getting tired from staring up. It was time to go.

"Fred? Tell Mom I'm okay, would you?"

"I will. Unless I have to bring you down. Then all bets are off. Why are you doing it, son?"

No answer. Finally, "Fred, will the hospital talk to you? I've been trying to find out about Sylvia, but they won't tell me anything."

"It's not good."

"She died?" Andrew's voice rose. Maybe it was finally hitting him that they weren't immortal.

"Not yet. She's in a coma."

"Oh, God." With what sounded like real feeling.

"Andrew, do you know anything about her family? We're trying to reach somebody to be there for her. Or did she keep her emergency contact information up there? Someone local would be good, even if it wasn't her family."

"She never told me about her family, and I didn't notice anything like that. I'll ask Skirv. Don't know when I'll get through to him—he's kind of weird. A little wild-eyed, you know? But I'll try."

"Good. I have a call in to her sister, so I'd better get off this phone."

"Thanks, Fred."

"Sure." He walked back to the car, enjoying the crunchy cushion of the many layers of leaves under his feet until he hit the bare soil of the clearing. Although the trees weren't leafed out yet and even the oaks had dropped their last stubborn hangers-on, he could feel the temperature rise between the woods and the bright sun.

Ketcham was snoozing in the car, but he woke when Fred touched the passenger door. "He okay?"

"Yeah."

"You ask him about Sylvia's family?"

"He doesn't know anything. He'll ask the man who took her clothes away, but I don't think he's likely to get much help from that direction. If you're looking for a password again, you might try *butterfly* or *luna*. But I'm thinking we found all there was to find about her family." His cell phone rang while he was fastening his seat belt. "Lundquist."

"I've been calling and calling! What's the matter with Sylvia?"

"Linda Smith?" He met Ketcham's eyes. Ketcham, who had reached for the ignition key, sat back.

"Yes. Who are you? What's wrong?"

"I'm Lieutenant Fred Lundquist, of the Oliver Police Department. Your sister's in the hospital, and they want you to come right away."

"What happened? An accident?"

"Yes."

"It's not fair! She's such a careful driver."

"It wasn't that kind of accident. You know what she's been doing, don't you?"

"No, what?"

So he had to tell her about the tree sit as well as Sylvia's plunge to the ground. "It's not a police matter," he ended. "But we're all worried about her. How soon can you come?"

"Can I call her?"

"I'm afraid she's still unconscious, but they hope your presence will help her." And them, if someone needed to make life-or-death decisions for her.

"Poor Sylvie. Her heart's in the right place, but she always did get into these harebrained deals. I'll come as soon as I can. I have to arrange for someone to take care of the children and the dogs, and oh, there are a million things I have to do before I can leave."

"Will you need a ride from the Indianapolis airport? We could help with that." On a slow day like today.

"Do you really think I should fly? It's so expensive, and with all the delays these days, I might as well drive."

"It's your decision, of course, but the hospital is concerned about her."

"Yes. I'll do my best."

Sure she'd decide to drive, he had to leave it at that. Could hardly force the woman, and who knew how much difference it would make to her sister anyway? He gave her the direct number for the Intensive Care Unit's nursing desk. "They'll tell you what they can, and they'll be glad to know you're coming. They'll also ask you about her family doctor and her medical history—any seizures or fainting spells."

"I don't think so. She probably doesn't even have a doctor. Thank you, Lieutenant."

The next morning, Joan woke early. It was still dark, but the birds had begun to twitter. Through the open window a light breeze wafted spring air, moist after a long overnight rain and already unusually warm for early April. In short, it was perfect weather for morels. She hoped Andrew's shelter hadn't leaked. It was hard to think of anything much more miserable than lying in a wet sleeping bag.

Leaving Fred gently snoring, she rolled out of bed and pulled on jeans, boots, and a long-sleeved shirt. No need to dress for work. She'd be back in plenty of time to change clothes. The best time to go 'shrooming, as Oliver natives called it, was early morning. And what better place than Andrew's woods? She wasn't fooling herself about her real reason for going out there. If she waited a couple of weeks, even in southern Indiana, she could expect to find a lot more mushrooms, though the paper had run a feature a week ago about a man who claimed his early patch always yielded the first delicious morels of the year. But even after Fred's description of Andrew's sensible behavior, she had to see for herself how he was doing.

She downed a quick breakfast and tucked a couple of mesh onion bags into her pocket, just in case she succeeded in finding any "sponge" mushrooms. The mesh would let the morel spores fall back to the ground for next year's crop.

By the time she was in the car, her watch read 6:45 A.M., and the sun was up. She parked her car in the clearing and took her long walking stick out of the wagon's wayback. She'd use it to explore rotting leaves and twigs for the delicacies hiding under them. Even though she didn't seriously expect to find any yet, she might get lucky.

No sign of life in Andrew's tree. But he wasn't lying broken underneath it. Let him sleep, she thought, and with a light heart she began to search the underbrush for the first subtle but unmistakable golden sponge poking up from the forest floor.

Nearby, past a couple of shagbark hickories, she was poking her stick in the leaves along the rotting trunk of a fallen walnut tree, a likely spot for morels, when she was distracted by another unmistakable bit of her childhood. But what was it doing in these woods? Morels grew all through the Midwest, she knew, but the smooth gray pebble shining up at her from the bed of wet leaf litter had no business in southern Indiana, much less in a woods. Yet here it was. Nothing else looked quite like the misshapen hexagonal, cell-like patterns on a Petoskey stone, and because this one was wet, the white lines outlining the cells showed up clearly, as did the darker spots in the centers. Sudden suspicion stopped her hand from automatically picking it up. She couldn't help thinking of the five smooth stones David took along with his slingshot to slay Goliath. They would probably have been bigger than this one, for a giant. It was not quite two inches long.

They'll probably laugh at me, she thought.

But why else would a stone made of fossilized coral be here? Besides, its size and shape matched what she remembered of that spot on Sylvia's temple.

Staring down at it, so close to Andrew's tree, she wished she could memorize its location. A real woodsman could, she thought, but if I go after Fred now, I'll never find it again.

She pulled the phone Andrew had given her out of her pocket and dialed home. Wake up, she thought, as she listened to ring after ring. Finally, Fred's groggy voice answered.

"Fred, it's me."

From the bed's creaking, he had to be rolling over and sitting up. "Where are you?"

"In Yocum's Woods."

"Is he all right?"

Bless you, Fred. "I think he's still asleep. But I found something near his tree. Will you come out here? I think it's important. I'm afraid to pick it up."

"Afraid it'll hurt you?" He sounded wide awake now.

"No." Afraid to touch it or even to broadcast what I say about it. "I think you need to see it here. It might have something to do with what happened here yesterday."

"Sit tight. I'm on my way."

She stabbed her stick into the ground a few feet from the stone, sat down on the wet leaves, and leaned against the trunk of a tulip poplar. Even its relatively smooth bark dug into her back. Why hadn't she thought of using the stick earlier? She could have tied her handkerchief to it, like fake flowers on a car antenna. She didn't need to guard the stone. If it had been under the leaves that long, it wasn't likely to disappear now.

But she was glad he was coming.

When she heard the Chevy, she went to meet him, picking her way carefully at first. She didn't trust the greenbrier and grapevines not to trip her. But once she reached the clearing, she ran.

Fred had thrown on yesterday's rumpled clothes, and he hadn't bothered to shave, but he looked good to her. His stubble rasped her cheek.

"So, what's this great find of yours?" His eyes crinkled down at her.

"I'll show you. It's just past Sylvia's tree."

"Oh?" But he followed without pushing her to tell him more.

Joan was glad she'd left the stick to mark the spot. "Here it is," she said. With a twig, she lifted the wet leaves by the log. "There. Look at that!"

He looked blankly. "That what?"

"That Petoskey stone." She pointed the twig at the gray, oval pebble nestled in the leaf mold.

"What's a Petoskey stone?"

"A kind of fossilized coral. When they're polished or wet, like this one, they're easy to spot. I used to find them on the beach when our family spent vacations on Lake Michigan, especially up by Petoskey, where they developed. It's the waves of the lake that make them so smooth. But this is a long way from the beach—it didn't get here by itself."

"You brought me out here to show me a lake pebble?"

"I wanted to take it to you, but I was afraid I'd be destroying evidence."

"Evidence of what?"

She took a deep breath and blurted it out. "I think some-one shot Sylvia with it. It looks just like a spot on the side of her head. The right size and shape, I mean."

"You and Andrew didn't hear a shot."

"No, but with Andrew talking and the birds carrying on, we couldn't have heard a slingshot. Andrew used his Wrist-Rocket—it's a kind of powerful slingshot—to shoot a line over the platform."

"You're serious?" He squatted down to look at it.

"Yes. It's smooth enough that it might have fingerprints on it. I was afraid I'd destroy them. Besides, if I moved it, you wouldn't see where it landed."

"You're not the only person to go to the beach. People down here like Lake Michigan, too, you know. Maybe it was a special souvenir to Sylvia, and she had it on her platform. It could have fallen off when she did."

Joan thought about it. "I don't see how. She landed only a few feet from the tree, over there. Why would it fall here, on the opposite side? But if it was shot from a distance, couldn't it keep going after it hit her?"

Still squatting, he looked up at her. "What's the range of that thing?"

"A Wrist-Rocket? About a hundred yards. That's why I took Andrew's away from him when he was shooting at cans in our neighborhood. I couldn't afford to fix any more windows."

Fred stood and looked through the trees, and Joan followed his gaze. Even without leaves, the tree trunks seemed to cluster together in the distance.

"So someone could have stood far enough away that you might not have seen anything," he said. "It's possible, I'll grant you that. Even so, this rock could have come from some kid shooting out here, like Andrew and his cans. Nothing to do with Sylvia."

"So you're not going to do anything about it?"

"Not much to do." But he pulled a camera out of his jeans and snapped several shots, including a couple that showed the distance of the stone from Andrew's tree. Then he pulled plastic gloves from another pocket, picked up the stone, and put it in an evidence bag, which he marked before tucking it in the pocket. "Just in case."

He came prepared, she thought. So he had taken her seriously. "If someone did that on purpose, or even by accident, I think we ought to know, don't you?"

"You planning to join the force?"

"Oh, Fred." At least he wasn't laughing at her. Or was he?

"Come on home, woman. Feed me breakfast."

All right, he was, but she didn't care. Arm in arm, they walked past Andrew's tree and out into the clearing. Still no sound from Andrew. Fine. He didn't need to know she'd been checking on him.

8

*S*howered and shaved, Fred arrived at the station only a little later than usual. When he walked in, Ketcham put down the phone and looked up, his eyes serious behind his wire rims. "She's dead."

"Who?" But he knew.

"Sylvia Purcell."

"Any word from her sister?"

"According to the ICU nurse, she decided to drive and didn't make it in time. The nurse thinks she'll arrive later today."

"Too bad. You told her not to release the information until she gets here?" Not that hospitals needed to be told about privacy these days, but Sylvia was news, and leaks happened. Hearing it on the car radio would be a hell of a way to learn your sister was dead.

"Yeah," Ketcham said. "And I called Henshaw."

Dr. Henshaw was Alcorn County coroner, in charge of investigating accidental deaths, homicides, and any death under dubious circumstances. Fred appreciated his quiet competence. Not every county elected a coroner who knew what he was doing. For that matter, not every county had a forensic pathologist available to elect. But Henshaw lived in a small college town by choice and didn't seem to mind being called out of bed to the scene of a bloody highway accident. No longer young, he'd said more than once that he hoped to die with his boots on.

"The nurse was kicking herself," Ketcham said. "She talked to the doctor and told Linda Smith they thought she had time to drive."

She may not be the only one kicking herself, Fred thought, if it wasn't an accident, after all. He held out the evidence bag containing the smooth gray stone with the markings like cell walls on a microscope slide. It was about two inches long. "Get someone to check this for prints." The thing looked smooth enough to take them. "Then turn it over to Henshaw for comparison."

"A Petoskey stone?" Ketcham said.

"You know about them?"

"We go up there sometimes. My wife used to polish them, when she was on a jewelry-making kick."

"This one was in Yocum's Woods. Near the tree sit."

"Odd. Could be someone's souvenir, even Sylvia's."

"I'm hoping we can find her prints on it."

"But?" Ketcham always could read his mind.

"It's possible she was shot down with the thing, from a powerful slingshot."

Ketcham nodded. "My oldest kid had one of those Wrist-Rockets. Drove us nuts till I finally made a target for him, out back, away from anything else."

"If she was shot down, we might even find some DNA evidence, though I'd expect the rock that hit her to be closer to where she landed."

67

"Maybe even on the platform."

Which would mean Andrew had spent the night in the middle of a crime scene. They'd have to get him down sooner now, rather than later, and send up a young, agile officer to search the thing. Chuck Terry could probably handle it. Or Jill Root. As long as he'd been up there, though, Andrew had likely already touched everything on his platform. The scene was already contaminated, both in the tree and below it, first by the EMTs who had taken Sylvia to the hospital and then by Andrew and the others who'd helped him up to take her place and Skirv, whoever he was, who had carried Sylvia's things away with him. Not that the shooter had stood that close to the tree. Joan and Andrew hadn't seen anyone.

One thing at a time, Fred thought. With the advantage of the first hours already lost, he waited to hear about the stone they had in hand. The amazing thing was that anyone had spotted it at all, much less recognized it as not having any business where it had fallen. Might as well hope it belonged to Sylvia.

The good and bad news came from Henshaw, who phoned early in the afternoon. "That rock you sent over? It's not a match for her fingerprints."

"So there was a print on it?" Hardly surprising, since the thing hadn't walked to southern Indiana.

"We lifted a couple of partials. A thumb on one side and a finger on the other side. But they're not hers."

"Great." It had been too much to hope for. Partials were better than nothing, but you couldn't check a partial fingerprint against all the prints in the computer. Holding the phone to his ear, Fred caught his toes under his desk for security and leaned back against the wall in the old wooden swivel chair that threatened to dump him.

"The good news is that the shape of the thing fits a bruise on her temple. Looks like your projectile, all right."

"That's what killed her?" Hard to believe.

"I haven't done the autopsy yet. My first guess is the fall killed her. But if you want to know why she fell, it's a good bet. Was she standing up?"

Fred thought back to what Andrew and Joan had told him. "Yes. And letting her basket down. Probably leaning over."

"Seventy feet off the ground?" The whole town knew that much.

"Yes."

"Well, then. Whatever made that bruise hit her with enough force to throw her off balance. Startle her, at the very least. Maybe even knock her out. All the other injuries visible at first glance look like the result of the fall. I say your rock sent her over."

Fred thanked him and sighed. Whatever the age or intent of the shooter, they were dealing with a homicide.

Ketcham stuck his head in the door of Fred's office. "Linda Smith's here."

Fred's feet thumped onto the floor. "Bring her in." He stood to meet her.

Ketcham made the introductions and then left. Fred nodded at him when he raised his eyebrows to ask whether to shut the office door, and he closed it unobtrusively.

Linda Smith wore a denim jumper and turtleneck. Her hair was speckled with gray that he didn't remember from the photos, and her eyes were red and swollen. "Thank you for seeing me, Lieutenant."

"Ms. Smith, I'm very sorry for your loss," he said, and meant it. "Won't you sit down?" He held the visitor's chair for her. "How can I help you?"

"Tell me what happened!" She twisted the sodden handkerchief in her hands. "They wouldn't tell me anything at the hospital, except that she never woke up, never spoke to them. They sent me to you."

"I doubt that they knew much more. I've spoken with the coroner—"

"The coroner!"

"In Indiana, he's automatically called for any death that may not be from natural causes. He had to look at Sylvia's body." Inside and out, but he didn't want to add to her distress by mentioning the autopsy. "We can take you there to see her." In fact, he was glad she would be available to make a formal identification. Not that there was any doubt.

"She's in the morgue?" Her voice threatened fresh tears, but they didn't spill.

"In the funeral home—Oliver's so small that we use it, instead—but her body will be released to you soon, as her closest relative, and you can make whatever arrangements you prefer. Or maybe she told you what she wanted?"

"She never talked about dying. She's a young woman!"

"You were in close touch?"

She shrugged. "I thought so. But then you call and tell me she's been living up in an oak tree, and I realize that I don't know anything about her. I haven't seen her for years."

"When's the last time you heard from her?"

"Well . . ." She paused to think. "Probably a couple of months ago. She didn't say anything about it then. She was working hard, she said, and playing in an orchestra. She played violin. Did you know that about her?" She managed a smile.

"Yes, I did." He smiled back. "My wife plays in the same orchestra. Did she mention any friends?"

"Only a woman from work. Another violinist. Kind of old-fashioned name."

"Birdie Eads?"

"That's the one! I ought to see her."

"She was very concerned about your sister when I spoke with her yesterday."

"Does she know she died?"

"Possibly, now that you're here. We don't like to release that information until the family has been notified. But the whole town knew that she fell. Her tree sit was big news in Oliver. I'm sure she'll make the news again this evening if she hasn't already. You may have the press coming around. Are you staying in Sylvia's apartment?"

She looked vague. "I hadn't thought that far. I suppose I might as well, if I knew how to get in."

"I think Sergeant Ketcham may still have her key. When we were trying to reach you, her friend Birdie lent us her copy. The electricity and phone were working."

"Is it a disaster? Sylvia always said there were more important things in life than polishing furniture."

He smiled. Sylvia had put her life where her mouth was. "Not much there to polish, but it was neat when I saw it. Unless her friends have dumped her tree-sitting things there since then. I don't know whether they had a key."

"Do you know her friends? Have you seen where she fell?"

"I know the young man who took her place. And yes, I was there after she fell."

"Could I go there?"

"Of course. What do you want to do first?"

He could see her girding herself. She firmed her jaw, put the wet handkerchief in her jumper pocket, and said, "I want to see my sister. Then where she fell. Then her place."

He had time for it this afternoon. And he might learn something from her. "I'll be right back." Leaving her in his office, he went out to ask Ketcham to check whether Henshaw was in the middle of the autopsy and, if not, to warn him that they were coming to view the body.

When he got the all clear—Henshaw hadn't begun yet—he returned to Linda Smith. "They're expecting us."

"Is it far?"

"No, just down the street."

"Then let's walk. I've been sitting all day."

He made sure she'd locked her luggage in her car before walking her over to Bud Snarr's funeral home. Gil, Bud's son, who ran the business these days, met them at the door of the big old rock-face limestone building with its distinctive roughly chipped look, which had to have been home to a large family at some time in its history. Or maybe it had been built to give that impression to grieving families.

Fred knew Gil had been Joan's sixth-grade classmate when her father had brought the family to Oliver for a sabbatical year. Now Gil held the wide door for them. "I'll take you back," he said.

They followed him down a long hall, its once-elegant carpet faded, to a cold back room with white cinder block walls, a tile floor, and two tables, one white porcelain and the other stainless steel. On the white table lay a still form covered by a white sheet. Fred was grateful on her sister's behalf that Sylvia wasn't in a body bag. But not even the faint fragrance of several funeral bouquets in one corner could disguise the overwhelming strong fingernail polish remover smell—acetone for the embalming fluid they used here. Probably easier for her sister to smell than the formaldehyde he knew from other places.

Linda's hand reached out shakily toward him. When he offered her a steady arm, she held on.

"Ready?" he asked.

Lips tight, she nodded, and Gil drew the sheet back from Sylvia's face. Only a few scratches and the dark bruise on her temple suggested what had happened to her. Someone, Fred assumed the nursing staff at the hospital before she died, had washed her and braided her hair. Remembering what she'd landed on, he was glad for her sister's sake that she'd lived long enough for them to do that. Gil wouldn't be able to work on the body until Henshaw finished the autopsy.

"Poor Sylvia," Linda said, and wiped her eyes. She looked for a long moment and then turned away. "Thank you," she told Gil.

He escorted them out, with none of the intrusive sympathy affected by some funeral directors. Not that he needed to push his services. Snarr's was the only funeral home in Oliver.

"I wish I'd made it in time," Linda said on the walk back to the station, where Fred's car was parked. "I know it wouldn't have mattered to her, but I wish I'd seen her alive."

"Yes," Fred said, glad to inhale the fresh spring air again.

"And you'll take me to where she fell?"

"It's not far," he told her, and opened his passenger door for her.

On the way, they passed a man selling roses out of a panel truck parked at the side of the road. A rough hand-painted sign advertised DOZEN ROSES $5. A plastic tub outside the truck held bunches of roses in water. On this cool day, they hadn't begun to droop.

"Oh, stop, would you?" Linda begged.

Fred pulled over. She hopped out and returned with a single red rose. "I had to talk him into selling me just one."

"We're almost there." He turned at the gravel road, rounded the curve, and pulled into the clearing. Inside the car, the scent of her rose was overwhelming the subtler odors of spring, but when he opened the door, he inhaled the contrasts of muddy earth in the clearing and the damp leaf mold a few feet farther on.

He led her into the woods and pointed up. "There it is." Ropes hung here and there from the platform that had been Sylvia's last home, but he couldn't see the things Andrew had said were hanging above it.

"She stayed up there?"

"For a week."

Andrew's dark head poked over the edge. "Hey, Fred!"

The cell phone in his pocket rang. "That's Andrew Spencer, who helped Sylvia and then took her place in the tree," Fred told Linda. He spoke into his phone. "Andrew, this is Sylvia's sister, Linda Smith."

"How's Sylvia doing?"

"I'm sorry, son. She died this morning."

"Oh, no." He was silent for a moment. "Do you think I could talk to her sister?"

"I'll ask her." He relayed Andrew's question and held out the phone.

"Of course," she said, taking it. She listened, thanked him, and gave the phone to Fred again.

"I'm going to take her over to Sylvia's place now," he told Andrew.

"Give her my cell phone number, would you? In case she thinks of something she wants to ask?" He rattled it off.

"Sure." Fred wrote it down for her and in his own little notebook.

Linda laid her rose at the base of the oak, and they went back to the car.

"He seems like a nice young man," she said.

Fred nodded. He had to tell her the rest. "There's one more thing you should know," he told her. "We don't think Sylvia's fall was an accident."

"I don't understand. Sylvia would never . . ." Her voice trailed off uncertainly. "I suppose I don't know what she would do."

"There was nothing to suggest that she took her own life."

"You think she was murdered?" Her face crumpled. "But who would kill Sylvia? And why? And how?"

"I don't know."

"Yesterday you called it an accident!"

"We didn't know yesterday. We're not absolutely sure now, but we're treating her death as a homicide. That's why I asked you about her friends. We need to learn all we can about your sister."

Her grief turned to anger, but she wasn't much help. "I thought I knew her," she kept saying. "I wish I could help you catch the person who did this to her. Promise me you'll catch him."

Or her, Fred thought. Could some woman have been jealous of Sylvia?

9

$\mathscr{D}$ etective Chuck Terry and Officer Jill Root were in the station house when they returned. Chuck was taking down a new complaint from a man who showed up regularly. He'd been carrying on a feud with his neighbors for years. Nodding as he filled out a form, Chuck let the man air his grievances as if he'd never heard them before. Fred knew that in the end the man would back down. He was glad Chuck had the patience to hear him out.

Ketcham approached them, a folded paper in his hand. His face looked grim. "Lieutenant, can you spare a moment?"

"Is it urgent?"

"Yes, sir." The formality was a tip-off.

Fred nodded. "I'll be in my office in a moment."

"I've taken up enough of your time," Linda said, as he meant her to. "You've been very kind."

He called Jill over and introduced them.

"Officer Root will take you to Sylvia's apartment now," he said. "If you see anything that strikes you as wrong, or if you can suggest anyone else we might talk to about your sister, she'll want to know."

"Ms. Smith, we're all so very sorry," Jill said.

"Did you know her, too?"

"No, ma'am, not personally, but we were all concerned about her, way up there by herself."

They left together, and Ketcham followed Fred into his office.

"What's up?" Fred asked.

Ketcham, standing in front of the desk, dropped the formality. "Altschuler heard it on the radio and split a gut."

"Already?" Fred rounded the desk and sat down heavily. He had counted on telling Captain Warren Altschuler, their chief of detectives, himself. "How did it get out so soon?"

"The hospital told the media once her sister arrived."

"That she was murdered?"

"No, that she'd died. But someone must have leaked it." His jaw tightened. "I'm gonna find out who—maybe someone eavesdropping at Snarr's, maybe someone on Gil Snarr's staff—but it damn well better not have been one of ours. And now they're speculating about all the people who would have had it in for Sylvia. They've already asked him for a comment."

Fred groaned. "I'd better go see him." But it was too late. Through his office window, he saw Altschuler heading toward him, his homely face distorted. Fred managed to get to his feet before the door crashed open.

"What the hell do you think you're doing, hanging me out to dry like that?"

Nothing to do but take it. "It shouldn't have happened."

"It didn't *happen!* You held her sister's hand and left me to take the flak. Where was your head, man? Where was your sense of duty?"

Fred stood silent, waiting until his chief wound down. It

wouldn't take long. Warren Altschuler was a reasonable man, supportive of his force, and a friend. He'd stood up with Fred at his wedding. But that didn't mean he'd stand for arguments. So Fred waited.

"Oh, all right," Altschuler said at last. "Tell me now." He sank down in the old leather chair he usually chose.

Fred leaned back carefully on his old swivel chair. "You know anything more?" he asked Ketcham, still standing near the door.

"Not yet. Nothing yet from Henshaw."

"Let me know."

"Yes, sir." Ketcham looked grateful to leave. He closed the door behind him.

Fred turned to Altschuler. "You probably know by now that my wife and her son witnessed the fall."

Altschuler raised his bushy eyebrows. "The news didn't mention that."

"Maybe they didn't know—Joan doesn't use my name. When I arrived, I met the ambulance on its way to the hospital. From the scene and what she and Andrew could tell me about what they saw and the conversation they'd had with Sylvia Purcell, there was nothing to indicate anything but an accidental fall. But this morning Joan was back out there, because Andrew took Sylvia's place in the tree."

"The kid who gave his mother away at your wedding."

"Yeah." More or less.

"She was poking in the leaves, looking for morels, and she found a rock she knew wasn't from around here."

"She a rock hound?"

"No. But she knew it came from Lake Michigan. Some kind of fossil, but nothing like a trilobite or crinoid that you might find in this area." Fred, having grown up in northern

Illinois, gave himself points for that bit of local lore. "Ketcham recognized it, too, when I brought it back here. The partial prints on it aren't the deceased's. And Henshaw said it matches the bruise on the side of her head."

"Henshaw thinks this rock killed her?"

"He hadn't done the autopsy yet. But he guessed it probably triggered her fall, and the fall killed her."

"Not much to go on."

"I was waiting for more. But I should have informed you."

Altschuler was past worrying about it. "You learn anything from the sister?"

"Not really. She ID'd the body. But she didn't even know Sylvia was up in the tree, and we'd already spoken to the only friend Sylvia had mentioned to her. At that point we were only helping the hospital locate her family while she was still alive."

"You'll have to interview them both again."

"Yes. And look for someone with a powerful slingshot."

"Could be a kid," Altschuler said.

"Yeah." A possibility Fred hated to think about.

"Or someone who hates tree huggers."

"The construction boss, for one." Tom Walcher had to be a suspect.

"You didn't talk to her after she fell?"

"She never came out of the coma."

"You're going to have to lean on Andrew."

"I know." Maybe Sylvia's death would be enough to make him open up about the others who supported her cause.

"Or get him down."

"Yeah." Nothing like a murder to destroy family harmony.

"It's going to polarize public opinion in this town, with everybody blaming whatever group they already hate. Keep me informed." He stood.

"Yes, sir." Fred stood, too.

"Don't click your heels at me, Fred. You know me too well."

"Thanks, Warren."

Relieved, he called Ketcham into his office.

"You said your son had a Wrist-Rocket. Where'd he get it?"

"Mail order. These days he could buy it off the Internet. Or right here in Oliver."

"Where?"

"Over by the campus. That store with all kinds of gadgets. Caters to students, of course, but doesn't turn down anyone's money. Owned by Matt Skirvin. Grew up around here, but left town for about ten years. Came back a couple of years ago, lives out in the woods somewhere, over toward Brown County. I've been keeping my eye on Matt."

"Any particular reason?"

Ketcham scratched his head. "Not exactly. He got in enough scrapes as a kid, but nothing all that serious. Just a kind of general recklessness about him. Skates on the edge of the law, but not so's you could haul him in. We could probably get him on pot, but I don't know that he distributes it."

Fred nodded thoughtfully. "Andrew called the man who collected Sylvia's clothes 'Skirv.' "

"That's Matt. Skirv's Stuff is his shop."

"Of course. Looks like junk."

"Some of it is. But there's new stuff, too. And probably some drug paraphernalia, though he doesn't have that out for general inspection. So far we don't have any hard evidence that he's done worse than smoke a few joints."

10

The news spread through Oliver like a bad case of poison ivy.

Someone brought it through the front door of the Oliver Senior Citizens' Center before lunchtime.

"And they're saying it *wasn't* an accident," Annie Jordan told Joan as they stuck address labels on a mass fund-raising mailing for the adult day care.

"Who's saying?" Joan slapped the next label on crooked. How had that gotten out?

Annie shrugged. "I don't know. Radio, I suppose."

"Not the police?"

"Wouldn't Fred tell you if someone killed her, with your boy up there and all?"

Joan had told Annie that much. She made herself stick the next label on straight. Eventually, she thought. Depends on how busy he is. And how mad he still is at Andrew. Or maybe on how trapped he feels about talking to me when Andrew's tree sitting. Can he even talk to me? If it really is murder and Andrew's right there in the middle of it, involved who knows how with Sylvia and her group, how much can

Fred take me into his confidence? Andrew changes everything, that's for sure.

"I'm sorry," Annie said. "I shouldn't have worried you."

Joan sighed. "I worry all the time these days, Annie. Not much you can say to make it worse."

"I care about him. He's a sweet boy."

"I know you do." And I know he's a sweet boy. Why do I keep remembering him as a baby?

The day dragged on. Joan deliberately did not turn on the radio they kept in her office mostly for weather warnings. She hoped Andrew had enough sense to come down if a tornado was on the way, or even a thunderstorm—she planned to phone him if she heard a warning. So far he'd only had to deal with rain. With the sun shining outside her office window, she felt free to ignore the radio.

Ignoring the comments around her was harder. Most of them were the same things people had said earlier, but now they were looking for villains among their friends. No one took seriously the idea that Cindy Thickstun would murder anyone to get her daughter and grandchildren out of her house, but more than once Joan heard muttering about the hot temper of Bert Barnhart, unemployed husband of the woman who cleaned for Annie. Alone in her office at last and paging through her phone book, she found him listed at a rural address. Not surprising, she thought. Living a little way out in the county often cost less than living in town. She supposed he might practice taking potshots at squirrels with rocks, too. Cheaper than shooting with bullets. He'd have plenty of time on his hand, with no job. And good reason to resent Sylvia—and now Andrew. Had they spent time in Michigan? She asked Mabel Dunn.

"Where are the Barnharts from, do you know?"

"She grew up here, but he didn't. I think he's from some-where in Michigan. Don't take my word for it, though."

She'd have to tell Fred. When she tried, using his private number, the man who answered said he was out but offered to take a message.

"No, thanks. I'll see him later." Surely later would be soon enough. Except for her son. She dialed Andrew's cell phone.

He sounded so cheerful that she wasn't sure what he knew. But then he said slowly, "I suppose you've heard the news."

"Yes. Turns out somebody may have killed her, after all."

"How? I mean, we were right there. Did you see anybody?"

Rats. She hadn't meant to lay that on Andrew if he hadn't already heard it. Never mind. He'd hear it soon enough. Better from her.

"You know I didn't. But this morning I found a stone near your tree."

"You were out here this morning?"

"Early, looking for morels."

"It's too soon for mushrooms, even in southern Indiana. You were checking up on me, weren't you?"

She was glad he couldn't see her blush. "I suppose so. But I found a Petoskey stone, instead."

"And?"

"There aren't any Petoskey stones down here. Andrew, I think someone with a slingshot like yours shot it at her."

He didn't laugh, for which she was grateful. "You tell Fred?"

"Of course, and he came out and got it. You keep your head down!"

"You're really worried."

"Worried doesn't come close. I'm scared to death that you're up there, now more than ever. I just heard a guy I wouldn't want to have mad at you is upset at the construction delay."

"Old Walcher doesn't scare me."

"He scares me, but I didn't mean him. Somebody killed her, Andrew!"

"I'll be careful. And I let down the tarp to the walls more than Sylvia did."

She hoped he meant it.

"But not all the way, or all the time. I'd get claustrophobia on this dinky platform if I couldn't see around me some. And not at night, unless it rains or I'm freezing. They're not going to shoot at me in the dark. And you wouldn't believe the stars I can see from here. This far away from the lights in town, they're really awesome, even through the trees."

Her urge to warn him had been so strong that it hadn't occurred to her to wonder whether she'd told him too much, but now she worried that she had, even if it didn't seem to be sinking in that he was in real danger. "Andrew, you'd better not mention the Petoskey stone to anyone else."

"Why not?"

"It's the kind of detail the police sometimes don't release."

"So nobody but the cops and the murderer would know it, you mean?"

"Exactly. Fred and I didn't talk about that, but if I hadn't been so scared, I would have known better than to mention it to you."

"You know I didn't do it. You were there."

"I would have known that anyway. But yes, it's good you and I can witness for each other."

"You think anyone would believe us if we did?"

"I think it's never going to come up. Just be careful, okay?"

"I promise."

"And let other people tell you what they think happened. They won't expect you to know anything."

"Right." He was tolerating her.

She gave up, for now, anyway. "You have enough food?"

"Yes, Mom. I'm doing fine. And I suspect the whole protest will get a lot more attention from now on. Sylvia would have liked that."

She would, Joan thought. "How well did you know her, Andrew?"

"Not as well as you did—I wasn't in love with her, if that's what you're thinking—but I agree with what she was doing."

"You think it's worth it?"

"Worth dying for? I don't want to die. But I'd rather die for this beautiful land and wildlife than a lot of things they give out medals for. And no one had the right to do that to Sylvia! I'm standing up for her, and for her commitment."

She wished his father could hear him. He would have been so proud. But she hoped Andrew wasn't literally standing up on his dinky platform. How did the mothers of people on active duty in the military bear it, knowing that at any time their children might be killed? She couldn't answer him.

"They've already got big equipment in that clearing where we buried her basket. It'll serve 'em right if they dig it up." The grin on his face came through in his voice.

"It's no joke!"

"I know, Mom, but I've gotta do it."

She wondered during the afternoon whether he was right about the attention the protest would get. On the way home after work, though, she knew he was. A straggly crowd, mostly young, was already marching though Oliver, beginning at the Oliver College campus and apparently headed for city hall, or maybe the police station.

"Who killed Sylvia?" they were shouting, and, "Don't kill the trees!" Fists pounded the air to the beat of the shouts.

Joan paused at a corner to watch, as did a couple of men who'd been playing pool at the senior center. Several uniformed police officers also were watching, but not attempting to interfere with the march. Probably wise, she thought. A little shouting wouldn't hurt anybody. But she hoped they weren't dismissing the march as campus nonsense. She thought it was in dead earnest. And if those fists started pounding anything besides air, Fred might be in for a late night. For that matter, he probably was anyway, if the police were investigating Sylvia's death. As the detective first on the scene, he'd be sure to end up with the case.

The intensity of the demonstration was picking up. She was glad Yocum's Woods wasn't within easy marching distance. A confrontation out there could turn ugly fast, if Mr. Walcher enlisted any of his construction crew.

"Those kids are spoiling for a fight."

Joan jumped. Intent on the marchers, she hadn't noticed Annie Jordan behind her.

"You want a ride home? I'm parked right over there." Annie pointed at her elderly Escort.

"No, thanks, Annie. You know me. I like to walk."

"Better not hang around here much longer, then, unless you've got a flashlight."

In the depths of her shoulder bag, Joan kept a slender flashlight for just such situations, but she nodded. Annie was right. There was no point hanging around.

"See you tomorrow," Joan said. Turning her back on the

marchers, she started toward the park that made her daily pedestrian commute a pleasure.

As she'd expected, Fred didn't make it home for supper. She scrambled eggs, zapped fresh broccoli spears in the microwave until they were just past raw, and toasted a couple of slices of Fred's sourdough oatmeal bread. A real Andrew supper—she couldn't help wondering what he was eating tonight.

After supper, alone and with no excuse not to, she pulled out her viola and attacked the Britten. The viola section's lush solo wasn't actually too hard, if she could just keep a smooth legato tone, but the fugue took real work. An hour later, she thought she could pull it off, if not as fast as Alex probably would take it. Even so, making her fingers comfortable with fingerings that worked for her would help when she tried to bring it up to speed.

It felt strange to go to bed alone, but with no sign of Fred, she picked out a book and crawled in. To her surprise, considering all that was on her mind, she fell asleep before Beethoven's Violin Concerto, playing on the college radio station, came to the last movement.

Sometime in what seemed the middle of the night she felt Fred's arms around her. "When did you get in?" she murmured.

"Hours ago. Phone probably woke you."

She rolled over and forced her eyes open. In the faint light coming through the window she could just see the outlines of his face. She didn't remember the phone ringing. "At this hour? What's wrong? Is it Andrew?"

"Far as I know, he's fine."

"Then what?" But her muscles were relaxing again. Nighttime phone calls weren't all that unusual for Fred.

"Vandals. That was your friend Tom Walcher. Seems that

when he got to work at six this morning, someone had damaged his construction vehicles."

"It's six? I just went to bed."

"Six fifteen. All right if I turn on a light? I can pull my pants on in the dark, but since you're already awake . . ."

"Oh, sure." She watched his efficient movements. Like a firefighter, he always kept his clothes within reach when he went to bed. "Want some breakfast?"

"It'll wait. A cup of coffee?"

"Sure." She pulled on a robe and put a couple of cups of water to boil while she ground Starry Night beans in the electric grinder Andrew had given Fred for Christmas. Tucking a filter into the funnel that fit over his big mug, she waited for the kettle to whistle. The coffee had dripped by the time he came out of the bathroom. Joan handed Fred his steaming mug and a couple of slices of his sourdough oatmeal bread, toasted and buttered.

"Thanks." He sandwiched the toast together, washed down a couple of bites with his first slug of coffee, and took the rest with him. "I'll see you when I see you." For a man who'd thrown on his clothes, he looked remarkably put together. The tie that stuck out of his jacket pocket could make him totally presentable for the station—or for cameras, if it came to that. Only the roughness of his cheek when he kissed her gave away the fact that he hadn't shaved since the night before. He'd told her when they were first married that he liked to shave at bedtime, just in case. It helped to be blond, she thought.

11

*E*ven though he'd answered Joan's question casually, Fred felt anything but comfortable about Andrew's safety. He'd left word at the station that he wanted to be called immediately about any problems at Yocum's Woods. Johnny Ketcham, of course, knew why. Fred let anyone else think it was only because of Sylvia Purcell.

Two uniformed officers met him at the edge of the clearing, Jill Root and Kevin Wampler, a tall, skinny kid who was newer on the force than Jill. Hard to think of her as experienced enough to work with a new officer, but she'd do a good job of it, if Wampler didn't get on his high horse about a woman partner.

Until now, only the tracks of large construction equipment in the clearing had suggested what Sylvia had been protesting. This time nothing had budged from those tracks. Men in denim and hard hats stood in clumps, talking and smoking. No skin off their noses if they were paid for doing nothing. Tom Walcher wouldn't look at it that way, Fred was sure.

"So, what's up?" he asked.

"They sabotaged the equipment," Jill said. "Walcher's ready to kill whoever did it."

"He won't have to look far," Kevin said.

"What do you mean?" Fred asked.

"They signed it." Kevin stood back and pointed.

Emblazoned on the bulldozer behind him were crudely painted black letters a foot high.

" 'EFF,' " Fred read. "That anything like ELF?" The radical group Earth Liberation Front, he knew, had been linked to acts of vandalism in the name of environmental causes around the country and often left graffiti of its initials. But EFF was new to him.

"I don't know," Kevin said. "Maybe it's like a typo."

Jill raised her eyebrows. "Every time?" She pointed to the same initials on a hydraulic excavator—a huge backhoe on Caterpillar tracks—and a tub grinder that stood ready to grind up the very trees Sylvia and Andrew didn't want them to take down. "I don't think so. In a day or two, if they're anything like ELF, they'll probably take credit for it and tell us their full name."

Which didn't mean that individuals would step forward to take the blame, Fred knew. Meanwhile, of course, people would get a kick out of talking about the "effing" vandalism. And he would have to deal with what had to be Tom Walcher, heading for him. In his forties, maybe five eight, Walcher was all muscle, obvious even through his denim jacket. But the flaming hair Joan had described couldn't compete with the fire in his eyes.

"Bad enough they have to camp out in my trees," he said. "Now they're sabotaging my equipment."

"Detective Lieutenant Fred Lundquist. I'm sorry this happened, Mr. Walcher. Our crime scene people are on their way."

"They'd better be! It's a good half hour since I called you guys. You have any idea how much this is costing me by the hour?"

Not to mention repairing these babies, Fred thought. "You'll want to file the police report with your insurance company."

"No way. They'd hit me with a rate increase you wouldn't believe."

Fred couldn't argue with him. "Can you tell me what happened?"

"I've already told those two." He jerked a thumb at the uniforms.

"It's a nuisance, I know, but I need to hear it directly from you."

"We were supposed to start work at six, on another job. I've been storing my equipment here overnight." The thumb jerked again.

"Yes."

"First we saw the graffiti. Then nothing would start—we saw right away they cut all our fuel lines. God only knows what else they did that we can't tell yet. I called 911 immediately, and I've been waiting ever since. If they'd set fire to them, instead, it would've been worth filing with our insurance. We would've lost the whole damn woods by now. Of course, the kid in the oak tree would've gone up with them." The thought clearly didn't bother him as much as the money he was losing.

Maybe that's why they didn't, Fred thought, but he suspected EFF would be more concerned about trees than about Andrew. He climbed up and peered at the severed diesel fuel lines to each cylinder of the massive engines. Presumably EFF was on the same side as Andrew and Sylvia. But he didn't trust the judgment of whoever had immobilized the earthmovers. Who knew what they'd pull next time?

"We were here in five minutes, Lieutenant," Jill said when he climbed down from the equipment.

"We secured the area and took statements from all the workers," Kevin said.

Secured the area was a joke, Fred thought. The construction workers were still walking around freely, and their tracks and the many tracks left by their vehicles and by Andrew and Sylvia's supporters on previous days, not to mention Joan's and his own visit yesterday, would give the crime scene people fits.

"This is gonna cost me anyhow a day, even if there's no more damage than we can see and we can get replacement parts right away," Walcher said. "You still need my guys? It's Saturday—I'm paying them overtime for doing absolutely nothing. I need to send a couple of men up to Indy for the parts. I can't afford to wait until Monday, if the parts we need for these machines are even in stock—they're not exactly new. It'll end up costing us more time if we have to order them." He tightened his mouth and shook his head.

"They've all given their statements, Lieutenant," Kevin said. "And we have their names and addresses."

"Sure," Fred said. "They can go."

Walcher charged off toward his crew.

Time to talk to Andrew. Fred pulled out his phone and walked into the woods.

A tousled head poked out from under one of the side tarps, cell phone to its ear. "Fred? What's going on?"

"Haven't you been listening?"

"You woke me up. What did I miss?"

"Someone sabotaged the bulldozers." He gestured toward the letters.

"All ri—" He peered down at the graffiti, and his tone changed. "Oh. That's going to make trouble, isn't it?"

"We already had trouble, but up until now, you've been okay, even if you were trespassing."

"A little paint changes that?"

"It's not just paint. They did real damage—cut the fuel lines. So it's time to tell me who's working with you."

"Those guys wouldn't pull that kind of stunt."

"You sure?"

"They'd know better than to stir up that much trouble."

Maybe. After dealing with the hotheads marching on city hall last night, Fred wasn't so sure. And would Andrew have said it in different company?

"You know anyone in EFF?"

"Never heard of it. I'll ask around. Maybe someone I know knows more than I do." Andrew's refusal to rat on his friends wasn't likely to weaken. "I'll tell 'em to call you if they do."

"Right." And I'll do some checking on Matt Skirvin.

"But hey, Fred, late last night I think I spotted something you might be interested in. That's why nothing woke me up this morning."

"You don't mean you heard someone down here messing around?" But from Andrew's first reaction, he already knew that wasn't the case.

"I would've told you."

"Then what?"

"I saw flashlights in the woods. At least they looked like flashlights. Maybe lanterns. Fred, I think there's a cave out there."

"What do you mean?"

"The lights bobbed around in more or less a straight line,

or as straight as you can walk when you have to dodge trees and rocks and stuff and go up and down those hills. Then they disappeared, all of a sudden. After a while, they showed up again at the same spot and went back the way they came. Sometimes it was one light, sometimes more, but they all did the same thing at about the same place."

Could be a cave. This limestone area was, after all, full of them.

"You think they've got a still or something out there?" Andrew asked.

"More likely 'or something.' Like a methamphetamine lab. They've found them farther out in the county. Exactly where were these lights when you saw them?"

Andrew sat up and pointed into the woods. "Over that way. Want me to draw you a map?"

"Could you see that clearly?"

"It's all different at night. But the moon was full, and some of those big trees over that way are easy to spot when you've been staring at them long enough. They make good landmarks. Hang on a minute." He ducked down where Fred couldn't see him.

Looking back over his shoulder, Fred saw the crime scene techs pulling into the clearing. Good.

Andrew sat back up. "This is the best I can do. Pretty rough, but it might help." He flipped his phone shut and fed down a light rope from which a basket hung, a twin of the one Sylvia had smashed.

Reaching up for it, Fred took out a map, cleanly drawn in ink on notebook paper. Immediately the basket rose beyond his reach.

He looked up. Andrew was waving his phone again. "The X marks this tree, see?"

Fred nodded, still not oriented.

"The wiggly line is the creek over that way." Andrew pointed. "I don't think you can see it from down there, but trust me, there is one. There's a house on the other side of the creek that I'm sure you can't see. You can probably see the big old sycamore on this side, though. Splotches on the bark make it stick out. I marked it with an *S*."

Fred spotted the tree and turned the map. "Got it."

"The dotted line is where I saw the lights. Where it stops, in the middle of the map, is where they suddenly disappeared. If there's a meth lab, that's where it's hiding. It was so sudden, like a cave."

"That's great. I'll see that it's followed up on. Probably by the sheriff." Andrew was thinking like a cop. He might do more. Couldn't hurt to ask. "Any chance you'd be willing to watch the construction equipment tonight, in case the vandals return?"

"Why would our side want to help their side? I mean, I wouldn't do that myself, but you can't expect me to be sorry someone else did."

Fred scuffed his toe in the leaves. "Think about it, would you? If I could tell Walcher you were keeping your eyes open, he'd be a lot less likely to come after us to get you down."

Silence in his ear. He wished he were close enough to read the expression on Andrew's face.

"If you put it that way . . ."

"Call 911. Or me."

"Maybe. If I get enough sleep today. I sure didn't get much last night."

"Good enough. How late were you awake last night, watching those lights?"

"I didn't shine a light to check my watch—didn't want

them to notice me—but it must have been two or three by the time I fell asleep."

"And you didn't hear anyone in the clearing during that time?"

"No. If they were trying to be quiet, though, I might not have heard them."

"Maybe not, but you'd probably have seen lights around the equipment. Odds are good they came after you fell asleep. I'd go with the odds, Andrew. If you can, watch for them during the second half of the night."

"I'll try."

Better than he'd expected. Fred waved at him and walked back to the clearing.

"Anything?" he asked the two techs.

"We took scrapings of the black paint," one said. "Sorry to disappoint you, but it looks like the kind of stuff you can get in any hardware store."

Probably was. "Prints?"

"Nothing by the graffiti. They're wiped clean. Otherwise, the machines are covered with 'em."

"Mostly just smears on the fuel lines, but we got a couple of partials."

And they had partials from the Petoskey stone. Not likely to match, but worth checking.

"About a million footprints. Some in the diesel on the ground."

They'd do their routine, but Tom Walcher's crew had been tramping all over that ground this morning. Any recognizable boot prints were bound to belong to them. Fred didn't hold out much hope of finding the saboteurs by any physical evidence they'd left.

. . .

On the way to the station, he wondered, Would whoever merely cut some fuel lines be likely to kill as well? And why Sylvia? Unless they planned to blame her attack on the construction people? It was a stretch. Worth keeping in the back of his mind, though.

Even if they hadn't gone after Sylvia, what if Andrew asked the wrong person about EFF? Had he put his stepson at greater risk?

Or was he already at risk from watching the lights in the woods? Is that what Sylvia had done? If people cooking meth out in the woods realized they had a spy in the sky, had they also cooked up a way to get rid of her? And wouldn't they monitor the tree for the next sitter?

Back at the station, he called Andrew's cell phone again. "I was wrong, son. You're not a cop. It's too dangerous. Come down."

"No."

"What you're doing—"

"What I'm doing is peacefully protecting these fragile woods. I'm not hurting anything."

"You're watching bad guys who don't want to be watched."

"I told you, I won't turn my flashlight on."

"People know you're up there. Come down, Andrew. I shouldn't have asked you to stay up there and keep watch. It's not worth it."

"I'll watch EFF, the way you asked, but it doesn't make any difference. I'm staying until they drag me down."

Or knock you off, Fred thought.

"Then promise me you'll let me know the minute you see anything suspicious, no matter who's doing it."

"I promise." He said it almost too quickly.

"That means anyone, Andrew. Even if it turns out to be a friend of yours."

"I don't have friends cooking meth in the woods!"

"You don't know." Skirv had been helping him—Skirv, whose store catered to college kids and maybe sold drug paraphernalia. If he wasn't cooking meth in the woods, that didn't mean he wasn't picking some up there to pass on to the age group that used it most. Skirv was worth keeping an eye on.

"All right, I promise."

Fred hoped he would. Had Sylvia recognized someone and kept a silence she should have broken?

12

The mystery of the EFF attack on Walcher's construction equipment was only slightly less mysterious by the time the senior center's board of directors met that afternoon. Most of their meetings were held during the ordinary workweek, but Alvin Hannauer, their president, had asked to postpone this week's meeting to Saturday. With no one else in the building, Joan felt free to attend in jeans.

The noon radio news had read a statement by Earth Freedom Fighters, a new organization, it seemed, that claimed credit for "stopping the forces bent on destroying our fragile environment in their Caterpillar tracks." The overnight damage at the construction site was only the beginning, EFF asserted. It promised to do by stealth whatever was necessary "to free Earth's environment from the terrorist ravages of greedy capitalism."

"I'd like to give them greedy capitalism!" Annie Jordan, newly elected to the board, said. "If they met Cindy's grandchildren or Diane's Bert, they'd have to think twice."

"Who are they, anyway?" board secretary Mabel Dunn asked. "The announcer said they took responsibility for messing up those machines, but I don't hear them taking any responsibility at all. Seems to me they're just hiding behind speeches."

Mabel generally wasn't so outspoken. For her, this amounted to a passionate outburst. And Joan had to agree with her.

"They want the credit, not the responsibility," Alvin Hannauer said. "You're not going to see any of them coming forward in person, not like the tree sitters. Whatever you think of that protest, those kids let you know who they are. I have to respect them for that." He smiled at Joan.

Joan thought he was probably right about EFF, but she was particularly grateful for what he'd said about the tree sitters. Did he know Andrew had taken Sylvia's place? When Joan's old teacher, Margaret Duffy, had proposed her to the board, Alvin had voted to hire her. A retired Oliver College professor, he was an anthropologist, as her father had been. They'd even worked together briefly. Alvin probably had fatherly feelings toward her, but she didn't think they'd cloud his judgment in this case. Still, he didn't need to say anything. And the smile gave him away. He must know about Andrew.

"You're right," Mabel said. "And they don't damage other people's property." She, too, smiled at Joan.

The whole board probably knew, or soon would. Andrew might want them to, but Joan felt shy about telling the group, especially after what Mabel and Alvin had said. She'd thank them later for their support.

Alvin called the meeting to order then, and the subject was dropped as they dealt with the center's business.

Joan caught her mind wandering to the things that concerned her far more than the persistent discoloration of the center's roof, even after they'd installed zinc strips to prevent that staining. But she tuned back in again when the subject changed to kids who chose their smooth parking lot and ramps for skateboarding.

"They look like freaks," Annie said. "And have you heard what comes out of their mouths?"

"We all know those words," Alvin told her. "They won't hurt you, Annie."

"Maybe the words won't, but the boards can," Mabel said. "The boys jump off when they're about to fall, and the skateboards go right on. I couldn't dodge if one of those things flew at me."

"But we have to have ramps," Joan said.

"Suppose Oliver built those kids a skateboard park of their own," Alvin said.

"How much would it cost?" Annie always got to the nub of things.

Alvin pushed his wire rims back up his nose. "More than most people want to spend on what Vernon calls 'a bunch of fool kids,' but if we put it to the mayor as a safety issue for the rest of us, we might get somewhere."

"It's not just about old folks, either," Mabel put in. "Little children and babies in strollers are at risk, too."

"We need an advertising campaign," Annie said.

"We could sponsor one," Joan said. "Maybe together with the hospital. Do they keep statistics about that kind of injury?"

Alvin promised to do some checking and report back to them. "I kind of doubt it," he said. "But even a few horrid examples would say more than bare statistics."

"Nobody's going to tell you anything these days," Mabel said. "It's all I could do to fix it so my doctor can talk to my family."

Alvin twinkled at her. "You're forgetting my powers of persuasion. I know some of those nurses pretty well."

"And I could ask Fred," Joan said. "The police might have better luck with the privacy regulations."

When the meeting broke up, she called him, but skateboards were the least of her worries.

Fred picked up on the second ring.

"You all right?"

"Hassled, but yes," he said.

"I heard what happened out there this morning."

"Andrew's okay."

Bless him for answering what she hadn't asked.

"I enlisted him to stand guard tonight," Fred said.

"You what?"

"He slept through it this morning—that's another story. But if he'll be a pair of eyes for us from now on, maybe I can keep Walcher off his back."

"I don't know, Fred. . . ."

"I don't want to run him in. You have to know that. And EFF sounds like outsiders. I suppose it's possible they don't even know he's up there."

Was he whistling in the dark? He didn't sound convinced. "You don't think they'd hurt him. . . ."

"Nobody wants him hurt, least of all me. You can't even see the ropes that support him unless you leave the clearing and go into the woods. Besides, so far EFF hasn't shown any tendency toward violence. Not to people."

He *was* worried, she thought when she hung up. And she'd forgotten to mention the skateboarders. How could she think about skateboarders with visions of Andrew staring into the darkness like a cop? She hoped Fred was right. Andrew's an adult, she told herself. Other mothers' sons are cops at his age. Why was it so hard to let go?

On her walk home the sun was warmer than when she'd left. Here and there daffodils still bloomed in people's flower beds and in the middle of the grass, many tulips were out, and Virginia bluebells were showing color. Her spirits lifted.

When she walked into the kitchen, she flipped on the college radio station for *Prairie Home Companion* but heard the end of a local call-in talk show. Community reaction to the EFF sabotage was both lively and mixed. Then the show's young moderator announced excitedly that Herschel Vint of the Indiana Department of Natural Resources was going to make a statement.

Joan turned the radio up. Was the DNR going to get involved?

Vint spoke passionately about the need to preserve the forests, even while using their resources wisely. "We are often criticized for cutting any trees at all, but good forest management requires harvesting mature trees to allow the young trees beneath their canopies to grow. It's essential, though, to choose wisely what to harvest. There's a critical difference between such wise selective timbering and clear-cutting wild areas that should be protected for the common good. The construction in Yocum's Woods has no business in this fragile area. Its streams, sinkholes, and underground caverns make it totally unsuited to development, even if its wildlife were not at risk. Although the DNR doesn't own the land, and the landowner has the legal right to develop it, we must strenuously object to such an inappropriate use of our state's precious natural resources.

"That does not mean, however, that we endorse the

destructive tactics of the organization that calls itself Earth Freedom Fighters." He went on for some time about EFF.

Presumably he'd also be against shooting tree sitters, Joan thought. Actually, the DNR hadn't forced down the ones in Yellowwood State Forest a few years ago. But as Vint said, this woods was private land, where they had no authority. Even so, he'd come out on the side of the angels as far as Andrew was concerned. She wondered whether Andrew listened to the radio. Maybe someone from the group supporting the tree sit would tell him. Did those people even know one another? She felt totally isolated from the others who had backed Sylvia, except Birdie, of course, and she had no idea whether Birdie would do anything to help Andrew. She couldn't see herself asking the orchestra for help, as Sylvia had.

She fixed supper automatically, throwing her leftover broccoli into leftover chicken vegetable soup with no idea whether Fred would come home to eat it or be stuck at work. People who sneered at leftovers mystified her. Fortunately, Fred wasn't one of them. He always said homemade soup improved with age, like fine wine and beautiful women.

He rolled in while she was finishing her coffee.

"Smells good. Any left for me?" His kiss landed on her ear as he pulled a chair up to the place she'd set at the old oak kitchen table that had been her Grandma Zimmerman's.

"If you sweet-talk me like that, how can I resist?"

She drank a second cup of coffee and waited while he ate. Eventually, he began to talk.

"We've been sifting through the evidence we brought back from the EFF tampering, but it hasn't helped us at all. The work crew walked all over any footprints before we got there, and either they smudged or EFF wiped off pretty much all the fingerprints around the damage. We didn't find

much else, either. Talk about a contaminated crime scene."
He sighed.

"You said 'pretty much all'—does that mean they found some fingerprints?"

"Couple of partials. They'll probably turn out to belong to the work crew, though not to anyone who stayed around Oliver today. I sent someone out there tonight to check the guys who drove up to Indianapolis after parts. They're working overtime on repairs."

"They don't match the partials from the rock, do they?"

"No. I checked that, but it was a long shot. These guys won't stop, and we'll catch them on something. It's just a matter of time."

They were settled on the big couch together when the phone rang. "Damn," Fred said. "Probably for me."

Joan slid out of his arms and reached for it. But she shook her head at him and mouthed, "Alex."

He rolled his eyes.

"We've lost another one!" Alex roared in Joan's ear.

"Another what?"

"First violin. Birdie Eads just called me in tears. Says she can't bear to play the concert. We're in big enough trouble without Sylvia. We can't do it without her, too!"

"Alex, she and Sylvia were very close. It's understandable."

"Doesn't she know we need her now more than ever?"

And don't you know people have feelings? No, of course not. Joan kept silent, prepared to let her roar. But she wasn't ready for what came next.

"Joan, you have to go talk to her. She wants someone to hold her hand, and I can't do it. When I told her why not, she cried even more." Alex's voice turned from angry to coy. "She was probably jealous. I'm going out with Jim."

"Jim?"

"You met him. Jim Chandler, the narrator for the concert."

"You're dating Jim Chandler?" Amazing. She'd never known Alex to be interested in any man. But what did she know?

"Oh, yes," as if it were nothing out of the ordinary. "He'll be gone all day tomorrow, visiting his mother in Tell City, but tonight we're going dancing at Mike's."

"Mike's?" Joan felt like a broken record.

"Mike's Music and Dance Barn, over in Brown County. I'm going to learn to line dance." The coy voice returned. "Jim says I'll be good at it."

Your natural sense of rhythm, Joan thought. "Okay, Alex, I'll do it. You and Jim have a good time." She hung up before her laughter erupted.

"What on earth?" Fred asked.

Joan managed to stop laughing, but she felt it bubble just below the surface. "It's Alex. I think she's in love."

"Really?" His eyebrows rose. "Alex, the tyrant?"

"Oh, Fred, I don't know. It's great, really, if she's found someone. Or even if she's just having a good time. Might make her act more human to the rest of us. But I can't imagine what Jim Chandler sees in a grouch like her. He's taking her line dancing tonight, and he's already telling her about his mother, for heaven's sake—he's going down to Tell City tomorrow to see Mom. If he's talking to her about Alex, too, that could be serious."

"I assume she didn't call just to share girlish confidences with you."

"No." Remembering the problem sobered her. "She says Birdie Eads is so upset she wants to quit the orchestra—well, for this concert, anyway. We can't afford to lose her, too—she's one of our best violinists. I promised to go over and see her."

"Want me to come along?"

"You'd do that?"

"I wouldn't mind seeing her, without my cop hat on."

"But with your cop mind."

"Kind of hard to leave that behind." His eyes crinkled down at her.

"I'd love it. Let me call her. I don't think we should take her by surprise."

Of course, Birdie said, she'd be glad to see Joan and her husband.

She lived about half a mile past Joan's house. They could walk over in the crisp evening air. Joan pulled a heavy sweatshirt over her jeans, and Fred changed into khakis and a ratty old sweater. If she could ever slow life down, Joan thought, she ought to take knitting lessons from Annie and make him a new one. Fat chance, at this rate.

Birdie, filling out her bright red sweats, looked startled when she opened the door. "Oh! It's you!" Pushing her tousled blond hair back with her fingers, she was staring up at Fred. "But I thought . . ."

"This is my husband, Fred Lundquist," Joan said. "Fred, this is Birdie Eads, one of our best violinists."

"We've met," Fred said.

Must have been with his cop hat on, Joan thought.

Birdie held the door for them to enter. "Please, come in."

While they muddled their way through why Joan and Fred had different last names, Joan looked around Birdie's house. Like hers, it was a small two-story frame building in this older part of town. Hooks hanging from the porch ceiling suggested that some of the plants now crowded together on a low table near the front window soon would move outdoors. She wondered whether any of them were Sylvia's. The rest of the living room had furniture with clean, simple lines. Teak and oiled walnut predominated. Nothing fancy, but nothing cheap or cutesy. Linen hung at the windows and covered the cushions. In a corner, Birdie's violin case rested beside a music stand.

"This is beautiful, Birdie," Joan said. She sat down on a comfortable love seat next to Birdie while Fred took a matching chair opposite a fireplace with a wooden mantel and glass doors. Behind the doors, the ashes were cold, and no new fire had been laid.

"Thank you." Her hands folded in her lap, Birdie looked from one to the other.

"I wanted to thank you," Fred said. "You gave us all the information we needed, and with the key, we were able to find Sylvia Purcell's sister. She's staying in Sylvia's place now."

"I know," Birdie said. "She called me at work." Her eyes filled with tears. "But she didn't make it in time. And I never saw Sylvia at all."

"You were good friends, weren't you?" Joan said. She wasn't surprised to see the tears spill out.

"Yes. I wish she'd never gone up that stupid tree! It never would have happened if she'd just minded her own business!" Her whole face crumpled now.

Joan wanted to hug her but hesitated. "I'm so sorry."

"Everybody's sorry, but sorry doesn't bring her back! She was a good person, and it never should have happened!"

Now Joan reached out her arms. Birdie leaned into them and wept on her shoulder.

"She didn't just fall out of that tree," Fred said quietly. "You've probably heard we think someone killed her."

Birdie raised her head. "You really do?"

"Yes." He handed her a clean handkerchief and waited for her to swipe at her eyes before continuing. "If you can think of anyone who would have wanted to hurt her . . ."

Mascara streaking her round cheeks, Birdie said bitterly, "She should have stayed on the ground."

Joan waited, but Fred didn't push it. Finally, she said, "Birdie, I came because Alex told me you didn't want to play the concert."

"I can't!" Her eyes looked wild.

"I know how you feel, but we really need you."

"You don't know how I feel! Nobody knows how I feel!"

"I'm sorry," Joan said. "Of course you're right. I can only tell you that I care. And I hope you can see your way clear to playing through your grief. Is there anything I can do to make it possible for you?"

Birdie looked at her. "Anything? You mean that?"

"Yes, if I can."

"Put me in the back."

"The back?" Joan would have understood if she had demanded to sit first chair, but last? Only shy viola players vied to hide in the back, even if it meant being deafened by trumpets close behind them.

"I don't want to sit up there."

"I know Nicholas can be a pill to sit by, and I'd hate to be under Alex's nose, too, but you're too good. We don't want to bury you in the back. We need your strong playing up there to help lead the section."

Birdie's lips and round jaw tightened, and the tears threatened again. "Put me in the back."

Joan ached for her. "Of course, if that's what you really want. When you come to rehearsal Wednesday night, take whatever seat you choose. I'll fix it with the others." And have a special word with Alex and with Nicholas, she thought, to be extra sure they don't give her a hard time about it.

Walking home, Joan turned to Fred. "You think she knows something?"

"She's keeping something to herself, no question about it. Whether it has anything to do with Sylvia's death I don't know."

13

$\mathcal{B}$ack home, Fred checked his watch. "I promised Altschuler I'd watch the news tonight. Seems the mayor's going to sound off."

"The mayor? Why?"

"It's an election year. He doesn't need a reason."

"But how could he get on the news, and what does it have to do with you and Captain Altschuler?"

"That's what I'm about to find out."

She curled up on the sofa with him. Mayor Deckard's bald spot shone—he must have resisted the makeup person's ministrations, or maybe the college station hadn't offered him so much as a powder puff. The perfectly groomed young woman sitting opposite him described the EFF attack in Oliver. As she was speaking, they saw video footage of the vehicles EFF claimed to have stopped, at least for the day.

"Mayor Deckard, do you have any evidence linking this group with the murder of the protester who was sitting in an oak tree in Oliver?"

Joan caught her breath when the screen showed the platform on which Andrew was living.

The mayor didn't stumble as he so often did. His interviewer must have primed him for the question. "Not yet. At this point, the death of Sylvia Purcell must be considered totally unrelated. But we're leaving no stone unturned in our search for the person or persons who cut down this helpless young woman trapped in a tree."

Fred groaned.

"There's no doubt that she was murdered?"

"That's the premise on which we're basing our investigation. Personally, I have no doubt at all, and I am resolved to see her killer brought to justice." The mayor's eyes stared sternly into the camera, leaving no doubt about his resolve. "We hope to hear from any member of the public who can throw some light on this outrageous act."

"Thank you." The young woman looked intently into the camera. "If you have any information, please call the number shown on your screen." Joan recognized the number as the one she called to reach Fred at work.

When the newscast moved on to a story about the new college athletic director, Fred clicked off the television.

"That tears it."

"You didn't know he was going to do that?"

"No, and Warren Altschuler must not have, either. He would've warned me. You have any idea how many people will ignore that phone number and call 911 instead? It'll swamp the switchboard. Heaven help anyone with a real emergency."

"Will you have to go?"

"Maybe. They know to tell me if there's anything that sounds like a real lead. But even if there isn't . . ."

"I'll see you when I see you."

He nodded. "Could be a long night."

"Want some more coffee?"

"Not yet. I'd better grab a little sleep while I can." Pulling off his shoes, he stretched out on the sofa. He was snoring lightly before she'd begun to undress. She brought a quilt out from the bedroom to spread over him. Without opening his eyes, he smiled, burrowed into it, and in only seconds produced another gentle snore.

She climbed into bed with a book, but she wasn't even close to ready to turn out the light a few minutes later, when the phone rang. Even so, Fred beat her to it.

"I'm on my way," he said. He brought the quilt back to her. "Thanks. Gotta go."

She reached up for his kiss and soon heard the door slam behind him. She didn't mind not knowing the details he couldn't tell her. That part of the job she could accept easily. And she knew that anytime he left the house, he could be facing danger. So why did it worry her more at night?

"I'm sorry, Lieutenant," the 911 dispatcher said when he arrived. "I hated to call you. But you did say you wanted to know anything that came in about Yocum's Woods." She held out a sheaf of messages.

"Thanks, Virginia."

"No prob—" She stopped abruptly and spoke into her headset. "911 Emergency."

Fred waved at her, carried the messages up the steps to his office, and began returning non-emergency calls she had received. The first several citizens had dialed 911 not to provide new information, but to express an opinion or complain about the dirt the construction vehicles were depositing on their roads.

"They never cover their truck beds," the first man said. "Their gravel cracked my windshield. I say it serves 'em right what happened to those machines. They don't care about nobody else. Just the almighty dollar."

"I'm sorry that happened, sir," Fred told him. "Did you get his license number?"

"How'm I supposed to get his number when I can't see out the windshield?"

He had a point. "We'll try to get that stopped, sir," Fred said, already looking at the next message. "Thank you for calling."

"Do you have any idea what time it is?" an outraged woman squawked several calls later. The message said her name was Patricia Nikirk.

"I'm sorry, Mrs. Nikirk. This is Lieutenant Lundquist, Oliver Police. What's the nature of your emergency?" Knowing that there wasn't one, he wouldn't have thrown her 911 call in her face if she hadn't given him a hard time. He also knew her name, Patricia Nikirk, and her address, on the far side of Yocum's Woods from the clearing where EFF had done its damage.

"It's not my emergency, for heaven's sake. It could have waited until morning. I told the woman that. But the mayor said you wanted to hear about what's going on in Yocum's Woods right away."

"Yes, ma'am, we do. What can you tell us?" Tilting his chair carefully, he leaned back against the wall.

"I live across the crick from those woods, and I see lights out there most every night."

Fred's feet hit the floor. Hers must be the house Andrew saw from the tree. "Tell me about them."

"Not much to tell." She yawned in his ear. "Just lights, you know?"

"Where are they?"

"They move around in the woods, like someone's carrying 'em."

"How big are they?"

"How would I know?" She was getting her dander up again.

He tried specifics. "Do they look like spotlights? Car headlights? Christmas tree lights?"

"Oh, no, more like flashlights. They're white, like headlights, except there couldn't be headlights in those woods. And not so big."

"Uh-huh. And they're moving, you say. Anywhere in particular?" He pulled Andrew's map out of his desk, but it was too much to hope that this woman would be able to say anything he could connect with the map.

"I'm not for sure. But it looks like they're going to the cave."

"Cave?" Yes!

"I could show you tomorrow where it is. We used to play in it when we were kids. But I'm not going into those woods at this hour. No telling what they're doing out there."

"Can you see the lights now?" It was too much to hope.

"Not right this minute. I could when I called. They come and go. They kind of turn off when they get to the cave, but then that's what it'd look like, wouldn't it, if the people went in?"

"If we send somebody out there, you could point to where they went?"

"They can see for themselves. I'm not going out there at this hour."

"I'll report this to the sheriff, ma'am."

"I don't know why you'd drag the sheriff into it. I live in the county, but that cave's in the city."

The sheriff was going to love this one. And so was Altschuler.

"I think this may be connected to a case he's been working on," Fred said. "We try to cooperate with the county." And the state police, whose meth task force was less active than in the past.

"All right, you call him. But you tell him I'm about to go to bed. If he waits more'n a couple of minutes, I'm not coming to the door."

"We'll probably wait until morning, when you can lead us to the cave." Fred didn't give her time to object to that, too. With luck, between her information and Andrew's, they could stake out the cave Sunday night. Better get a warrant first. But they didn't need to bother a judge at this hour on a Saturday night. He left a message for the sheriff.

Nothing useful about Sylvia or EFF, for that matter. By midnight, even the crank calls had stopped dribbling in, and he went home to bed.

Leave it to Alex to dump a job on her Saturday night and then wake her on Sunday morning. Startled, Joan's first thought when the phone rang was Andrew. Her second was the urge to murder.

"Alex, it's only"—she looked at the clock—"eight o'clock in the morning."

"I know, but I forgot to mention this last night. I'm sorry. When I'm with Jim, I forget all kinds of things." That coy voice again, so totally unlike Alex. Or was it? How well did she know the woman, after all?

"And it's important enough to call me at this hour on a Sunday?"

"Well, it has to do with church."

Alex had never struck Joan as a churchgoer. They'd certainly never discussed religion. She devoutly hoped they weren't about to begin.

"Sylvia Purcell's sister wants music at her funeral. You need to talk with her."

Here we go again. "What kind of music?" And why me?

"I told her I was sure we could provide a quartet. I don't know what music she has in mind, but you have our music library. And whatever church it is ought to have something."

You'll want me to scrounge up the quartet, too.

Alex didn't miss a beat. "And you're our manager. You know who will be available. I don't even have that list."

Joan sighed. "When is the service, and where?"

"You'll have to ask her sister. Can't remember her name. Lois, Louise, Lori, something like that. It started with L, I'm pretty sure. But you have her phone number. She says she's staying in Sylvia's apartment."

"I'll talk to her. But Alex, I'm not promising."

"Thanks." She sounded so happy Joan wasn't sure she'd even heard the part about not promising.

She looked over at Fred, dead to the world beside her, and wondered what time he'd come home. Sliding out of bed, she headed for the kitchen. Sylvia's sister would probably not be in a hurry to hear from her, or would she? Did she have a family to go home to? It had to be lonely for her, holed up in Oliver with nothing to do but think about her murdered sister. Did she even know Sylvia had been killed? Had Fred told her? He'd said she hadn't made it in time to see Sylvia before she died.

Joan didn't have the heart to wake him, but a few minutes after she sat down to breakfast, she heard the shower. Maybe the smell of coffee reached him, or maybe he hadn't worked all that late, after all.

"You learn anything?" she asked him when he emerged, barefoot and wrapped in his bathrobe, his wet hair clinging to his scalp.

"Not what the mayor wanted." He settled down at the kitchen table with the Sunday paper and his first cup of coffee.

"I need to talk to Sylvia's sister," she said. "Alex says she wants some of us to play for the funeral. But she can't so much as remember her name, only that she was staying at Sylvia's."

"Linda Smith." He buried his head in the paper again.

"Thanks." Leaving him to it, she called Sylvia's number.

"Hello?" Linda sounded faintly like Sylvia, even after years of living apart. When Joan explained who she was and offered to visit in person, Linda took her up on it immediately.

This time, she drove. A few minutes later, she was ringing one of the bells on Sylvia's shabby front porch.

Linda opened the door immediately. Her face reminded Joan of Sylvia, but her hair was salt-and-pepper, and her jeans, sneakers, and plain rose turtleneck were more conventional. She held the door wide. "Come in. I'm glad to see a live human being. This place isn't very big, but it feels awfully empty without her."

Joan's eyes were drawn to the violin case in one corner. Who would play it now?

Linda shook her head, and Joan smelled lavender. "I can't bring myself to touch it. Sylvia was so proud when she finally could afford a good violin. She saved up a long time for it. Not rare or anything, but so much better than the one she learned on."

Joan knew how much difference even a good student instrument could make. Remembering its clear sound, she thought Sylvia's had cost her thousands. Maybe more than a few. From the simple furnishings of her apartment, it seemed that she hadn't spent much on anything else. "Do you play?"

"No. Our dad did, and he taught Sylvia on his old fiddle. She fell in love with the classical stuff in high school and kind of taught herself after she got out. She was the only musical one of us girls, but I have hopes for one of my children. Sit down, please."

Linda perched on the sagging sofa, and Joan chose the old oak rocker that reminded her of her grandmother. "Alex tells me you're planning a service."

"I thought I ought to." She didn't sound as if it were a matter of course.

"Was Sylvia religious?" It had never come up in the contexts in which Joan had known her.

"I don't think so. But I thought the people who knew her here ought to have a chance to say good-bye. Sylvia would appreciate having music be part of it, the kind of music she liked to play. And I'd like some old hymn tunes."

"Alex mentioned a quartet."

"Is that possible? Maybe her friend Birdie and some others?"

"I hope so. Birdie's really grieving, though. I'm not sure she could do it."

"I understand. It's probably too much to ask of anyone." Linda's shoulders slumped.

Joan melted. "I'll try hard to find you a quartet. It seems the least we could do. I thought a lot of Sylvia. She was a mainstay of our first violin section, and we already miss her dreadfully."

"I can't understand why anyone would do that to her. The police told me they think she was murdered. I'm probably not supposed to talk about it, though. I don't think they're discussing it yet."

"They tend not to," Joan said, but how could it matter, when the whole town knew? Had they told her more than that?

"I'm so far from my family. You're a good listener. I'm afraid I let it slip."

"Will your family come for the service?" Joan was glad to change the subject.

"I don't think so. The girls are too young, and my husband didn't know Sylvia all that well."

"When do you want to have it?"

"Whenever I can. They haven't told me yet when they'll release her body. And I suppose I ought to talk to a minister." Her voice rose, as if she hadn't ever talked to one before. In Oliver, of course, she wouldn't know anyone.

"It's not required, you know, unless you want it in a church. It's not like getting married, where you need someone authorized by the state."

"Really? Could we do it anywhere?"

"What did you have in mind?"

"I was thinking of that tree. Where she sat?"

A vision of Tom Walcher yelling at a crowd of mourners was almost too much for Joan.

"That would be hard, if many people came. And it wouldn't be good for stringed instruments." Though the weather was beginning to warm up these days. It might not be a problem. "Or the tree, of course."

"Oh, that's right." Crestfallen, Linda shrank into herself.

"But you could have a memorial service somewhere else with or without a minister. With or without her body, for that matter. If you don't mind cremation, you could scatter her ashes around the tree. In fact, if you didn't want to wait in town until they were ready, I suspect my son would be glad to do that for you."

Linda frowned, and Joan worried that she'd gone too far. "Your son?"

"He took Sylvia's place in the tree. He wouldn't come down, but we could ask him to scatter her ashes from up there."

"I spoke to him when Lieutenant Lundquist took me out there. I'd like that very much."

Joan wrote down Andrew's cell phone number and her own phone number. "Let me know when your plans are definite. Everyone in town knows what happened to Sylvia. I'm sure you won't have any trouble finding someone willing to do her service. Meanwhile, I'll hunt up some people to play." And hope they'll be available at the time you choose, she thought.

Her own house was empty when she returned to it. No note from Fred, but she didn't have to wonder where he'd be.

She pulled out the orchestra list and started calling to find four players. Might as well start at the top. Nicholas Zeller, concertmaster and Sylvia's stand partner, was the obvious choice to play first violin, but he was less than enthusiastic.

"You expect me to play for Sylvia? The woman drove me nuts. Always came in late, turned pages at the last possible minute, kept turning around to talk to Birdie while the conductor was talking. Alex only kept her because she played so well."

"I know she had her faults, but she's dead."

"I hear she was murdered. I can understand why."

"Nicholas!"

"Sorry." But he didn't sound sorry.

"Will you play? We need you."

"Oh, all right. You asking Birdie?"

"Yes," she said slowly. "But I don't know what she'll say.

She's still pretty broken up about her. First she didn't want to play our concert, and when she gave in, she insisted on sitting at the back of the section. I told her I'd arrange it." Kill two birds with one phone call, she thought.

"At least she's going to play. We need her. Did you find anyone to sub for Sylvia?"

"I hope so, if the woman doesn't have her baby before the concert. I don't know whether she'll play next season, but at this point, I'll be grateful to get through this concert."

She girded herself before dialing Birdie's number, but to her relief, Birdie sounded touched when she heard that Sylvia's sister had specially asked her to play at Sylvia's service. "Tell her of course I'll play. Just let me know when."

Joan felt a twinge of guilt for not mentioning that Nicholas would be playing next to her, but maybe for this purpose Birdie could face it. And not sharing a stand should help. They'd both be turning pages for themselves.

Now for a cello. Joan had taken flowers from the orchestra to the little first cellist, Charlotte Hodden, after her baby was born and had ended up taking Charlotte's cello to the violin shop for her. Since that time, Charlotte had always been particularly friendly, and she, too, agreed readily to play. That left only a violist.

For the first time, she struck out. All three violists who sat in front of her in the section begged off. The first chair was setting off on a trip and would miss the next orchestra rehearsal anyway. The second had some kind of family emergency of her own. And John Hocking, Joan's stand partner, pleaded a heavy work schedule. "It's all I can do to come to rehearsal. You can do it. Pick music you can play, and you'll be fine with a run-through beforehand."

He was right, of course. Sorting through the music, she

chose the "Pastoral Symphony" interlude from Handel's *Messiah*. Everyone would know it, and the notes weren't difficult, if they could agree how to approach them. A few simple hymns would do for the rest. Lots of Bach chorales in hymnbooks. If the service was in a church, they could use their hymnals. If not, she could borrow books from the Community Church she sometimes attended and where she and Fred had been married.

So the music was easy. But had Nicholas meant what he'd said about Sylvia? Did Birdie have a reason for wanting to keep her distance from him?

Joan couldn't believe she was even thinking such a thing. Being impatient and obnoxious didn't mean he'd kill. But someone had killed Sylvia. Could it have been for simple dislike? Did people kill for no more reason than that?

Was it true that anyone could kill? She remembered the chant her southern Indiana Grandma Zimmerman had taught her when she was a little girl. First, she'd quickly cup her hand over a spot on the wall. Then she'd say, "Poor li'l fly, sittin' on the wall. You ain't got no clothes on at all. No shimmy shirt, no pettiskirt—ooh, you must be cold! Poor li'l fly, are you sick? Poor li'l fly, are you tired? Poor li'l fly, are you goin' to see God when you die?"

Then Grandma would grin fiercely and squash the imaginary fly into the wall. "Well, see him then!"

Joan had thought it was funny. But Grandma also would wring a chicken's neck in seconds, leaving its body to flop around the backyard in a way that still turned Joan's stomach to remember. Her brother, though, had gloried in the blood and feathers. And now Joan could disjoint a chicken without wincing.

How hard would it be to let a rock fly at someone you

resented? Would you have to mean to kill her? Had it been an accident? She suspected they'd never know. Meanwhile, of course, the mayor was pressuring the police to find out, and she wasn't likely to see much of Fred until they did, or until they gave up.

She'd kept her distance from Andrew long enough not to be a hover mother. Surely Sunday afternoon would be a natural time to go out to see him. Should she call first? No, she'd just stop by. And fresh-baked cookies probably wouldn't insult him. She pulled out the chocolate chips.

14

*F*red, too, had decided to pay the woods a visit. Rather than take the quickest way, he intentionally passed the road that was within the city limits in favor of the one beyond the creek, where the woman lived who'd seen flashlights headed for a cave. The sheriff's territory, for sure, and the sheriff hadn't returned his call yet. But getting the lay of the land could hardly be called interfering on the sheriff's turf.

The woods were, if anything, denser on this side of the creek. He knew Andrew could see this far from his perch, but down here on the ground, hills and curves and tree trunks restricted his view of the occasional houses and the road itself, often to less than a hundred feet. Rounding a curve, he slowed when he saw flashing lights immediately ahead.

Two sheriff's patrol cars blocked the road, and two uniformed deputies stood talking. Beyond them a green sport-utility vehicle had missed the sharp left curve and plowed into a tree. Amazing that it hadn't tipped over, as those things were prone to do. Now Fred could see the glass strewn on the road. One of the deputies held his palm out in the universal stop sign. Fred pulled over.

The young man started toward him. Fred had seen him around the courthouse but couldn't name him.

"Oh, hi, Lieutenant. Sorry about the delay. You'll probably want to turn around."

"I'm in no hurry. Abandoned wreck?"

"The driver's still in there, but he didn't make it. We're waiting for the coroner."

Fred nodded. The sun was out, and the road was dry. On Saturday night, he would have figured the driver for drunk. But Sunday afternoon? The license plate was an Alcorn County number, so the driver probably knew the road. Speeding? But why hadn't he braked? No skid marks on the dry pavement.

"You know him?" Fred asked.

"He looks familiar, but I can't tell you why."

"Mind if I look?"

"Be my guest." The deputy stood by while Fred walked up to the SUV and peered through the broken driver's side window. The air bag had deployed, but it hadn't protected the man inside from the tree that had clobbered the left side of the car and of his head. He had stopped bleeding some time ago—the blood on his face was already congealing. Dr. Henshaw would be able to approximate the time of death from that before doing the full exam.

Fred didn't recognize him. Ordinarily, he wouldn't have hung around, but he was intrigued. Could this be one of the meth gang? Why think that, at this hour of the day? Those guys had to be long out of here. More likely someone who lived down the road.

Hearing a motor stop, he looked behind him. Dr. Henshaw, bag in hand, was climbing out of his pickup. Not a fashionable mode of conveyance for a physician, but practical for a coroner.

"What've we got here?" he asked. "Man versus tree?"

"Hi, Doc," Fred said. "The tree won."

"Looks like it." Dapper even in a flannel shirt, the doctor strolled over to the SUV. "This your case?"

"No, the county's."

The deputies advanced on him. "Citizen down the road heard the crash, and we were closest," said the one who'd stopped Fred. "He was dead when we got here."

Dr. Henshaw looked into the car. "Herschel Vint!"

"You know him?" Fred and the deputies chorused.

"Sure. He's with the Department of Natural Resources. Gave a speech the other day about the EFF business in Yocum's Woods."

"I heard that!" one deputy said. "He made it sound like the tree sitters were in the DNR's pocket."

"But he sure gave it to EFF," the other one said. "If we'd found him with a hole in his head, now, I wouldn't be looking any further than them. But this is obviously an accident."

Fred and Henshaw exchanged glances. "That's what I thought when Sylvia Purcell fell out of the tree," Fred said. "Humor me, and treat this as a crime scene."

"You touch anything yet?" Henshaw asked.

They shook their heads. "Just walked around. We could see he was dead. We waited for you."

"Good. Get the cameras out of my truck, would you?"

"How many cameras do you use?" Fred asked him while one of the deputies went after them.

"I want a Polaroid, so I'll know right away what I have."

"Sure." Henshaw wasn't a young man. Fred wondered how long it would take him to try a digital camera.

"But it's too grainy for the kind of detail you sometimes

need, so I use a couple of 35 millimeters, too. I like both black-and-white and color. We're not going to get another chance at it."

All too true. Once the body was moved, they could never reconstruct exactly how it had looked. Even if Fred had been on the spot in time to see how Sylvia had fallen, he couldn't have asked the EMTs to wait for him to photograph her. The rock Joan had spotted wouldn't have been in the picture anyway. It was a minor miracle that she'd seen the thing at all.

"I suppose you've been tramping all around here," Henshaw said almost casually.

The deputies looked stricken. "We went over to the car," said one.

"Had to make sure he was dead," said the other.

"Of course. You touch the car? Reach in through that broken window to take his pulse?"

"Yes, sir," said the first man. "But he'd already stopped bleeding. So we called you instead of the EMTs."

"Didn't even check his ID yet," said the second.

"Anybody go over on the passenger side?"

The deputies looked at each other and shook their heads.

"Good." He took shots of the ground all around the car. "I don't see much, but you never know." Then he beckoned to Fred. "Come look in this side, would you?"

Fred went over and stared down into the SUV. A small, round stone with markings like the ones on the Petoskey stone Joan had found stood out against the dark blue floor mat. "You thinking what I'm thinking?"

Henshaw was snapping pictures. "Yup."

Even at this distance and through the closed window, Fred could see a spot of what looked like blood on the stone.

. . .

Joan arrived at the woods in a car filled with the irresistible fragrance of Andrew's favorite cookies. So far she'd taste tested only two of them, unless you counted the broken ones, which she didn't. She'd always considered broken cookies low-calorie food. At the last minute, as a nod to good nutrition, she had added a bag of Fuji apples to her basket. She suspected Andrew's supporters tended toward pizza rather than fresh fruit or vegetables.

That must be one of them now. A skinny man with a scrawny mustache and a ponytail was pushing a ratty old bike out of the clearing. When she pulled even with him, she recognized him as Matt Skirvin, who was playing percussion for the children's concert. Or would, if he showed up. She never knew about Matt. He must have volunteered when Sylvia asked the orchestra for help. But he was still here for Andrew—she had to give him points for that.

"Hi, Matt."

"Joan, good to see you. I can't stay—just stopped to check on Andrew. He seems to be doing okay up there."

"Thanks."

He reached the road, gave her a wave, and pedaled off.

The clearing was empty now, the ground even more deeply rutted than she remembered. She picked her way across the ruts. Tom Walcher must have found someplace he considered safer to store his equipment. She supposed that meant he'd repaired the EFF damage—where could he have found a tow truck big enough to haul a bulldozer out of there?

She was relieved that Andrew wouldn't be on night duty anymore. How could Fred even have asked him to do such a thing?

"Mom!" His voice floated high above her.

She shielded her eyes and looked up into the sun. For the first time, Andrew wasn't sitting or lying on the platform but standing tall, hands to his mouth.

She waved the arm that wasn't carrying the basket. "Hi, Andrew!"

Her cell phone rang. She fished it out of the basket. "What's up, Mom?" he said into her ear.

"Nothing much. I brought you a little food."

"Thanks." He let down his own basket, and she transferred the apples and cookies to it, valiantly resisting the temptation to snitch one more cookie. She watched them rise safely out of her reach and was relieved to see Andrew sit down to unload them.

"Oh, wow, this is great!" His words slurred with the unmistakable sound of a full mouth. "And fresh fruit!"

"Glad you like them."

"I have a lot of time up here to do nothing," he said. "Kind of like being stranded on a desert island—I keep thinking of food I don't have and can't get. I'm not hungry, but even pizza gets a little old. I'll make these last."

"You know where to find me."

His voice changed from appreciative to resentful. "Now you're on my case, too?"

"What do you mean?"

"Fred keeps trying to talk me down."

Glad to hear it, Joan backpedaled. "You'll have to work that out with him. I've told you how I feel, but I wasn't trying anything. I only meant you could call me if you run out of cookies—or anything else, for that matter."

"Thanks, Mom. I didn't mean to jump down your throat. So, what's going on in the outside world?"

"Don't you have a radio?"

"I mean ordinary stuff."

"Not much. Fred's working overtime, but what else is new?"

"On Sylvia?"

"Yes. The mayor's putting on the pressure."

"So you're bored enough to make cookies."

"In between coming up with a string quartet for Sylvia's funeral. Her sister asked Alex, who dumped it on me. But for a change, she has a reason."

"She needs a reason?"

"Doesn't seem that way, does it? But she's fallen for a man."

"A man? Who's going to fall for Alex?"

"That's what I thought—she says he's teaching her line dancing, for heaven's sake."

He chuckled into her ear. "Maybe if she's not so frustrated, she'll let up on you guys."

"Don't count on it. Besides, when he's had enough of her, I'm afraid we'll pay." Her neck was beginning to ache from peering up at the platform at such a steep angle. She'd have to lean against something next time, if she wanted to carry on a conversation with him. "I'd better go before I get a crick in my neck."

"Thanks, Mom."

"Sure." Then she heard a car. Turning, she couldn't see beyond the clearing. "Andrew, can you see who that is?"

"It's Fred," he said, just before the Chevy pulled into the clearing and stopped beside hers. "Did he know you were coming?"

"No, but he does now."

Fred strode across the clearing and into the woods. Giving her scarcely a glance, he reached for her cell phone. "Andrew, you've got to come down."

Joan couldn't hear Andrew's answer, but Fred's face gave her the general idea.

"Because we've had another one, that's why."

"Another what?" she said.

"Another murder out here trying to look like an accident. An SUV ran off the road into a tree."

Overhead, Andrew waved his free arm.

"Because we found another Petoskey stone, the kind of stone your mom found near the tree."

Andrew was gesticulating again.

"This stone was inside the car. Looks as if someone shot it at him, made him crash into the tree."

"Oh, Fred, no!" Joan said.

"That's not for public consumption, though," Fred said into the phone. He nodded. "Right. We don't want this guy to know what we have on him. And the victim is Herschel Vint. Yes, the DNR man. You heard him, too?" He was looking up at Andrew. "Whoever did it, or why, we can't overlook the connection to these woods, and maybe, even probably, to Sylvia's death. You're at terrible risk up there, son."

All Joan's worries flooded back. Until now she'd tried to tell herself that the motive for shooting Sylvia must have been personal. Something to do with her, not with the woods or with Andrew. But whoever went after Vint, who had practically endorsed the tree sitters, had to have reasons connected to the woods or to the construction project that would destroy them.

Andrew had said he didn't want to die, but this was a cause worth dying for. Was it a cause worth giving her son for? How could he be so brave when she felt so wimpy? Or was he? Had he, too, been in denial? Would he welcome Fred's authority now? Should she beg him to come down?

"If we have to haul you down, it may kill the tree, and the trees around it, sooner than the construction crew would," Fred was saying. "You've made your point. Can't you see how much you're worrying your mother?"

Below the belt, Fred, Joan thought, but if it works, I'm glad you said it.

"I can't stay and argue." Thrusting the phone at Joan, Fred looked up one more time. Then he turned his back on them both and made his way back across the rutted clearing.

Was it her imagination, or were his shoulders sagging? She put the phone to her ear.

"I'm sorry, Mom," Andrew said, and broke the connection.

Joan called his number back, but after several rings, she gave up. Churning inside, she carried her empty basket back to the car. On the road home, she expected to come across the wrecked SUV, but she didn't see so much as broken glass. It must have happened past the turnoff to the woods. No point in going to gawk. She'd only be in the way.

All the way home, she tried to persuade herself that Fred was wrong. The only connections between Herschel Vint's death and Sylvia's were the Petoskey stones and where they happened. If someone out there with a stash of Petoskey stones was using them to aim at people, didn't it suggest a kid messing around in the woods, as the man at the center said he had done as a child? Who knew how many people this young woodsman had used for target practice or how often he had missed?

If there was such a kid, she wondered how he must be feeling now. Guilty? Proud? Both, she thought, all mixed up together.

Would two deaths convince him that it was time to stop? Or would the thrill of it all tempt him to take potshots at Andrew next, if he hadn't already? If he'd hit Sylvia, he was bound to connect with Andrew eventually. Once had been enough for Sylvia.

15

Fred's thoughts were running in a different direction as he drove to meet Sheriff Newt Inman, who'd finally called him. Although the call from the woman who thought she'd seen lights in the woods hadn't inspired the sheriff to give up his day of rest, the coroner's request to investigate a possible homicide near those very woods had. He'd leave the Vint case long enough to join Fred in checking out the woman's story, he said, but he doubted that it would come to anything. If it did, Fred could do the follow-up. The woods were, after all, inside the city.

Fred couldn't help suspecting a connection to Vint and to Sylvia. Tenuous, maybe, but it made sense to him.

Andrew had seen the lights from his perch. Had Sylvia? And had something, maybe the glint of her binoculars, given away her location to what Fred suspected were people manufacturing methamphetamine in one of the underground limestone caves dotted around this karst land? A perfect hiding place for a meth lab. Or it soon would be, when the trees were leafed out. Already, a green haze suggested they wouldn't wait much longer.

If not a meth lab, then some other illegal activity, Fred was sure. And when Herschel Vint, working for the state, had come too close, he, too, had been eliminated. Would Andrew be next? When would the risk to him in forcing him down be less than the risk of leaving him where he was?

But Fred hadn't told the sheriff all his concerns, much less floated any theories he couldn't back up. Persuading him to bring his experience with meth labs to bear on whatever was going on in Yocum's Woods would do for the moment.

When Fred pulled up, Sheriff Inman was waiting in Patricia Nikirk's long driveway, his car facing the road, motor running. Driver's side to driver's side, they rolled down their windows.

"Newt."

"Fred."

"You talk to her yet?"

"Thought I'd wait for you. Give her a good look at me." Inman removed his hat and sunglasses. As dark as Fred was blond, Inman still had a full head of wavy hair at forty-something, a trim waistline, and a sharp jawline.

A curtain flicked in the window of the small cinder block house. "She sees us," Fred said. "Let's go."

The door opened before they could knock.

"You took your time coming." Wearing jeans and lace-up boots, the wiry little woman in the doorway looked ready to lead them into the woods. She also looked to be about seventy-five. She didn't invite them in.

"I'm sorry, ma'am," Inman said. "We had a fatality on the road."

She sniffed. "Damn drunk drivers. Carry on all hours of the night. Saturday night's always the worst."

"Yes, ma'am." Inman was letting her assume that he'd meant last night.

"No witnesses? That would surprise me. People on this road are too damn nosy, if you ask me."

"We haven't found anyone yet. You didn't hear the crash?"

"All the other racket they make, I don't know how I could."

Fred doubted there had been much other racket on a quiet Sunday afternoon.

"I take it you know your neighbors farther down this road?" Inman said.

"Aren't many past me. That Jim Chandler won't be much help."

"Oh?"

"Man's a womanizer. Always in and out with some woman, usually on the pudgy side, like the one he had last night." She shook her head. "No accounting for taste."

Right, Fred thought. Alex wouldn't be mine. And if Patricia Nikirk is right about Chandler's womanizing, Alex is in for a disappointment.

Mrs. Nikirk eyed Inman's lean physique and ran her hands down her own trim jeans. "But that's not what you come about."

"No, ma'am. I'm Sheriff Inman, and—"

"I know who you are. I didn't vote for you." Crossing her arms across her flat chest, she dared him to make something of it.

"And this is Lieutenant Lundquist, of the Oliver Police," he went on in the same bland voice. "He says you've been seeing lights in the woods. Can you tell me about them?"

"Not much more to tell than I told the police last night." She nodded in Fred's direction. "These lanterns or flashlights or whatever they are, they meander through the woods toward that old cave we used to play in. Then they disappear. Directly, they come back out. I don't know what they've got stashed in the cave, but whatever it is, they don't want people to see 'em going in and out. I figure that's why they do it of a night."

"You've seen them before last night?" Inman asked.

"Sure. Thought it wasn't none of my business. But when the mayor asked people to call last night if they knew anything about Yocum's Woods and said it might have to do with that poor girl killed sitting up in the tree, I decided it was my bounden duty."

"We appreciate that," Fred said. "Last night I gathered you might be able to lead us to the cave you're talking about."

"No might about it. I know these woods like the back of my hand. Let me get my stick." She disappeared into the house, shutting the door behind her and leaving them on the front step.

When she came back, the stick in her hand was not a fragile old lady's cane but a hiker's gnarled staff. A sheltie bounded out with her.

"Heel!" she commanded, and the dog obeyed without losing any of its bounce.

Fred didn't hear the latch click when she shut the door, and she didn't turn to lock it. He could feel his eyebrows rise.

She looked up at him. "You think I'm foolish not to lock it? Nobody out here locks up. But there's a German shepherd in my house twice the size of this dog that'll make anybody breaks in sorry he tried it."

Fred hoped so.

The stick and the sheltie led the way briskly along a ridge, down into a gully, and up another ridge. Yocum's Woods didn't look all that big on a map, but the ups and downs added considerably to the distance a person on foot traveled, not to mention the energy expended climbing and negotiating the rough ground. Limestone outcroppings revealed the nature of the land beneath the trees and brush. When they reached the gully after the third ridge, Patricia Nikirk paused. Fred, wishing for a stout staff of his own, welcomed the respite, but she wasn't even puffing.

"You can see it from here," she said, pointing her stick at the side of the next hill.

Fred couldn't. The sheriff also looked baffled.

She chuckled. "That's what makes it a good hidey-hole. Come on; I'll show you."

They followed her along the gully and started up the hill.

"This is about where I see the lights disappear," she said.

And suddenly, in a tangle of rocks and tree roots, Fred saw an opening large enough to admit a full-grown man if he bent over. It was mostly hidden by brush that didn't look altogether natural. A little too convenient. The smell was powerful, as if a herd of cats had been using the woods for a litter box. That was enough for Fred. A different kind of herd had been cooking meth here, he was sure, with anhydrous ammonia one of the main ingredients. If they moved the brush away, they'd probably be able to see into the cave, but he didn't disturb it. Foot traffic had already worn enough of a path to make the entrance obvious, now that he knew to look for it.

"Well, I'll be," Inman said. "I thought I knew this area pretty well, but I didn't know this was going on."

"Surprised you, didn't I?" Mrs. Nikirk was enjoying herself.

"You smell it, too?" Fred asked Inman.

"Oh, yeah," Inman said. "This is where we back off. Nobody's going in there without protective gear. The fumes alone can be toxic."

"One of us should stay here," Fred said. "Anyone who heard us coming will take off the minute we leave."

"Or come out shooting," Inman said. "We need more backup."

Fred knew he was right.

Mrs. Nikirk had been waiting quietly, the dog lying at her feet showing no interest in the cave, in spite of the odor. "I never see anyone going in and out of a daytime," she said. "Only at night. Besides, if they heard us, they're long gone. This cave has a back door, you know. I can show you that one, too."

Now she tells us, Fred thought. But we didn't ask. Serves us right for not taking her seriously.

"Yes, ma'am," Inman said. "We'd appreciate that. Just one back door?"

"Far as I remember. Of course, I don't remember the way I used to." Her eyes sparkled.

Uh-huh, Fred thought. More likely you didn't want to show us everything you know right up front. Maybe you still don't. Some limestone caves went off in several directions, he knew.

"If they heard us, it's too late. Best we'll do is shut this one down," Inman said as they followed her and the dog up the hill. "But if nobody was home just now, we might just get lucky tonight."

Fred was glad the sheriff seemed to have forgotten about city–county boundaries. They were both following up ongoing investigations, and cooperating could only improve their chances of success. Inman was talking as if he'd be taking part in the next step.

The back door, on the far side of the ridge, turned out to be small enough that a man escaping through it would have to crawl out. Good, especially if Mrs. Nikirk wasn't holding out on them about still another opening.

They began the trek back to the road in her wake.

"I didn't mention it before," Fred told Inman, "but our tree sitter saw those lights, too."

"The woman who got shot down?"

"No. The one who took her place. My wife's son."

Inman shot him a glance. "That's rough."

"We've had some tense moments about it. He's basically a good kid."

"But?"

"I can't talk him down. Hope I don't have to haul him down. And I don't think he really knows the people he's mixed up with. He's full of high ideals, and the devil take the consequences."

16

*J*oan was glad Fred took time out for supper, but he seemed preoccupied and said almost nothing. He left again as soon as he'd eaten. "Late night," he threw over his shoulder as he walked out the door. "Gotta check out some lights Andrew's been seeing."

She turned on the porch light for the other members of the quartet, who would soon arrive to rehearse the music for Sylvia's funeral. She put four chairs in the middle of the living room under a good light and set up her folding music stand. She hoped the others would remember to bring their own. In a pinch, two players could share one. Certainly two of them could play out of one hymnal, but the Handel parts would be squeezed if more than one player used one of those little stands. Telling herself not to borrow trouble, she went to brew coffee.

Birdie Eads arrived first. "I'm glad you're doing this," she told Joan. "I've been feeling so helpless. I don't know her sister, really, don't know what to say to her."

"It's hard, isn't it?" Joan said. "But she seems to feel better since she's been able to make plans. The coroner says she can hold the service after tomorrow." He had vetoed cremation, though, Linda had said. Probably better not even mention that to Birdie. "She was in a hurry at first, but now she's decided to wait till Thursday, so that her husband and children can come."

"If this means something to her sister, then maybe it would to Sylvia, too." Birdie's eyes looked misty, but she kept it under control as she unpacked her violin and set up her stand. "Where do you want me?"

"Over here." Joan pointed to the second violin spot. "Nicholas agreed to play." She held her breath.

"I'm surprised. He and Sylvia never got along." Birdie took the second chair without objection.

"No, they didn't." *But it was you who fell apart about sitting with him,* Joan wanted to say. Not that I'd blame you.

Nicholas blew in next on a gust of wind and dumped his violin case on the sofa. He gave Birdie the merest nod. "Where's the cello?"

You're not in charge here, Joan thought. "I'm sure she'll be here any minute. I hope you remembered a stand."

Looking insulted, he pulled it from the zipper compartment of his case and set it up by the first violin chair. He started to tune.

Joan offered him her tuning fork, but he shook his head.

"I have perfect pitch. I'll show you." He tuned his A string and then hit the tines of her tuning fork on his knee and held its foot against his violin. The resulting clear tone exactly matched the sound coming from his A string.

"I'm impressed." Joan meant it. She often could come close by ear but was often a hair off. She was about to check her own strings when the doorbell shrilled again.

"Sorry I'm late." Charlotte Hodden looked frazzled by

more than just the wind. "I couldn't get the kids calmed down for their dad. Finally had to leave the baby crying. I felt like a mean mother."

"God, I don't know how you put up with kids," Nicholas said. "They'd drive me crazy."

The way you act, I don't think it's ever going to be a problem, Joan thought. But who knows? Some women like men who push them around.

While Charlotte unpacked her cello and stand and found a spot in the rug for the cello's peg, Joan passed out the *Messiah* parts and the hymnals she had borrowed. They might as well warm up on the hymns. How hard could they be?

She found out on "Abide with Me" when she automatically began playing the alto part she usually sang.

"No, that's my part," Birdie told her. "The first violin plays soprano, and the second plays alto, so the viola is the tenor."

"You'll have to bear with me," Joan said. "I haven't read bass clef since I quit piano lessons. I must have been all of ten."

Nicholas sighed. She remembered the night he had marched over to the string basses to correct their playing—and he'd been right. But that didn't make him any easier to take.

"You'll remember," Charlotte said. "Like riding a bicycle."

Easy for you to say, Joan thought. You're not playing in a foreign language. The B flat below middle C was easy enough, and she could find the next few notes by interval alone, but after that it was hard.

Right. All Cows Eat Grass, those are the bass clef spaces. I can't believe I'm going back to that. And the lines are Good Boys Do Fine Always. Miss Whatsis would be proud of me for remembering. Or shocked that I needed to.

They moved on to "The King of Love My Shepherd Is,"

a version of the Twenty-third Psalm set to an ancient Irish melody that Joan loved. This one took the tenor part down another note, to the D on the C string. If the tenors sang much lower, she'd have to play an octave higher than what was written—that C was the lowest note on her viola. She still missed many of the notes, but she was getting the hang of it. By the time they played "Lead, Kindly Light," she was feeling a tad more confident, and she almost enjoyed the moving parts of "In Heavenly Love Abiding," totally unfamiliar to her but one Linda Smith had chosen.

Last, they played "For All the Saints."

"You don't want this one to drag," Joan said. Even if she couldn't find the notes fast enough—the tenor part in this hymn was written at the bottom of the treble clef. In most of her viola music, treble clef was used only for higher notes. For some of these notes, several lines below the staff, she had to decipher lines and spaces all over again. But it went well, all things considered.

"Let's open with it," Nicholas said. Joan hesitated, but the others agreed.

They took a brief break before starting the Handel. Joan poured mugs of coffee and directed Charlotte to the bathroom. Pregnant again? Maybe, though she wasn't showing yet.

By the time Charlotte picked up her cello, Nicholas and Birdie were debating how to take the long-short-longs in the Handel. Nicholas started it. No matter what Handel had written, he said, it was established practice to play the shorts only half as long as they were written and to double dot the longs.

"In the overture, yes, but not here," Birdie objected, and the two of them went at it hammer and tongs. Charlotte rolled her eyes, but Joan was surprised and pleased to see Birdie stand up to him. Agreeing with his musical, if not his human, approach, she was relieved when Birdie caved in and they could get on with the rehearsal.

By nine o'clock, she was fading fast. They'd worked through the Handel several times, coming as close to an agreement as she thought they were capable of, and she was making mistakes she hadn't made half an hour earlier.

"Let's take it straight through from the top one more time," Nicholas said.

"Sorry," Joan said. "I can't."

"Sure, you can."

"I'm too tired. This has been quite a week for me, and I just ran out of spizz."

"Something happen to you?"

Birdie kicked him in the ankle. "She was there when Sylvia fell, you jerk. She practically caught her."

"You did?" Nicholas looked at her with new respect, and Joan could see the questions forming in his mind. But he shut his mouth.

She loosened her bow, dusted the rosin off her viola, and tucked them into her case. "I'll see you all Wednesday night. I'll sort out the bass clef between now and then, and I suppose we could run through the Handel once after orchestra rehearsal. Or during the break."

"We'll be fine," Charlotte said. "You take it easy for a few days."

"Thanks, Charlotte."

Nicholas didn't contradict her but packed up quickly and whipped out the door.

Birdie, last to leave, gave her a hug. "I'm glad you asked me. I didn't think it would help me, but it's going to."

Joan didn't want to mention Nicholas or ask Birdie to go back up and sit with him at the children's concert. Leave well enough alone, she thought. But she no longer felt so worried that Birdie would back out. She returned the hug and heaved a sigh of relief when the door finally shut behind her.

If only she could feel sure Andrew would be safe. The music had pushed that worry out of her mind for a while. She considered phoning him. He might hang up on her again. Or maybe he was already asleep out there in the dark.

But if Fred expected to be late checking on the lights Andrew saw, Andrew must have seen them at night. And it wasn't ten yet.

It's just my stupid pride, she thought. Curling up on the big sofa, she called his cell phone.

He picked up on the second ring. "Hello?"

"Andrew, it's Mom." She held her breath.

"Hi, Mom," he said as if nothing had happened. "What's up?"

"Not much. Practiced some music for Sylvia's funeral. Linda wanted a quartet."

"When is it?"

"Thursday morning. I don't suppose you'll come." She kept her voice light.

"Not unless they drag me down. But I'll think of her then."

"You see Fred?"

"Tonight?"

"He mentioned checking out some lights you saw."

"Really. I wasn't sure he believed me."

"You think they had something to do with Sylvia?"

He was silent for a few moments, and she thought she could hear wind in the trees over his head. "I suppose it's possible."

"Andrew, don't let them hurt you!" It burst out of her in

spite of all her promises to herself not to voice her worries to him.

But he didn't fuss at her, and he didn't come back with some flip response. "Not much I can do if they're determined. But I'm keeping a low profile. And I'm not using so much as a flashlight myself. I don't want to remind anyone that I might be up here watching."

"Good. The paper hasn't mentioned you. It's as if when Sylvia died, the tree sit ended. You think they don't know?"

"They didn't get it from me. Still, it's no secret. And you can see the platform a long way off. I'll be glad when the trees finally leaf out."

"Andrew, how long do you expect to stay up there?" When did oaks and maples and such leaf out, anyhow? She couldn't remember.

"I don't know yet. So far, no one else is offering to take over."

And you'll stay until someone does? That's not the way you made it sound at first. But she held her tongue this time.

"Mom? You mad?"

"Not at you."

He was right, though. The thought of Andrew up there, unable to defend himself against a sneaky assailant, filled her with rage.

"I feel that way about the guy who got Sylvia. If he showed up, I'd drop out of this tree so fast. . . ."

"You really cared for her."

"I don't know. Maybe I would have. I'll never find out now, will I?"

The sadness in his voice gave her new reason to rage against Sylvia's killer. In taking her life, he had stolen not only her future but also the futures of others who might have become involved with her. Never mind whether Sylvia would have made a good life partner for her son.

But none of that came close to the rage she felt at whoever would endanger Andrew himself.

And who would? she wondered. Tom Walcher, the angry construction boss? If Fred was right, and she believed he was, someone had intentionally caused Vint's accident—almost certainly the same someone who had caused Sylvia's fall. Bert, of the fierce temper? She needed to meet that man. The people Fred was checking out tonight, whose lights Andrew had seen? Whatever they were doing in the woods, it seemed they didn't want witnesses.

"Mom? You still there?"

"Sorry. I was thinking."

"Me, too. Did Fred mention whether he ever got Sylvia's things from Skirv? He carried off her sleeping bag and coat and stuff that was up here."

"I can ask him. How well do you know Skirv?"

"Not too well. He's kind of strange. You always have the feeling he has some other agenda."

"I know."

"You know him?"

"Sometimes when we need an extra percussionist, Matt Skirvin plays. If I'm lucky. He's good, but totally unreliable. Never bothers to cancel. Never even makes excuses. Seems to me he shows up when he feels like it and lets us go hang when he doesn't. So I try not to depend on him. I was surprised to see him out there this afternoon. I'll have to tell Fred I have his phone number."

"Good." He yawned audibly.

Even over the phone, it was catching. Fighting back a yawn of her own, she said good night and looked for her orchestra list to write Fred a note with the number before sleep made her forget.

Matt Skirvin was still out there checking on Andrew, or that's what he said, anyway. Why had he volunteered for Sylvia in the first place? Andrew claimed not to be in love with her, and Joan was inclined to believe him. But Matt was older, probably older than Sylvia. Was *he* in love with her? Did she turn him down? What if he thought she and Andrew were a couple? Would he have reacted like Wozzeck, in the opera? "If I can't have you, then nobody will!" he tells Marie. And then he stabs her.

Had Matt killed Sylvia? And was he waiting for his chance now to take revenge on Andrew?

She shook her head, hard. Don't let your imagination run wild, she told herself. Just give Fred the phone number. But her hand shook while she wrote it down.

17

Joan had read most of the paper over breakfast by the time Fred, freshly showered but bleary-eyed, dragged himself into the kitchen.

"Herschel Vint's obituary is in already," she told him. "And an article about the crash, with a picture of the car. Nothing about its being a suspicious death."

"Mmm." He poured himself a cup of coffee.

She stuck some bread in the toaster, passed him the front sections of the paper, saving the funnies for herself, and waited.

Eventually, he told her about staking out the meth lab. "We waited till midnight, but not a soul showed. Finally, we went in. They'd been cooking meth, all right. There was plenty of evidence left behind, even some of the finished product, but they were out of there. Either someone warned them, or someone was in there when we found the place earlier in the day, and they cleared out in a big hurry."

"Too bad." Joan poured him another cup of coffee. He was going to need it. She hadn't heard him come in, but he couldn't have had much sleep.

"At least we shut it down. Sheriff Inman will have someone check on it from time to time, but I don't expect them to risk going back."

"I guess that's something."

"Yeah, but not enough. They could pop up anywhere. People have been known to cook meth out of car trunks, would you believe that? It's harder to get the ingredients than it used to be. Maybe that'll help."

"They're expensive?"

"Not for these guys. Farmers use tanks of anhydrous ammonia in fertilizer, and meth cookers would steal it." He laughed. "But with this new GloTell stuff, they can't get away with it as easily."

"What's GloTell?"

"A new pink dye developed specially for this purpose. Even if you wash it off, it shows up in ultraviolet light for days. If you touch it, it stains your hands pink, and if you use it in methamphetamine, it turns the meth pink. People who snort it or shoot it end up pink, too. They're not going to want to buy meth made with stolen ingredients. But it's so addictive, we may even catch a few that way."

He really was wound up. She wondered whether the coffee had been a mistake.

"The saddest thing we found out there was a child's raggedy teddy bear. Can you imagine cooking that stuff in front of little kids?"

She couldn't. She wondered how many children of the people who used the stuff were affected, too. Probably plenty.

"Inman says it's not unusual to find kids at these labs when they make arrests. They have to hose them down to decontaminate them and throw away all their things—teddy bears, blankets, clothes, such as they have—before they can put them in foster care."

"The poor things!"

"You have any idea how many kids end up in foster care after their parents are arrested for meth? Or how sick they sometimes get?"

She shook her head.

Fred drained the cup and stood. "The good news is that Andrew's no threat to these guys now."

She'd forgotten her own child. "That's right! So they're no threat to him. But we don't know . . ."

"No, we don't. It might not have had anything to do with them in the first place. If I were Andrew, I'd get the hell out of that tree now."

She looked him in the eye. "Whenever anything you're doing is dangerous, you quit?"

His eyes crinkled down at her. "Yup."

Joan sighed. "I guess if I can let you go to work, I ought to be able to let him do what he thinks he has to do."

"Is it so hard for you, what I do?" He wasn't teasing now.

"Sometimes."

He reached across the table to her, but when the phone rang, he stretched out a long arm to the wall near the stove instead and listened a moment. "I'll be right there."

"See?" She smiled at him. It's really all right, she wanted that smile to tell him, because it really was. Just hard sometimes.

"Don't worry. That was Johnny Ketcham. I'm needed at the station house, but no one will be at my throat."

"You're coming home tonight?"

"Best I know." It was as close as he ever came to promising.

"And you saw the phone number I left on your dresser?"

He patted his breast pocket. "Got it, thanks. I don't expect to find much of anything in Sylvia's things, but it can't hurt. What do you know about that guy, anyway?"

"Matt Skirvin? Nothing much." And I'm not going to tell you what I was thinking about him last night.

"You've met him?"

"Oh, sure. He fills in on percussion for the orchestra, when he feels like it. Trouble is, I never know when he's going to feel like it."

"Andrew called him weird."

She thought it over. "Maybe. Or just flaky. He rode his old bike out there yesterday afternoon to check on Andrew."

"He ever sound a little wild?"

"He doesn't say much at all to me. Maybe to the other percussionists. You think he's done something?" Maybe she should tell him, after all.

"Probably not." He kissed her and went out whistling Scott Joplin's "The Entertainer."

Joan put the breakfast dishes in the sink and decided not to carry a brown bag to work. This was one day she wanted to hear the gossip around the lunch table.

She didn't have to wait for lunchtime. When she arrived, the bridge players were shaking their heads over the meth lab, which they'd heard about on the radio.

"It's not the first one in Alcorn County," Berta Hobbs said. "But it's the first one inside Oliver."

"Wouldn't be if they hadn't annexed so far out," said her partner, Ora Galloway, who'd been playing at the senior center since his wife of almost sixty years had died. "Makes no sense at all to say Yocum's Woods is in town."

"It does when you build apartments out there," Berta said. "Think of the property tax."

"They're supposed to be for low-income people," Ora countered. "Tax on new construction like that will drive up the rent."

"Not with government subsidies," Berta said firmly. "One heart," she bid.

"You think those apartments will attract more drug dealers?" said the opponent to her left. "Pass."

"Bound to," Ora said. "You cram that many poor people together like that, you'll see. Two clubs."

Joan hung up her jacket and slid her purse into her desk. At a table outside her office, Mabel Dunn and Annie Jordan were putting together the newsletter she had produced on her computer.

"I'm glad Cindy Thickstun can't hear them talk like that," Mabel said, folding newsletters before passing them to Annie to staple. "She'd really lay into them. She's so proud of her daughter, even if having them all at her house is hard on her."

Annie sniffed. "Cindy always did think her children could walk on water. But I wonder if she'd be in such an all-fired hurry to get those grandbabies out if she thought they'd run into drugs where they were going."

Joan climbed the steps to the room where the morning exercise group was gathering. Still waiting for their peppy young leader to arrive, they were talking about Herschel Vint.

"Nice young fellow," one man said. "Helped me when I had to sell off that stand of timber. The state wanted to buy it, and Herschel told me how much I could hold out for. The state got the woods it wanted, and I got a fair price. He didn't have to do that."

"He left a wife and three boys," a woman said. "I don't know why they had to print that picture on the front page. Why couldn't they think of those poor children? Bad enough they had to lose their daddy—they shouldn't have to see that car with the window all smashed in. Enough to give 'em nightmares."

"I don't know," Margaret Duffy said. "Kids sometimes find the truth easier to bear than what they conjure up in their imagination." Margaret would know, with all her years of teaching.

"Like murder?" someone said.

Joan's antennae rose. Why was anyone talking murder? Nothing in the story had suggested anything but a traffic accident.

"Maybe," Margaret said. "After that speech he gave, I expect EFF thought about it a time or two."

"He laid it on the line about them, didn't he?" The man who'd sold the woods chuckled.

"But I'd think the people who want to build that apartment would have been even more upset," said Alvin Hannauer. "He as much as said they were raping the land. Didn't claim to be speaking for the DNR, either. Just stuck his neck out. If someone murdered him, now, I'd look in that direction."

"Nobody murdered him, Alvin," Margaret said. "He hit a tree."

"On a sunny Sunday with a dry road, right." He gave her a professorial glare, which he'd probably used on Oliver College students who challenged him in class.

As Joan remembered, Margaret's sixth-grade classroom glare was even fiercer, but she didn't use it now. Instead, she raised her eyebrows. "You really mean that?"

"I hope the police are considering the possibility." He glanced over at Joan, who concentrated on not letting her face give anything away. Fred told her the little he did only because she had proved her ability to keep her mouth shut. "And I'd think first of the construction people. That's who's losing money every day they can't start this project."

"But why take it out on Herschel? All he did was make a speech." The man who was grateful to him had a point. "Nothing like those EFF people, who wrecked the machinery. Or the tree sitters. Isn't a young man up there now?"

A couple of people shushed him, and Margaret, standing beside him, spoke quietly into his ear. He looked at Joan and quickly looked away again.

But he was right. Why would someone go after a man who did nothing more than make a speech, and not Andrew? Or had Vint gone into the woods at the wrong moment and perhaps seen the killer getting ready to go after Andrew? Or seen something that linked him to Sylvia's death? Another Petoskey stone, perhaps? Would Vint have known one, if he'd even been able to see it? A slingshot? That would be easier to see and to recognize than a little rock. Matt Skirvin had been in the woods on Sunday. Had Vint seen him? Had killing Vint distracted him from his anger at Andrew? If so, for how long?

Or had Tom Walcher gone after both Sylvia and Herschel Vint? Walcher was plenty angry at Sylvia when he poked Andrew in the chest for supporting her. The way he'd seen it, she was endangering his livelihood. And Vint had accused the whole construction job of raping precious natural resources. Just how explosive was Walcher?

An unusual noise jerked her out of her thoughts. Someone was shouting downstairs. People generally didn't raise their voices at the senior center unless someone's hearing aid battery needed replacing, but these shouts sounded angry. She'd better find out.

The man in work clothes towering over Mabel and Annie with clenched fists wasn't especially tall, but he made up in decibels what he lacked in inches. He was twenty or thirty years younger than most of the center's regulars. Could he be the son of someone who usually participated in its activities? Or in the adult day care next door?

"Don't tell me she's not here! I got a right to see her!"

Joan, coming down the stairs, was at less of a disadvantage than the women sitting at the table. She said more calmly than she felt, "Can I help you, sir?"

"You damn well better! These—these women tell me my wife's not here, and I don't believe it for a minute!"

Annie shook her head and spread her hands to say, "I don't know anything about it."

"Who is your wife?" Joan asked.

"Diane Barnhart. Where are you hiding her?"

Diane—who cleaned for Annie and who needed the work the new construction would bring her. Then this must be Bert, the unemployed husband with a reputation for flying off the handle.

Joan drew herself up to her full five feet four and wished she hadn't shed her professional-looking jacket. The bridge players had fallen silent. She hoped Ora Galloway wouldn't try to jump to her defense.

"Mr. Barnhart, I'm Joan Spencer, the director of the Oliver Senior Citizens' Center. I assure you we're not hiding your wife."

"That Annie Jordan"—he jerked a thumb in her direction—"Diane said she'd be here working for Annie."

"Nobody works for Annie here. When Diane works for Annie, it's at Annie's house, not here." Inspiration hit, and she went on as if it were the most natural thing in the world,

"I assume you came to pick up her paycheck." On Monday? Could be. Annie probably paid Diane every time she worked.

"She tell you that?" he growled.

"No. I haven't seen her." Never met her, for that matter. "And I don't know where she's working today." Or whether she's working at all. Maybe the poor woman told him some story to get out of the house and away from him. "But if you could use a little ready cash, we might have a job for you."

Suspicion was written all over his face. "What kind of job?"

"It's not much, and I'm sure it wouldn't take you very long, but it would help us. The railings on the stairs and the ramp to the front door have rusted. They need to be sanded and painted with that paint that turns rust into metal. Then tomorrow, a coat of green paint to match the outside trim. Actually, we have several small jobs that need doing. It's hard to get someone to do that kind of upkeep. Of course, if you don't have time . . ."

"I wouldn't mind taking a look. Since I'm here 'n' all."

"Wonderful. Let me get my jacket, and I'll show you the railings and where we keep the things you'll need. I think we still have enough paint." If not, she could send him to pick up some more. That would give her time to think of the other jobs she'd just invented. But it was true about the railings, and from what Annie had said, Diane and her husband were willing enough if they could find work. The center could afford it, she knew, even though she found volunteer labor when she could.

When she came out of her office with her jacket, Bert was leaning against the wall watching the card players, and the buzz of conversation in the room had returned to its usual level. He was clean and sober; she gave him that. Needed a haircut, but so did half the men on the college campus. His denim jacket and jeans were less frayed than most students' clothes. He straightened and came toward her.

"I appreciate this, Miz—what did you say your name was?"

"Spencer, Mr. Barnhart."

"Sounds like my old man. I go by Bert."

"Bert, you can call me Joan. We're pretty informal around here." She turned to Annie and Mabel. "If Fred needs me for anything, I'll be checking the railings and then down in the basement getting paint. Back in a few minutes." Not that she was afraid of him, but it couldn't hurt.

Annie nodded emphatically. "I'll be sure he knows." And she'd be counting the minutes, Joan was sure.

She didn't care whether Bert got the point of that exchange. He followed her outside and ran his hand along the rusted spots as if he'd done that kind of work before.

"Not too bad," he pronounced, and eyed the length of the railing. "I ought to be able to do it this afternoon and finish the green in the morning."

She led him down the basement stairs, where he checked the paint like a pro and found the wire brush and scraper for the rust. "I have what I need for today," he said. "But there's not enough green paint. You want me to pick some up, or will you do it?"

Joan had walked to work, as usual, but she could buy it on the way into work the next morning. The only paint store in Oliver wasn't far from the center. "I'll do it."

She left him to it, transformed from the man who had raged into the center only a few minutes earlier. Could Bert in his fury have attacked someone he thought threatened his livelihood? She supposed he could, but it was hard to imagine him doing it from a distance. Still, what choice would he have with someone seventy feet up in a tree?

18

When Fred arrived at the station house, Johnny Ketcham was waiting for him and followed him into his office.

"There's good news and bad news." He leaned against the door.

Fred sat in the old swivel chair, willing it not to dump him. "I'll bite. What's the good news?"

"We got a match on the prints they lifted from Vint's car. They match the partials from the stone that hit Sylvia."

"Great." Fred waited.

"Name's Ward Utterback. Arrested in Benzie County, Michigan, fifteen years ago and charged with assault, but he got off and seems to have kept his nose clean since. Not so much as a parking ticket."

"So where is he now?"

"That's the bad news. Vanished. No sign of him in Michigan or Indiana—and not in any of the other states we've been able to check so far. No driver's license, nada."

"Could have changed his name. What does he look like?"

"Hard to tell. The photo is blurry—seems they had a leaky

roof right over where a lot of those old records were filed. And he's sporting a full beard that hides most of his face."

"Scars, tattoos?"

Ketcham shook his head gloomily. "Caucasian, five nine, brown hair, brown eyes, and that damn beard."

"How old is he?"

"Forty this year."

"He could look like half the men in this town, not counting the students."

Ketcham nodded.

"And he may have it in for tree people, or we may have a serial killer on our hands, just getting started."

"The other good news—"

"There's more?"

Ketcham grinned. "Captain Altschuler wants you to report to him ASAP. That's why I called you."

"That's good news?"

"Yeah, because it's you he wants, not me."

"Very funny." Fred sighed. "Keep on it. See what else you can dig up about this Utterback character." Ketcham would already have people working on it, he knew. Fred stood up and girded himself to face his chief of detectives.

Altschuler, his face as rumpled as his shirt, waved Fred into his office. His desk and the table behind it were piled high with papers. "Fred, just the man I wanted to see. Pull up a chair."

Might as well be comfortable while Altschuler flew off the handle. Fred eased himself into the twin of the leather chair in his own office, the one Altschuler liked.

"How did the stakeout go last night?"

Last night felt like years ago. "It was a meth lab, all right, but they'd already taken off. In some hurry. We found enough to suggest that they'd been there that day. So the best we can say is that we closed that one down. Sheriff Inman's coordinating with the state police. He'll keep an eye on it from here on. Easiest access is from the county side of the woods."

"Good, good."

"He'll probably take credit for it, of course."

"Let him. We'll get out the word that we're cooperating. Make us all look good."

"I agree." And we won't tie our people up, hiking in and out of those woods.

"So where do we stand on Purcell and Vint?"

"We finally have an ID on the prints from Vint's car, and they match the partials we had on the stone we think hit Sylvia Purcell."

"And?"

"It's a man with an arrest record for assault in Michigan, but he wasn't convicted and hasn't been seen since. White male, age forty, brown hair and eyes, five nine, no distinguishing marks. The photo's fifteen years old, water damaged. And his face is hidden by a full beard."

"Name?"

"Fifteen years ago he went by Ward Utterback, but there's no recent record of him by that name in Michigan or Indiana. Ketcham's keeping on it."

"Could be anybody. Could be Ketcham."

Now Fred grinned. "If we didn't know he'd lived here all his life. Or Newt Inman. Not you or me—I'm too tall, and you're too old."

"Thank God for small favors."

Fred crossed his legs. And that Altschuler was feeling so mellow today.

"Keep me informed," the captain said.

"I will. You want to release the name?" Fred hoped not,

but if Altschuler was going to do it, he'd rather know than be blindsided.

"I don't see any reason to. Do you?"

"No. At this point, he doesn't know we know it. So far it hasn't occurred to him to wear gloves. We can only hope he'll continue to be that confident—or that stupid."

"Nobody who's covered his tracks that well is stupid."

"We don't know that he changed his identity. He could have been anywhere. We haven't had time to check all the other states, much less Canada. It's a quick hop from Detroit to Windsor, Ontario, and you don't need a passport."

"That where he was arrested? Detroit?"

"No, Benzie County, over by Lake Michigan, pretty far north in the Lower Peninsula." Why did he remember where Benzie County was? One more bit of usually useless information stashed in his brain. "That figures, if he used a Petoskey stone. I just meant that Canada was close to Michigan. Who knows where else he's been?"

"Or who'll get it next."

"Yeah." That was the damnable part of it, Fred thought when he was back in his own office. With so little to go on, they might not find out anything more until he killed again, if he did. Unless Mr. Utterback became overconfident. He was a good shot, that was for sure.

He'd been in Michigan long enough to establish an identity there when he was arrested. But it made more sense to change his identity after he had a record than before.

Trouble was, plenty of people moved around in this day and age, and residents of college towns were more mobile than most. Fred checked his watch. Late enough to try the elusive Matt Skirvin in his shop. He wondered how old the man was. Joan would know. He picked up the phone.

For a change, she answered her own phone. "I'm glad you called," she said, but she sounded more anxious than glad.

"You all right?"

"Now I am."

"What does that mean?"

"We had a firsthand demonstration of Bert Barnhart's temper. For a little while there, I thought he was going to tear the place apart."

"Who's Bert Barnhart?"

"I thought I told you about him. His wife cleans for Annie Jordan, and Bert's run out of unemployment. They were counting on getting the contract to clean those apartments, but of course that's been delayed. They're really up against it, Annie says."

"That's rough, but why was he mad at the senior center?"

"He got the idea somehow that his wife was working here, and when we told him she wasn't, he thought we were lying. I'd heard he had a hot temper and a short fuse, and it's true."

"You threatened to sic me on him?" He wouldn't put it past her.

"No, I offered him a job." No longer anxious, she sounded amused.

"You what?"

"He's outside now scraping the rust off our railings before he paints them. I figure I'll pay him by the day. I can cover this job out of petty cash, and then, if he does good work, I'll ask the board to consider hiring him on a regular basis as our handyman. I'll admit I was a little nervous at first, but the minute he saw I was serious, he turned from nasty to businesslike. And I signaled Annie to call you if I got in trouble."

A soft touch, but with a practical side to her, that was his wife. "Do you need a handyman?"

"Well . . ."

"That's what I thought. So why are you glad I called?"

"I'm always glad; you know that." There was the flirting he'd missed at first. "But I've been wondering about old Bert. The way people talk about him, it occurred to me that he might be your man."

"Old Bert? How old?"

"That was a figure of speech. He might be my age. Maybe not. Why?"

Joan was forty-three, almost forty-four.

"Humor me. What does he look like?"

"When he's not throwing a tantrum, you mean? Pretty average. Average height and build, hair about like mine." Medium brown, in other words. "I didn't notice his eyes. He needs a haircut, but he was clean. Needs a dentist, too—poor people often do."

"If you can, find out how long he's lived around here."

"You know something." It wasn't a question.

"Maybe. And Joan, don't talk about it. Just find out what you can. Get other people to talk."

"I'm good at that. Annie's my best source."

"And tell me more about Skirv. How old would you say he is?"

"I have no idea," she said promptly. "He has that weather-beaten look that makes it hard to tell."

"Younger than Andrew?"

"Oh, I don't think so. And probably not as old as you."

So, between midtwenties and late forties. "Is he tall? Short?"

"Sort of average. But thin. So's his hair, but he ties it back in a ponytail, and he wears a mustache."

"Good enough." And Ketcham said he'd been out of town for about ten years.

As usual, she wasn't pushing him. He knew some cops whose wives chafed at being left out of what they were working on. Maybe it was those years as a minister's wife that had prepared her. He didn't know. Or maybe the minister was lucky from the beginning, too.

"Thanks, Joan." He hung up and told Ketcham where he was going.

"You want me to come along?"

"No, I'll just stroll over to pick up whatever Sylvia left in the tree."

Unlike Joan, he needed to drive to work. When he got the chance to walk during the day, he grabbed it. Skirv's Stuff was only a few blocks from the police station, on a side street near the campus. Ready to poison young minds, Fred thought. Or help kids find bedspreads with pizzazz. A collection of bright cotton spreads flapped in the sunshine outside the store. Tie-dyed, some of them, and batiks and colorful Indian prints, probably made in China these days. The selection would increase, he knew, when the new crop of students arrived in the fall.

The window was filled with a motley assortment of antiques, collectibles, and just plain junk. Mostly junk, he thought, but he could see the appeal of a worn wooden rocking horse, an almost hairless doll in a wicker buggy, and a beaded Indian headdress, genuine or not. A layer of dust suggested that they were window dressing, not merchandise Skirv ever expected to unload.

In the dim light inside the store, he had no trouble recognizing the man from Joan's description. His drooping mustache as thin as his hair, Skirv stood behind an old-fashioned glass counter framed in oak. Incense burning on the counter didn't succeed in disguising an illegal smell that didn't interest him at the moment.

"Help you?" Right size, and his eyes were brown.

"Mr. Skirvin? Lieutenant Fred Lundquist." He showed his shield.

Skirv tensed but stood his ground, his hands spread on the counter.

"Andrew Spencer said you were good enough to rescue Sylvia Purcell's belongings when he took her place." Fred could see the man relax his guard ever so slightly. "Do you still have them?"

"Sure. They're in the back. I didn't know what to do with them when I heard . . ." He called into a room behind a curtain that looked like one of his Indian bedspreads, "Paul, bring out that bag of stuff from the tree sitter." Turning back to Fred, he said, "Poor girl. Did they ever find out who did it?"

"We haven't given up yet."

"I hope you get the bastard. I mean, she was helpless up there. No way to defend herself. How's Andrew doing? He seems like a good kid."

"All right, far as I know."

"You know his mom manages the orchestra? That's how I knew Sylvia, from the orchestra. God, it sounds awful to say knew."

"How close were you?"

"We weren't. But you had to respect what she was doing."

The bedspread curtain behind him opened, and a teenager even thinner than Skirv himself—his son?—appeared with a black plastic garbage bag slung over his shoulder.

"Give it to him," Skirv said, making no move to touch the bag. "Or better yet, why don't you carry it out to his car?"

"I left my car at the police station," Fred said.

"No problem," Skirv said. "He can walk over there."

Damn, he'd hoped to see Skirv touch it. The man was bare-handed, even touching the glass counter, but Fred had no grounds on which to lift prints from the counter. Odds were good he'd used gloves when he brought the stuff back. It would have been perfectly natural.

Fred looked around for something he might conceivably be interested in buying, something that would take a fingerprint. That glass paperweight over there, maybe, the globe with the miniature snowman and children inside. He peered at it.

"You interested in something?" Skirv asked.

"My mom collects those things," he lied. "You shake it and it snows, right?"

"Sure. Go ahead; try it."

Reaching for it, Fred managed to knock it off the table crammed with junk he knew his mother would never have in her house. "Sorry! I hope I didn't break it."

"Doesn't look like it," Skirv said. He leaned over the counter but made no attempt to pick the globe up.

Fred bent down. "Guess not. Shook up the snow, though. How much you want for it?"

"There's a sticker on the bottom," Skirv said helpfully, still keeping his hands to himself.

Fred resigned himself to picking the thing up. Holding it by the edges of the bottom, he upended it. "Twenty bucks. That's pretty steep."

Skirv shrugged. "There's a market for those things."

"I suppose so, but I don't think Mom would want me to

pay that much. How about a glass vase? Or something crystal? She's big on those things, too. She likes milk glass."

Skirv waved at the table the paperweight had come from. "What you see is what we've got." The voice was friendly enough, but no way was Skirv going to hand sell anything to a cop. Meanwhile, young Paul stood holding Sylvia's bag.

Fred gave up. He'd have to send over someone whose demeanor didn't scream cop. Jill Root in plainclothes could pass for an undergrad if Skirv didn't know her, and she could probably pull it off, if she didn't take Kevin along. Maybe Joan—Skirv obviously had no idea she was his wife. He could send Jill with her, to preserve the chain of evidence. At the moment, he thought, Skirv was looking very good for it. And Joan had put him out there on Sunday. With his guard down, he might just give them what they needed.

"Thanks, anyway. And thanks for dealing with this. I'll tell Sylvia's sister." He could smell the mildew through the bag. No wonder, closed up in there for days. Unlikely they'd find anything useful, but as soon as the boy left, he'd get someone to take it into the station. "Okay, son, let's go."

19

Some time later, Joan was thinking about Fred's call. No question about it, he knew something. Asking how old Bert and Skirv were had to mean that he suspected someone in a particular age bracket. But why would that be the only thing he'd know about the man? He must be thinking of a man—he'd asked about Bert but not about his wife. Of course, she'd already told him about Bert's temper. But why had he asked about Matt Skirvin? Did he think Skirv had some underhanded reason to take Sylvia's things when Andrew went up the tree? Why would her killer want to be bothered with her stuff?

She'd met Matt out at the woods the day Vint was killed. Was his visit to Andrew window dressing, an alibi, in case someone connected him to Vint? But if jealousy wasn't his motive, why would he have it in for Sylvia and the DNR man?

"Good job, partner!" At the bridge table, Ora congratulated Berta on making four hearts. "You saw right through them."

Joan smiled her own congratulations, but her thoughts kept racing.

Had Sylvia seen something from her platform? Was that why she was killed? Was her killer afraid she'd left some evidence that could get him in trouble? If Skirv had killed her, he would have disposed of anything incriminating. A stone, maybe, if one had landed on the platform, and if he'd spotted it, of course. But if he was innocent, he might unwittingly have preserved evidence that would help find the man who had done it. She wished she could go along with Fred when he found out.

Skirv had volunteered for Sylvia and then for Andrew. Had he done it to get close to them? So they wouldn't notice him if he came near enough to hurt them?

Looking out her office window, she watched Bert, who seemed to be doing a workmanlike job on the railings. Briefly, he stopped scraping rust to greet someone coming to the center. But when the person—Joan couldn't see who it was—stayed to chat, Bert went back to work. He wasn't slacking off. Maybe hiring him would work, at that.

The door opened, and the person Bert had been talking to turned out to be Fred. Annie Jordan, still folding newsletters, greeted him. "She's in her office—the door's open. You making any progress on what happened to Sylvia Purcell, poor dear? We've all been talking about Herschel Vint, too."

"I'm glad to see you." Joan raised her face for his kiss. "You came to look Bert over for yourself?"

He closed the door. "That's one reason."

"Whaddya think?"

"Seems like a nice enough guy."

"You should have seen him a while ago."

"So you said. How about I take you out for an early lunch?"

She looked at the clock. Not so early at that. "Why not? I'll tell the cooks I'm not staying, after all."

He followed her out of the office, and she could hear him pumping Annie and Mabel about Herschel Vint. Not that they'd have much to tell him.

Eventually, when they were outdoors and out of earshot, Fred came back to the subject of Bert.

"Ask him to give you that can of paint he's been using when it's empty."

She raised her eyebrows. "Tell him I need to keep track of what he's used?"

"You can come up with something better than that. And pick it up by the bail."

"It's too small to have a bail." They didn't put wire handles on little cans.

"Fine. Just keep your fingers off the sides."

She finally got it. "You want his fingerprints. But all kinds of people have handled it."

"That's all right, as long as the prints on top are clear. We're not trying to find out which prints are his."

"Then why bother?"

"We've identified the prints we took from Vint's car, and they match the partial prints on the stone you found. If we don't find a match, I'm not going to worry much about Bert."

"If you've identified them, then you already know who it is. Am I missing something?"

"We've never heard of this man. But he could be using a phony ID now, or maybe he did when he was picked up years ago."

"Don't you have a picture?"

"It's damaged. No help at all. But you'll be interested to

know that he was arrested in Michigan, up north, and near Lake Michigan."

"So that's why he'd have Petoskey stones. And use them so casually—he didn't have to buy them in a rock shop."

"We don't know how long he was there, but from the age they have on record up in Benzie County, he'd be forty by now."

It wasn't much to go on. "And Bert looks like him?"

"Right size, right age. Could be. So could your friend Skirv. He doesn't know about you and me, does he?"

"Probably not."

"Good."

She kept her mouth shut, but it wasn't easy. They arrived at Wilma's Café then and would have had to stop talking about the case anyway. Even in Fred's favorite booth, where he could sit against the back wall and see everyone who came in, it was never safe to speak freely in a town the size of Oliver. The people they didn't recognize were bound to be related to or friends of anyone they mentioned.

She watched him scan the room, most of which was behind her. "You'd do better to bring Ketcham along," she told him. "He knows everyone."

His eyes crinkled, melting her. "I'd rather look at you."

Wilma appeared at Joan's elbow with a coffeepot and an order pad. She set the pot down on the table. "Hi, there. Take your order?"

"My usual," Fred said.

She nodded.

"What's Fred having?" Joan asked.

Wilma rattled it off. "Half-pound burger with fries, coffee, and apple pie à la mode."

Knowing Wilma's juicy burgers, she was tempted, but thought better of it, even if she could have eaten all that. There was a lot more of Fred than of her to feed, and she hoped to keep it that way. "Give me a BLT on whole wheat toast, please, Wilma, light on the mayo. And coffee."

"Got it," Wilma said, scribbling on the pad. She poured the coffee and disappeared. One of the reasons they'd have kept coming back even if Oliver had more restaurants was never to listen to specials of the day, much less to a kid in a bow tie say, "I'm Jeremy, and I'll be your server today. What can I get you guys to drink while you look at the menu?" After which, of course, he would vanish.

The food arrived in less time than Jeremy or Justin or whoever would have taken to bring them coffee. Joan's BLT stood tall, and Fred's burger with lettuce and slices of onion and tomato overlapped its huge sesame bun. He slathered mustard on it.

They kept the conversation general over lunch, about the food and her lack of progress in finding another violinist in case the sub delivered before the concert. Fred was eating the last of his pie and Joan was finishing her second cup of coffee when she suddenly found herself trembling.

"You think he's all right?" She knew he wouldn't think she meant Bert Barnhart.

"Scared?" He reached across the table for her hand.

She nodded. "For a while I'm fine, and then someone says something that sets me off. This morning Alvin Hannauer tried to pump me about what the police thought about the accident he read about in the paper, but of course I didn't answer. From there it went to the construction people, EFF, and Sylvia, and someone said a young man had taken her place.

The people who knew about Andrew shushed him. Bert's tantrum broke in then, which was just as well, and I didn't have time to think until just now."

"I can't promise you anything, except that we're working on it as hard as we can. I'd better get back to it."

"And I'd better go rescue that thing you want." It didn't feel natural to talk like this. She'd probably already said too much, but at least she'd kept her voice down.

"I'll walk you back."

"No. You go back to digging."

"Yes, ma'am." He took advantage of their back booth to kiss her hard before going up to pay the bill.

She followed slowly, and they parted at the door. She shivered. Was it her imagination, from watching Fred eat ice cream with his pie, or was it from worrying about Andrew? Or had the temperature actually dropped? Walking briskly back to the center, she warmed up quickly.

When she reached her office, three phone calls demanded her attention, and she made four more to find a substitute for the next day's speaker, who had come down with the flu after the flu season was supposed to be over. Two hours later, she remembered to look for the paint can Bert had used. He'd left without replacing it in the basement. Probably empty. She had no idea which brush he'd used, but they all looked clean. He probably wiped it off when he cleaned it. But when she took the lid off the big trash can behind the building, it, too, was empty. Why did the trash pickup have to be early the one day she needed it to be late?

She'd pick up a new can of the green in the morning. If she bought a gallon, there was no way he'd use it all on those railings. Fred would just have to wait. She went back in to call the paint store.

The rest of the afternoon ran smoothly until less than an hour before closing time. Joan was already looking forward to her walk across the park when the phone shattered her peace.

"Joan, it's Alex. I need you to run out to Fulford for me."

"You what?" Several members of the orchestra worked at Fulford Electronics, true, but running errands was not part of her job description as orchestra manager. "Why me?"

"I know it's an imposition, but this would really help the concert. You know how deadly the narration to the *Young Person's Guide* is."

She certainly did. And if adults thought so, what would children think? It had worried her all along.

"That kid who plays the piccolo part to 'Stars and Stripes' on the tuba—"

"Tory Isom," Joan supplied.

"Right, Tory. Well, he volunteered to pep up the words a little. I didn't expect him to pull it off, but what he just brought me is better, I have to admit. I want you to take it to Jim Chandler, to give him time to read it before Wednesday night."

"Won't you see him before then?"

"Joan!" Alex was all wounded dignity. "I couldn't throw myself at him like that!"

No, you'd rather steal my time from me.

"So you want me to come get it and then take it out to Fulford? Alex, I'm on foot."

"Oh, I don't mind dropping it off to you. I'll even give you a ride out there." Alex, conciliatory?

"Well . . ." She could walk home from Fulford.

"Thank you! I'll be right over." As usual, she hung up before Joan could object further.

She scarcely had time to ask Mabel Dunn to lock the building before she heard an imperious honk. Out in the parking lot, Alex was leaning on the horn of her Thunderbird.

"Keep your shirt on," Joan muttered, but she threw her bag over her shoulder and went out. When she slid into the passenger seat, Alex pulled out into traffic before Joan had finished fastening her belt.

Annoyed at herself for agreeing to go, she looked at the manila envelope Alex tossed into her lap. "This is Tory's narration?"

"Yes. Take a look at it; see what you think."

She did and was impressed. Rough spots notwithstanding, the boy's words were a considerable improvement on the original text. "I like it."

"Me, too. That's why I wanted Jim to see it before he had to read it in public, even to the orchestra. He's actually kind of shy, though you might not think so."

"No." The man who'd made the speech to the orchestra on his first night had seemed anything but shy.

At the edge of the parking lot, Alex pulled up. "I'm going to drop you here, all right?"

Talk about an unlikely shy person. "I'll be fine."

"You want me to wait?" Alex was clearly uneasy even to be that close to the building.

"No, I can walk home from here."

"Thanks, Joan." No sooner had the passenger door closed than the Thunderbird peeled off, firing bits of gravel that stung Joan's legs and were probably going to leave holes in her hose.

She tucked the new script in her shoulder bag and walked down the driveway to the front door.

20

Joan had never seen the inside of Fulford Electronics before, as often as she had driven past it. Only a rose on the receptionist's desk rescued the inside from being as plain as the outside. But no one was sitting at the desk. Was she supposed to call out? Hit a bell somewhere? She didn't see one.

She'd give it a few minutes. Taking a seat in one of the plain black chairs that lined the wall, she looked again at the new narration. Compared to the stodgy stuff they'd been listening to, it was a breath of fresh air. No story line, like *Peter and the Wolf,* but you couldn't have everything.

"I'm so sorry. Did you have to wait long?" A trim gray-haired woman was smoothing her jacket as she hurried down the hall. Now Joan saw the word "Ladies" on the second door past the desk.

"No, I just got here." She stood. "I'm Joan Spencer, manager of the Oliver Civic Symphony. I have something for Mr. Chandler."

"We're closing for the day, but you can go back and check. I think Jim's still here. Sales is the third door on the right after you go through the double doors." She pointed and then ducked behind her desk.

Joan thanked her and headed down the long hall. As soon as she opened the double doors, she heard him. But the voice that had caressed the words he read to the orchestra had a sneer to it now.

"They won't care if you quit. They know who brings in the money."

Somebody sobbed.

"Right, turn on the waterworks."

Joan stood transfixed. Before she could move, a door on the left slammed open, and Birdie Eads flew down the corridor toward her, gulping and blinded by tears.

"Birdie!" She spread her arms, and Birdie ran into them.

"He—he—" She couldn't stop sobbing.

"It's all right." Joan patted her back, wondering what could possibly be all right about working with a man like Jim Chandler after he'd obviously thrown her over for Alex Campbell, of all people. No wonder Birdie hadn't wanted to share the first stand with Nicholas in the orchestra. It wasn't about Nicholas at all. She didn't want to sit up there so close to Jim, but she still had to work with him. Poor child. Not that Birdie Eads was a child. Like her friend Sylvia, she was a grown woman.

Now she straightened up to her full five feet something and blew her nose. "Thank you. I suppose you heard all that."

"Not much. I'm glad I came along when I did."

"Why are you here?"

It didn't seem like the time to mention Alex. Was Birdie the real reason Alex hadn't wanted to come in? "I have to deliver something to Jim. The tuba player—the one who played the 'Stars and Stripes' solo—tried his hand at improving the narration for the Britten, and it's not too bad."

"But Alex didn't want Jim to stutter the first time he read it." So Birdie saw through Alex.

"Stutter? Does he, really?"

"No, but he has to practice to sound that good. It doesn't come naturally." Bitterness permeated her words.

"I'm sorry, Birdie."

"Thanks." Birdie wiped her eyes. "I'd better go fix my face."

"I'd offer you a ride home, but—"

"That's all right. I drove."

And I didn't.

"And you have to take that script to Jim," Birdie said. "Feed his vanity." She managed a smile. "Go ahead. I'll be okay."

Joan watched her head for the door. Then she squared her shoulders and turned to face Jim Chandler. She dreaded entering the room Birdie had escaped from.

She needn't have worried. He came out into the hall, and his handsome face broke into a charming smile.

"Joan!" he said. "What brings you here?"

Besides an urge to smack you? she thought, but she controlled it and held out the new script. "Alex asked me to bring this to you." Even if Joan hadn't promised, there was no way she'd tell this man Alex had dropped her off.

"You didn't have to go to so much trouble, but thank you." He flipped through the pages. "Does look a mite more interesting for the kiddies." A man who would bring Birdie to tears with his sarcasm talking about kiddies? Or was this more of the same?

"See you Wednesday night, then," she said.

"Don't hurry off. Is this your first time here at Fulford? Let me give you the grand tour."

"Sorry. I have to go." She forced a quick smile and left the way she'd come. Once out of the building, she felt her tight shoulder muscles relax.

The receptionist's light was off and her computer monitor shrouded in a dustcover, but the front door opened easily. Not seeing Birdie's car in the parking lot, Joan struck out on foot. Walking home from this side of town would take her maybe half again as long as from work, and without the park's green space to enjoy along the way, it would feel still longer.

She didn't care. The spring breeze washed her face, and even the exhaust of an Oliver College truck ahead of her was an improvement over the odor of Fulford. By the time she turned onto her own street, she was humming Sousa.

Her message machine was blinking when she walked into the house. She hit the button and heard Fred's voice. "I have to go back tonight. Call me if you'd rather I didn't bother to come home."

Silly man. She made a quick supper automatically and slung two of everything on the table. When Andrew finally came home, she'd have to remember to set the table for three again. When she and Fred were first married, she'd forgotten to set his place more than once. Habit dies slowly, she thought.

He walked in the kitchen door just when she finished grinding the coffee beans.

"Wonderful smell," he said. "Better than the coffee itself."

"I know. We could sit around and sniff it and skip the rest."

"Not tonight. Tonight might be another late one."

She knew better than to ask why and finished making the coffee. Fred hung his jacket on a hook and watched her.

"You bring me the paint can?"

"It got away from me, sorry. I'll bring you the one he uses tomorrow."

"Just can't get good help these days," he said, shaking his head.

"Not at this pay rate."

"But consider the fringe benefits." He nuzzled the back of her neck and nibbled her ear but then tore himself away. "I really do have to go right back. Maybe I won't be too late."

"Wake me when you come in."

Tuesday dawned cold and bright. Joan's first thought when the cold air hit her on the way to work was of Andrew. This isn't as cold as last week, she told herself. His sleeping bag is rated for much colder than this, and he has his parka and ski pants.

But when she picked up the green paint, the clerk reminded her to wait. "Don't use it below fifty degrees."

She thanked him and hefted the gallon can. At least the bail didn't dig into her gloved hand as it would have if she'd been bare-handed. By afternoon, she hoped, the sun would have warmed the air enough for Bert to finish.

But the sun went behind a cloud before it could do the job, and when Bert arrived, she had to send him home.

He wasn't happy about it. "I've painted lots colder days'n this."

"Maybe so, but I don't want to have to have it done over again. I'm sorry, but it's worth waiting one more day." She held her breath, but he didn't put up a fight. Merely hitched up his jeans and left.

Fred wouldn't be happy, but even Bert had worn gloves today. Letting him go ahead wouldn't have helped Fred any more than it would have helped the railing.

During the afternoon she found time to work at transposing the tenor part of the hymns for Sylvia's funeral to the viola's alto clef. With no staff paper, she drew her own with a ruler and pen, added the alto clef sign, and copied the page on the photocopier before adding the notes. She wrote the notes themselves in pencil, so that she'd be able to fix any goofs easily. Let Nicholas look down his nose. She'd managed to find more notes than she'd expected during their rehearsal, but the way she saw it, there was no reason to struggle. Playing for Sylvia's service was a favor for her sister, after all, not a test. And it should sound as good as Joan could make it.

She tucked the results into the hymnbook and stashed the book in her shoulder bag. She'd run through the hymns on the viola tonight, just to be sure.

But when she got home, Fred had other plans.

"I couldn't get Bert to handle the paint can today," she told him. "It was too cold to paint, and anyhow, he had gloves on."

"I figured as much. He'll keep. But would you drop in at your buddy Skirv's for me?"

"Matt Skirvin's store? Why?"

"He won't touch anything when I'm in the place, and I don't know which cops he recognizes. I want you to buy something he's handled."

"That's all?" She was relieved not to have to tell him what she'd been suspecting, after all.

"Well, it should be something smooth enough to hold fingerprints. He has plenty of glass and china things. Something round would be good, something he can't pick up by the edges."

"I'll get him to reach me something down from a high shelf."

"Good." He sighed. "This business of ruling out possibles is a nuisance, when there are so many of them. We can't ask half the men in town to come down and let us fingerprint them."

"At least you know it's a man. Older than Andrew, too, if you're zeroing in on guys the age of Bert and Skirv."

"Andrew was a little boy when this man was arrested in Michigan. But you didn't really wonder about Andrew."

"Oh, Fred, of course not."

"I'll meet you for supper at Wilma's when you're done. Don't worry, though. I'll have someone watching."

"Skirv wouldn't hurt me!" But Sylvia? Herschel Vint? Andrew? How could she be so sure he'd stop there?

"No, he won't." He smiled down at her. "Want a ride? I don't want him to see us together, but I can take you most of the way."

"Thanks." She dumped the hymnbook out of her shoulder bag and slung the leather bag over her shoulder. The poor thing looked the worse for all the abuse she heaped on it, but so far, it was holding up. "I'm ready."

A block from the store, he let her out to walk the rest of the way.

Skirv's Stuff greeted her with fluttering bedspreads hung outside. Joan, partial to Grandma Zimmerman's quilts, didn't bother to look them over.

In the dimmer light indoors, she recognized Matt Skirvin standing behind the counter.

"Welcome, Joan." His brown eyes smiled at her. "I'm kind of surprised to see you here, what with Andrew up in the tree and all. You have some problem with the concert, or what?"

"Hi, Matt. No, except for missing Sylvia in the first violins."

His face fell. "Wasn't that awful? I can't believe anyone would do such a thing. She wasn't hurting anyone up there. And you must be worried about Andrew, too. I was glad I could help him make it up into the tree. He seems like a good kid."

"He is." She wasn't about to invite Matt Skirvin into her worries.

"If there's anything I can do, I will." He sounded sincere, but who could tell? Wouldn't Sylvia's killer sound sympathetic when you met him? She tried to put the thought out of her mind.

"Thank you, Matt. As a matter of fact, there is something."

"Anything."

"This isn't for Andrew, and it's certainly not important. But I need to find a gift for one of the little old ladies who helps me at the center." Annie Jordan would skin me alive if she heard me talk about her like that. "I know she likes old things, antiques and such, more than new stuff. So I came here. What do you have that's pretty enough to give as a gift? Nothing too expensive, you understand, but really nice. And I'd want it in a nice box. Gift wrapped, even, if you do that."

He came out from behind the counter. "I ought to have something. What kinds of things does she like?"

"I don't really know. I'm hoping I'll know it when I see it. Nothing knitted or crocheted or embroidered—she does all that herself." And fabrics wouldn't be a good choice for Fred.

"There are some pretty things on that table." He gestured to a table full of china and glassware.

She looked as seriously as she could, picked up a few things, and then spotted something that might work and that he'd have to help her with. "Maybe those candlesticks up on the shelf? They look like crystal."

"I doubt it. If they are, they're seriously underpriced." He reached for one and held it out to her. Fingers and thumb right on it, good.

She took it delicately by the top and bottom and set it on the counter. "I like the simple lines and the little leaves carved into the base. How much are they?"

He flipped it over to show her the price tag on the bottom. "Ten dollars."

"For the pair?"

He flashed her a smile. "For you, sure."

"Okay." She pulled out her wallet. "Would you wrap them both, please?"

She watched him lift down the second candlestick. Fred ought to be able to get what he needed. She hoped the police would be willing to pay ten bucks for them. But maybe she'd rather keep them when this whole thing was over. They really did appeal to her. Or actually give them to Annie, who knocked herself out at the center for nothing more than a smile and a thank-you. While he was wrapping them in tissue and tucking them into a neat box only a little too big for them, she had an inspiration.

"Do you have any candles that would fit in them? Then it would be a real present."

He looked pleased at the prospect of another sale. "We have some scented ones."

"Lovely." She took her time selecting candles that would send the fragrance of vanilla floating through the air. Even now, she could smell it. They were attractive enough, white flecked with brown spots that might actually have been vanilla beans. Matt handled them freely, too, and wrapped them in tissue paper. Between the waxy candles and the plain glass, he had to have left plenty of prints.

Feeling more than a little smug, Joan paid him and tucked the two parcels into her capacious shoulder bag. "Thanks, Matt. You solved my problem for me."

"Any time." He escorted her to the door and watched her turn toward Wilma's. She was glad Fred hadn't asked her to meet him at the police station, though maybe it didn't matter what Matt thought, now that she'd succeeded in her mission.

A young woman in blue jeans and a denim jacket who had been looking at the dusty antiques in the window of Skirv's Stuff when she arrived fell into step with her. "Hello, Joan."

Suddenly she recognized Officer Jill Root. "Well, hi there. I thought you were a student."

"That was the general idea. Good job."

"You were watching?"

Jill nodded. "Orders. But you obviously didn't need me. You even got him to wrap them."

"I didn't want to worry about rubbing off his prints when I stuck them in my bag."

"I brought along an evidence bag, but I don't think we need it."

"Are you going to escort me all the way to Wilma's?" Joan was amused by the idea.

"Only to report to the lieutenant."

Funny, Joan thought. He'll trust me to bring him the paint can on my own, but for this, he needed a witness. Maybe he's taking Skirv more seriously than Bert.

"Come have supper with us, why don't you?"

Jill smiled. "Thanks, but I have a date." That was good news. The man she'd been in love with had been killed in a hit-and-run the previous year, and Jill had taken it hard.

"I'm glad to hear it," Joan said. "Have a good time." She

wondered whether Jill would risk dating another cop but refrained from grilling her.

At the restaurant, Fred came forward to meet them.

"I snagged a booth," he said. "Come on back, both of you. You can tell me all about it."

"Nothing to tell," Joan said when they were settled in the privacy of the back booth. "He sold me a pair of glass candlesticks and a couple of candles. Wrapped them and everything. I watched him hold them, so I'm sure you'll have his prints." She patted the bag lying next to her. "But Fred, are you sure?"

"Of course not. We're eliminating a lot of men, you know. It just takes time." He looked tired. "This guy may not even be anyone local. But Johnny Ketcham said Skirv sells Wrist-Rockets."

"Oh, no!" How could she have missed seeing them in there?

Fred put his hand over hers. "Don't jump to conclusions. After all, Andrew has one."

"Are you sure he sells them? I didn't see them." What bothered her more, the fact that Fred had reason to suspect Skirv or her own inattentiveness?

"If Ketcham says so, it's true. And if it makes you feel any better, I didn't spot them, either. Or the pot. The difference is, a slingshot doesn't smell."

"He sells pot, too?" She felt incredibly unobservant. All she'd smelled was vanilla.

"Not openly. But it explains why he'd be nervous around cops."

"You think he had anything to do with that meth lab out there?"

"We'll keep that in mind."

Was he humoring her? She couldn't tell.

"Suppose you hand over your prizes to Officer Root. She'll see to it that they're properly taken care of."

"Suppose I hand them over to you, instead. Jill has better things to do tonight."

Jill blushed. "I'll take them, Lieutenant."

Oops, Joan thought. I forget who's in charge. She dug out the neatly wrapped packages and handed them over. Jill was going to need that evidence bag, after all.

21

*I*t was still daylight Tuesday when Fred dropped her at home and went back to work. She hadn't seen Andrew since Sunday, when he'd talked to her normally, even if he hadn't called since.

Before she could change her mind, she grabbed a sackful of oranges out of the refrigerator. Not that he'd be in danger of scurvy after less than a week, but they couldn't hurt. He'd welcomed the apples last time.

The road out to the woods seemed shorter every time. Familiarity, she supposed. She was taking the curves like a native when she remembered poor Mr. Vint and slowed down. One of those curves had sent him to his death. No, not a curve. Another Petoskey stone. Did the next one have Andrew's name on it? Was anybody safe? She hadn't thought to tell Fred where she was going. At least she had a cell phone.

Fat lot of good that would do me if I were out cold, wrapped around a tree.

But she wasn't worried about herself as much as she was about Andrew. It was a relief to pull into the clearing. The temperature's already dropped out here, she thought when she left the car and walked toward the oak tree with her oranges.

Immediately the cell phone rang in her pocket. Fumbling for it, she could see Andrew's dark head above the platform. Now he was waving at her. She waved back, set down the bag of oranges, and answered the phone.

"Hi, Mom. What's up?"

"Besides you, you mean?"

"Funny."

"I brought you some oranges."

The basket began its descent, swinging in the breeze that was chilling the back of her neck, and she waited. When she could reach it, she loaded in the oranges, and he hauled it back up.

"Thanks, Mom," he said into her ear then. "You're the only one who brings fruit."

"Sure. What are mothers for?" Already she was reassured, just seeing him.

"Skirv called."

"He did?" Her antennae went up.

"He said you went shopping at his place today for some old lady."

"That's right; I did." Should she tell him why? Not without Fred's okay. Even if Fred would trust Andrew, and at this point she wasn't sure he would, she knew he wouldn't want her to broadcast the fact that the police had those fingerprints.

Andrew was waiting for more. Had Skirv been spooked by her purchase? What had he said?

"You know Annie, at the center?"

"The one who knits all the time?"

"Uh-huh. And does all kinds of things to help me, for no pay. I decided it was high time to thank her. So I went gift shopping."

"At Skirv's?" He sounded dubious, as well he might.

"Sure. I found some old candlesticks, not the kind of thing he has for students. They look like crystal, but if they are, I got more of a bargain than he meant to give me. He wrapped them and everything."

"You're not going to tell me, are you?"

"Nope." She put a smile in her voice. "And Andrew, let it drop. I'll tell you when I can, okay?"

"Okay."

"How are you holding up?"

"I'm fine, Mom."

"And you don't tell me everything, either."

He laughed, a genuine laugh that did her heart good. "Just keep Fred off my back, okay?"

"I can't control Fred. But he's not what I'm worried about. I play for Sylvia's funeral Thursday, and you took her place."

"I'm sorry, Mom. I'll keep a good eye out, and if I see anyone who looks the least bit dangerous, I promise to lie flat on my belly and call Fred."

"Good." There wasn't much more he could do, short of coming down, and she wasn't going to argue about that. But they hadn't seen anyone dangerous before Sylvia was hit.

"Thanks for the oranges."

"Anything else you need?"

"No, I'm good."

"I won't be here tomorrow. Orchestra night."

"See you, Mom."

She knew he was all right for the moment. Reassured, she turned and made her way out of the woods, only to see a pickup roar into the clearing and Tom Walcher's flaming shock emerge from it.

He had to be the right age, she thought. She wondered how much more description Fred had of the mysterious man whose fingerprints they'd identified. He couldn't have been a redhead, not if Fred thought Skirv might be a match, and she was sure Walcher was a natural redhead. The freckles and fair skin, his nose burned bright red where the bill of his cap didn't protect it, were a dead giveaway. But suppose he'd dyed his hair some other color before they arrested him in Michigan and then let it go back to its natural state in Indiana? It seemed unlikely, but it was possible.

He charged across the clearing toward her.

"Mr. Walcher," she greeted him. Below his rolled-up sleeves, even the hairs on his freckled arms were red.

"You again! I told you to get out."

"That was before our friend Sylvia was killed."

"Don't I know it. The place has been crawling with cops ever since."

"Really?" Not when I've been here.

He blushed as only a redhead can. "We—uh, we had some damage out here."

"Oh, the EFF people."

"Yeah. Lost more than a day of work on my other jobs. Had to find a new place to store my equipment, and I've been coming out here and checking day and night in case they have something else in mind. Now they've sneaked a man up in that tree. Not even knocking her out of it did any good."

She couldn't resist. "Oh? You knocked her out?"

"That's not what I said!"

She was tempted to tell him who was up in the tree now but decided it would make him madder. Better just leave.

"Good-bye, Mr. Walcher." She turned to go.

He didn't answer, but she could feel his eyes boring into her back. He was still standing there when she started the motor and drove off.

On the way home, she kicked herself for not thinking of a way to get him to leave his fingerprints on her car. Going back might do it. He was belligerent enough to lean on it to warn her off. If not, she could make it stall and pretend to have trouble starting it up again. That would probably work with a man so eager to get rid of her.

Leave the detecting to me, Fred would say. He was right, of course. The man he was looking for was dangerous. He'd sent Jill Root to Skirv's, and she didn't think he was concerned only with protecting Skirv's prints. She wouldn't be surprised to see Jill or someone else she knew turn up at the senior center tomorrow.

She was reading in bed when Fred came in. "You're early."

"I wasn't doing anything useful." He pulled off his jacket and tie.

"So Skirv's prints didn't match?"

"Nope."

Joan felt hugely relieved, not so much because she knew the man as because he was part of Andrew's support system and she hadn't even let Fred and Andrew in on her suspicions. *If Andrew had been killed because I didn't want to look foolish, I never would have forgiven myself,* she thought.

Fred sat down heavily on the bed and untied his shoes. "Call me when Bert leaves tomorrow, and I'll send someone over to check the paint can."

"But you don't think it's Bert."

"Ketcham knows him. He doesn't think the man's been out of Indiana in his life."

"Oh." But hadn't Mabel said something about Michigan?

"We'll check anyway. Ketcham could be wrong. Anyone with reason to resent delays to the construction is suspect, and at this point we're down to looking under rocks."

"Could he be a redhead?"

"Walcher?" He untied his shoes. "Utterback's hair was brown."

"Yes. Maybe he dyed his hair in Michigan."

"You're grasping at straws."

"Looking under rocks. Fred, what about the meth lab? Did you—?"

"We found plenty of prints in that cave. No matches." He was unbuttoning his shirt.

Of course they'd checked. She sighed. "I saw Andrew this evening."

"He okay?"

"He thinks he is. When he first went up there, I hated it that you and he were at each other's throats, but now I almost wish you'd drag him down."

"Not unless I have to. That's dangerous itself." He dropped his shirt on the floor.

"I know."

"It's like terrorism."

"It's what?" she asked.

"Our own terror turns our lives upside down, puts people at risk, way beyond what the terrorists do."

"I don't want to turn his life upside down. But I don't want him killed, either. You have to find this man!"

"We'll find him. Move over, woman. It's cold out here."

She lifted the covers, and he slid in beside her. His body was chilled and his feet icy, but the arms that held her and the eyes that crinkled down at her promised something much warmer.

Joan smiled back and turned out the light.

22

By Wednesday afternoon, the weather had warmed up to sixty, and Bert arrived sans gloves, ready to paint. He was making a neat job of it and whistling while he worked when Joan went out to check half an hour later.

"Looks better, don't it?" he said.

"It sure does. I'll have to make you some 'wet paint' signs, though."

"I could tape 'em to the steps with masking tape."

"Good idea." *I don't want him to be the bad guy,* she thought, and she remembered that she'd have to find some more work if she wanted to be able to keep him on the job.

After taking him the signs, she spent the next hour walking around the building with a clipboard. The adult day care area looked distinctly dingy. *Of all the people who need cheerful colors,* she thought, *those folks did.* She consulted Karen Hultquist, who ran that program.

"That's great," Karen said. "In fact, we could make it an activity, letting the people choose the colors they'd like to have here. Some of them have done some amazing paintings— I'd trust their color sense before my own."

"Do it. I'll have to clear it with the board when they meet this afternoon, but we have enough for that in the budget, I know. And it's upkeep."

By the end of the hour, she had collected enough jobs to keep a man busy for a few weeks, if he could take on small carpentry repairs as well as painting and cleaning.

She took her list back to her office and typed it into the computer to make copies for the board meeting.

The board members, of course, had to pass Bert Barnhart as they entered the building. Joan saw some of them give him a wide berth.

"Are you sure it's safe, having him work out there like that?" Mabel Dunn asked before the meeting began. "He scared the pants off me the other day."

"He's been behaving like a perfect gentleman since then," Joan said. "I think he was desperate for money."

"I don't doubt it," Annie Jordan said. "They can't survive on the little I pay Diane, that's for sure. And now with this construction falling through . . . Bert can do more than clean."

"That's what I wanted to bring before the board," Joan said.

"Well, let's call the meeting to order," Alvin Hannauer said. He dealt quickly with the routine and returned to the question of Bert. "Now, what do you have in mind?"

Joan handed out her list. "I'd like your permission to hire Bert to do these projects and use him regularly for upkeep, if he continues to do as good a job as he's doing on those railings. He's a good worker so far."

"He can't come in here and terrorize people," Margaret Duffy said.

"Of course not," Joan said. "I'll make him understand that. But the way he's been behaving, I suspect he's already ashamed of himself. And we'll have to decide on a pay rate, if he's going to continue."

"We're not getting the volunteers we used to for that kind of thing," Alvin said. "I vote we take him on. It will cost less than hiring contractors for some of these piddly little jobs, even if you could get them. You think you can get him to agree to be on call for emergencies?"

"If he knows how to deal with them, I'd think so," Joan said. When the meeting ended, she had her vote. Now if only Bert's fingerprints wouldn't put him beyond the pale. But there was no harm in letting him know he had work.

"You mean it?" he said when she told him, and she thought his eyes misted over. "You have any idea how long I've been looking?"

"I mean it. The board was pleased with your work. They took a vote this afternoon."

"You won't be sorry!"

They settled on the details. She paid him for the railing and showed him her list. "I want you to keep your eyes open for other things that need fixing or fixing up. This building gets hard wear."

"You want I should start on the inside walls next? That's top of your list."

She'd know before tomorrow whether he was dangerous. Still, why start with the indoor work? "No, I want to give the adult day care people time to decide on the colors they want in there. Start by clearing the winter trash off the lawn and the flower bed. You saw the rake and garden tools down there with the paint supplies. Just be careful of the bulbs. Right now you can hardly see some of the flowers under all that, but they're blooming, and a rake can wreck the petals."

"You got it. I'll start a compost heap in the back corner with what I take off. By fall, we can use it."

When Bert left, she called Fred. "He's gone for the day. I feel like Judas. We just hired him as our regular handyman, and I think he's going to be good."

"I'll send someone over. If he's not our bad guy, you'll get a free security check out of it."

"I suppose. Nobody checked on me."

"You don't fit the profile."

"Fred!"

"You had character references right here, remember? But you have to be realistic if you're going to hire people off the street like that. I wouldn't want to trust my mother to a place that used anyone the least bit dangerous."

"No, of course not. But I wouldn't be surprised if Helga could hold her own against Bert."

He laughed. "You have a point." Even though her mind was failing, Helga Lundquist, Fred's mother, was still a strong Swedish woman.

"Will I see you tonight?"

"Orchestra rehearsal, right? So I doubt it. I'll grab a bite sometime."

"Okay."

A few minutes later, Jill Root appeared at her office door. Today she was in uniform and looked like the mature police officer she was, not an Oliver College kid. "I've come for the paint can."

Joan walked her down to the supply room, where she found it, neatly labeled on top with the date, "Railing," and a stripe of the green color. "He did everything but sign it."

"I'll bring it back, unless it turns out to be evidence."

"Tonight?"

"Oh, sure. Is he still using it?"

"I don't think so. But he'd miss it. If his prints don't match, I don't want him to know we suspected him of anything."

"Him and most of the guys in this town," Jill said. "It wouldn't be so bad if we could tell people we needed to eliminate them. But we don't want to tip off this Utterback character."

"You think that's his real name?"

"If it is, he's living in a cave somewhere. I never heard of him, and we haven't found any record of a man by that name doing anything here."

"In a cave . . . I suppose that's possible. Out there in the woods, like the meth lab."

"Possible, but not likely. If that ever was his real name, it's not the one he goes by these days. He's walking around acting perfectly ordinary, except of course for killing people."

"You think he'll keep doing it?"

Jill shook her head. "I wish we knew. We're keeping watch out there, though. The lieutenant doesn't say much, but we all know it's your son up in that tree."

Joan couldn't answer.

Jill gave her hand a quick squeeze. "I'll be right back."

After she left, Joan surveyed the storage room. Already, Bert had done more than label the paint. All the paint cans stood in rows, as did the garden tools and the cleaning supplies, each in its own section of the room's rough shelving. Even the smells seemed to have grouped themselves. It hadn't been chaotic before his arrival, but even before knowing he had a job, he'd made order out of disorder.

I can't believe this man would casually shoot rocks at innocent people, she thought. Unless he didn't think of them as innocent. If Bert thought Sylvia and Herschel Vint were keeping him and his wife from the work they so badly needed, what would he do? Considering how he'd behaved the first time she met him, she couldn't put murder beyond him.

By the time Jill returned, Joan wanted urgently to know the verdict. Ah, she'd brought the can back, a good sign.

Joan took it from her. "It's not Bert?"

"No. Not even close. And the lieutenant said to tell you Barnhart's not wanted for anything, either. We've had a couple of domestic calls, but he was never arrested."

"That's good, right?"

"It might not mean much. Sometimes the woman gets cold feet when it comes to pressing charges. And sometimes she didn't call in the first place. A neighbor complains, but the woman loves the guy in spite of how he treats her."

Hard to imagine, but Joan knew it was true. "Thanks, Jill."

"Or the neighbor made it sound worse than it was."

"I hope so."

"He's never bothered anyone else. Shoots off his mouth is all."

She'd have to keep an eye on him, Joan thought, and ask Annie to watch out for his wife. After Jill left, she went down and replaced the can exactly where she'd found it on Bert's neat shelf. Time to dash home for a quick meal before rehearsal.

Walking home bathed in the sunshine still delighted her after a winter of walking home in dusk or even in the dark, especially when someone failed to collect a frail family member from the adult day care program on time. By midsummer, she knew, she wouldn't enjoy that sunshine so much, but right now, it was pure pleasure.

By now, too, the runners and dog walkers were populating the park on her way home, though during the winter she saw few of them. She exchanged greetings with people she never saw anywhere else and couldn't name, even though she recognized them from their regular evening walks.

At the edge of the park, she paused only a few moments to admire Laura Putnam's new puppy and sympathize with Ellen, Laura's mother. "You sure you're up to it?"

"No, but I think Laura needs him. Look at them together."

The little girl and the puppy, which looked like a fuzzy mutt, were rolling on the newly green grass together, Laura looking happier than Joan could remember seeing her for a couple of years.

"Good luck with him!"

Joan went on. Neighbors were out working in their yards or just admiring the bulbs blooming in flower beds. She waved at some, exchanged greetings with a few more, but didn't pause again. Not on a Wednesday.

Birdie was already glowering from the back of the first violin section when Joan arrived on the school stage for rehearsal. She could see why—Alex and Jim had their heads together near the podium in what might have been consultation over the new narrative. But even though she couldn't hear his words, Joan could imagine him whispering sweet nothings into Alex's ear, instead. True or not, it had to look that way to Birdie.

If Alex or Jim was the next victim, she'd have to suspect Birdie, as angry as she looked. But of course Birdie couldn't be the elusive man arrested up in Michigan. And she wouldn't have hurt Sylvia—or would she, if Jim had made a play for her, too? Never mind. The Michigan man with the Petoskey stones was the killer.

Besides, Joan thought, I get mad at people, too. That doesn't mean I kill them. I just wish I could.

She fielded a couple of personnel and librarian questions on her way to her own seat, and she still hadn't unpacked her viola when Nicholas stood up and pointed his bow at the first oboe to start sounding the A for each section to tune. Woodwinds first, then brasses, then lower strings, and finally the violins. The brass section needed a second A before Nicholas was satisfied, and in the end, Joan had her bow tightened and her instrument up by the violas' turn. Even though their strings were an octave higher, they tuned with the cellos, who also had a C string. Nicholas, satisfied, raised his violin to signal for the last A, and the rest of the fiddles joined him.

Alex climbed onto the podium then, but before raising her stick to begin, she tapped for silence.

"Tonight we're trying something different. I've had a number of complaints about the lame narration, and one person here tonight has taken it upon himself to do something about it. So ignore any cues printed in your music."

Jim Chandler, having had plenty of time with the new words, surely wouldn't stumble over any of them, Joan thought. Not that they were difficult. She wondered whether there was any truth in what Birdie had said about his stuttering. Or had that been her hurt feelings speaking?

Alex nodded at Jim, and he read from the new script. " 'Benjamin Britten wrote this piece to show off the orchestra. First, they'll play the same thing together. Then they'll take turns messing around with it. It's kind of a march.' " Joan agreed with Alex that Tory Isom's new beginning sounded more like a kid and had a better chance of appealing to the children at the concert than the old, boring one.

Alex raised her baton, and they started. The first violinist subbing for Sylvia seemed to be holding up her end well enough. At this distance Joan couldn't hear how well the woman was hitting the notes she was bowing so strongly, but Nicholas wasn't making faces, and the bulge of her pregnancy didn't seem to be getting in her way.

But something sounded different about Tory's words. What had he written for the flutes and piccolos, whose last trills flew by her now? Joan couldn't remember, but what Jim was reading wasn't the same as what she had read.

" 'Oboes cut right through you,' " he said now, before their individual passage, and she couldn't agree more. That's what Tory had written. She must have been mistaken about the flute words.

" 'Give them a chance, and the violins cut loose,' " Jim read. Watching the pregnant sub's bow flashing in unison with Nicholas's, Joan relaxed.

But what was Jim reading now? " 'A lot of musicians make bad jokes about violas. Listen to these violas play, and you'll know why.' " No time to react, much less wonder where that had come from. She needed to think calm thoughts about the viola passage she'd hardly practiced. So far, Alex hadn't chewed anyone out, but it couldn't last forever.

The violas escaped her wrath, though, as did the rest of the strings and even the horns.

" 'Nobody can shout down a trumpet,' " Jim read for the trumpet fanfare. Too true, thought Joan, from bitter experience of trying to hear her own instrument with the trumpets' raised bells blaring only a few feet behind her.

After the rest of the brass and then the percussion had their say, it was time for the fugue. Why had she worried about the slow viola solo? It was nothing in comparison with what came next.

" 'Now the whole orchestra goes after the tune in a fugue.

It's a cross between a round, like "Row, Row, Row Your Boat" and a wild chase,'" Jim read. "'Hang on!'"

Too late now, Joan thought, and they were off.

They stumbled through it in ragged fashion. Alex didn't stop them in spite of many missed notes, and instead of chewing them out at the end, she stood beaming. "Much better," she pronounced.

Who is this woman? Joan wondered. And what has she done with our conductor? Behind her, Tory Isom, the tuba player whose narrative she had carried to Jim Chandler at Fulford's, was muttering something to the trombone player beside him.

"Give a hand to Tory Isom," Alex said. "He came up with the new words, or most of them. Jim did a little tweaking of his own here and there." Smiling, she tilted her head up toward him, even while pointing at Tory, while the orchestra clapped, shuffled their feet, and tapped bows on stands. The viola section responded with less enthusiasm.

Beside Joan, John Hocking, her usually cheerful stand partner, said, "Who stuck in that viola crack?"

"Not Tory," she told him. "I saw his version. Can't remember what he said about us, but it wasn't that."

"It's not funny. Just insulting."

"You're right, but I'm not sure I can talk Alex out of anything Jim did."

John shook his head. "I almost liked the old Alex better than this lovesick . . . cow."

"You don't think much of Jim?"

He, too, seemed to hesitate. They did, after all, both work at Fulford. "He's competent enough, and his good looks probably help him in sales, as well as with women. But I wouldn't want my daughter to choose a man like him."

23

hen Alex announced the break, Joan managed to corral the members of the quartet for Sylvia's service. "Are you up to a brief run-through when the orchestra's done?"

"You're the one who wore out the other day," Nicholas told her.

"You're right. I feel reasonably peppy tonight, though. And I'm the one who most needs the practice." She didn't feel the need to tell Nicholas that she wanted to check the way she'd rewritten the hymnbook's bass clef tenor part into viola clef.

The others were willing. For simplicity's sake, they agreed to join Nicholas in the inner circle of the orchestra seats, rather than move chairs and stands to a nearby room and then have to haul them back again. Joan would be able to keep an eye on the music folders being tossed into her bin this way, too, and she'd be available to any orchestra member with a legitimate request for her attention. Or illegitimate, she thought. But I'm not offering rides home tonight.

At the end of the break, she told Alex she wanted to make an announcement.

"Keep it short," Alex said. "We're running tight on time." Almost her old self just then. Not that you'd want her old self, but it would seem more natural.

Joan stood before they tuned, and Alex tapped on her stand for attention.

"I wanted to tell you all that Sylvia Purcell's funeral is tomorrow morning at eleven, at Community Church. A quartet from the orchestra will play." Short enough, Alex? She sat down.

Someone raised a bow from the back of the seconds. "Can anyone go?"

Joan stood again. "Yes, it's public. And if you feel like making a memorial donation, the orchestra would be glad to set up a Sylvia Purcell memorial fund." She hadn't discussed it with Linda Smith, but Linda surely wouldn't object. After all, she'd asked for the quartet.

After rehearsal, Joan was glad to see the stage clear rapidly. The few players who were still packing up and chatting when the quartet opened the hymnals gave them a wide berth and kept conversation down to a respectful level they could ignore. Probably because of her announcement. Ordinarily, any attempt to work through something after a rehearsal was drowned out by chatter.

When they began "Abide with Me," she heard a clear, high tenor singing the words. Hugging his tuba, Tory Isom had paused at stage right to join in the old hymn. The boy was full of surprises.

Nicholas raised an eyebrow at Joan's handwritten pages but said nothing. She didn't care. She was relieved to find no errors in them, and they made playing the hymns vastly easier than fighting her way through bass clef.

Now that Birdie and Nicholas had agreed on the double-dotted notes in the Handel, it, too, went smoothly. Good, Joan thought. They'd be out of there by half past nine.

But when they finished, Charlotte Hodden was in tears. Joan held out a hand to her. "I didn't know you were close to Sylvia."

"It's not Sylvia. My sister's husband died this week. Herschel Vint."

"Ohhh." She couldn't say what she knew from Fred.

"And now they're saying he might have been murdered, too." Charlotte blew her nose loudly. "My sister has three children and a job that won't begin to support them. I don't know what she'll do."

"I'm so sorry," Joan said, remembering her own struggles after Ken's sudden death.

"He was a good man. Who would want to kill a man like that? He never hurt anybody."

"I thought he totaled his car," Nicholas said. "That's what the paper said."

"There's more to it than that, but I'm not supposed to talk about it," Charlotte said. "I'm sorry. I shouldn't have opened my mouth, but the music . . . and those poor little boys. I can't stop thinking about them. I mean, Sylvia was bad enough, but at least no one depended on her, you know?"

Birdie's not going to see it that way, Joan thought, avoiding Birdie's eyes. And I wouldn't, if Andrew were shot down. Her own eyes stung, but she refused to give in to them. "Does she have any support?" she asked.

"Oh, you know. People are bringing food now. And everyone says if there's anything they can do . . . but they can't bring him back, you know? And that's what they need—him back."

No, they can't, Joan thought. "Did he have any insurance? From his job, maybe?"

"I don't know. I hope so. She's so upset, I don't know if she's even thought to ask. He took care of that kind of thing. Didn't tell her much."

Some men, Joan thought. Why, if they think women are so helpless, would they leave them ignorant of the very help they'd need most if they were left alone like that?

She suddenly realized that she and Fred had never discussed the subject of insurance. Like Charlotte's sister, she had no idea what insurance her husband had through his job, much less whether he had a private policy of his own or, if he did, whether he'd ever named her as a beneficiary. Having been widowed once, she knew how much it mattered. How could she not have asked him?

"I don't even know if she can afford to bury him. The mortgage payment is due next week, and I can't help much at all." Charlotte's tears threatened to overwhelm her again.

Now it was Birdie who went to her and embraced her. "Being poor is the pits, I know."

You? Joan thought. From all she'd seen, Birdie lived comfortably. And she had a steady job, even if it meant coping with Jim Chandler.

Nicholas spoke up. "Social Security has a death benefit that would help a little. Tell her she needs to apply for it right away. My grandmother didn't, not soon enough to get anything when my granddad died, anyway. She missed out."

"His auto insurance ought to pay something," Joan remembered.

"Maybe not," Charlotte said.

Would murder void the insurance? Joan had no idea, but like Charlotte, she needed to keep silent about what she did know. She shook her head. This Ward Utterback, whoever he was, had a lot to answer for.

"What will they do?" Birdie asked.

"I guess give up the house and move in with my folks if they have to. But my sister never got along well with Mom when she was growing up. It'll be worse now. The only good thing is, Dad is crazy about the boys. He'll sit on Mom."

Poor Mom, Joan thought, even while feeling for Vint's widow.

"Are we done here?" Nicholas asked abruptly.

"I think so," Joan said. "Bring your stands tomorrow, would you? I forgot to ask what the church has. I'll be sure there are seats. The service is at eleven—say half past ten to set up?"

"Good enough." Nicholas, already packed, slung his instrument over his shoulder and left. "Orchestra black tomorrow?"

"We don't need to wear black," Joan said. "And not a tux. Just something subdued. A jacket and tie, and dress shoes, not sneakers."

Charlotte zipped the soft case over her cello. "Thanks, you guys."

"Sure," Birdie said. Laying her violin in its battered case, she fastened the Velcro straps across its neck to hold it in place and loosened her bow. She was still slowly packing up when Charlotte left.

Joan closed her own case. "Birdie, thanks for your understanding. You knew what she was really worried about."

"I felt for her sister and those children. I remember when I was growing up, money got so tight, and my mother wouldn't take a handout from anyone. Once the only thing we had in the house was one can of green beans. We kids just cried."

"What did she do?"

"I don't know what she would have done, but that night someone brought us a big sack of groceries. Rang the bell and left it on the porch. When she went to the door, there it was. Then she cried."

"Poor Mrs. Vint. Bad enough to have to throw yourself on your parents after you've lived on your own," Joan said.

"Good that she has parents who could take her. Without my job, I'm on my own." Charlotte's voice went dead. "Before I got it, I was unemployed for a long time, and it was rough. The only thing I had of any value was my violin. More than once, I came close to selling it. But it belonged to my father, and music is the one thing that sustains me through terrible times. It wouldn't have bought as much food as it gives my soul."

"Are you afraid of losing your job?"

"You don't know what it's like! Jim's right. They'd let me go before him."

"I had to leave a job once." Joan's bitterness at the man she'd successfully fended off with a letter opener had long since faded, but she remembered well enough how desperate she had felt. "I had to leave town. Nobody in that town would have believed me over him. Anyway, I didn't have the courage to find out."

"What did you do?"

"That's when I came to Oliver. And this orchestra. They needed a librarian, so there I was."

"You couldn't survive on that!"

"No, I found something else, too. Old friends helped." And eventually I found Fred, but I can't tell her that.

"My only friend just got herself murdered."

Joan expected more tears, but Birdie kept the waterworks dammed up this time. Or maybe she'd cried herself out.

"She wasn't your only friend, Birdie. I care what happens to you, and I'll do all I can if you need help."

"Thank you. I appreciate it, but it's not the same as Sylvia."

"I know. Are you sure you'll be all right tomorrow?"

"No, but I'll try."

"Good." Now Joan could see the school janitor at the edge of the stage. "We'd better leave. We're about to get thrown out of here."

"It's all right. I'm okay." Birdie closed her case and tucked the music into the zippered pocket. "Let's go."

24

$\mathcal{F}$red shook his head wearily. "You ever get the feeling that all we're ever going to come up with is negative?"

"Don't be so hard on yourself," Captain Altschuler growled. He was sitting in Fred's office with the door closed. "Maybe Mayor Deckard can produce results out of thin air . . ."

"But the rest of us can't. I know."

"Deckard can make it sound good with the public. Buy us some time."

"Wish I thought that would get us anywhere." Fred sighed.

"Look on the bright side. Last time it got us a meth lab."

"Those guys will stay in business. They'll just move the business. We're keeping our eyes on a man we think might be one of their customers and hoping he'll lead us to them someday. Deckard got us a lead to that lab, but not to the killer. Who's killed again since then." He ran his hand through his thinning hair. "What really gets me is having an ID that's totally useless."

"Not totally," Altschuler said. "When you find him, you'll know you have the right man."

"Who'll kill who knows how many more before then. I can't begin to fathom dealing with a serial killer in a place this size. We don't have the manpower for it, for one thing."

"As close together as Purcell and Vint were, you're jumping the gun to talk about serial killers. It's more likely to have something to do with the woods."

"I hope so," Fred said, wishing Andrew weren't still sitting in a tree in those very woods. "Feels more like someone warning people off his particular patch, anyway. If old Mrs. Nikirk showed up with her dog and a slingshot, now, it would make sense. She grew up in those woods."

"But she's not Ward Utterback, whoever he is these days."

"No. And she got a kick out of showing us the cave she knew as a child. Not that he might not enjoy showing off."

"You think?"

Fred shrugged. "The EFF vandals did, though not in person. But nothing we found on that equipment matched the prints on Vint's car and the rocks that hit him and Purcell."

"A long shot at best."

"We're lucky to have that much. No witnesses. It's pretty remote—only reason we connected them was that Joan found the Petoskey stone in the woods and then Dr. Henshaw noticed the stone in the car. No reason for Utterback to think we spotted either of them."

"He has to be thinking he's home free."

"Maybe these are just his two latest. No way to tell how many he got away with."

"Now you're back to a serial killer," Altschuler said.

"Not yet. Not around here, anyway. We don't have any mysterious deaths that fit the pattern."

"You look at traffic accidents?"

Fred nodded. "And we asked the sheriff and the state police. Nothing suspicious, and no accidental deaths in this area in the past year. As I said before, everything we're coming up with is negative."

"I want you and Ketcham at both those funerals."

Fred nodded. "And checking out anyone else who knew either of them. It'll be our last chance at Sylvia's sister, too."

"No other family coming?"

"Only her husband and kids."

Joan didn't try to go to work before the service, as she would have done if she'd only been planning to attend it. She'd told the others to arrive by half past ten, and she'd promised to be sure chairs were ready for them. Stands, too, if she could find any. Might as well call ahead about that. It would be good not to have to carry one along.

The church secretary reassured her. "Oh, of course we have music stands, the good heavy black kind. You need four, right? I'll have the custodian set them up. Where do you want to sit, in the front or up in the balcony? The sound carries better from the balcony, they say, but people might like to watch you play, and they hate to have to turn around, especially at a funeral. You can park your cases in the choir room, behind the pulpit."

Joan agreed to sitting up front. It would be more intimate, especially if not very many people came. She had no idea how many friends Sylvia had. And Linda Smith might want to see the orchestra members who cared enough about her sister to play.

Fred took off for work at his usual time. "I'll see you there," he said. "Give you a ride home, if you want to walk over."

"I'll probably go on to work, but maybe you'd take the viola home afterward." The case was heavy, and by the end of the day she'd be glad not to have to haul it back across the park.

"Sure." He kissed her and was gone.

Before ten she checked her strings and her emergency supply of old strings, already stretched to tune. Even if they didn't sound as good as when they were new, they'd be a godsend if she suddenly had to change one during a concert. Only once had they rescued her, but that one time she'd been very glad to have them.

The sky was overcast, but judging by the thermometer outside her kitchen window, she wouldn't need to wear a coat. She slung her viola case across her back and her bag over her shoulder and started walking. The low-heeled shoes she'd chosen for the hike across the park would do fine for the service.

At the church, she climbed the front steps and walked down a side aisle. She was glad to see a semicircle of four chairs and stands waiting in the center of the chancel. She set her viola down and went through the door behind the pulpit. An upright piano, racks full of choir robes, and shelves full of sheet music told her she'd found the choir room, where the secretary had said they could leave their cases.

When she returned, the others had arrived. Together, they took their instruments to the choir room and unpacked. Back in the chancel, they checked their tuning to Nicholas's A.

Now people were coming into the church carrying white

papers the right size to be orders of worship. Joan went down
to beg an usher for four.

On the front was Sylvia's name and her birth and death
dates. Inside was a simple program, which didn't mention the
music.

"We're free to play in any order we like," Joan said.
"What do you think?"

"Hymns first," Birdie said. "That'll get the church people
in the right mood. Then Handel, for people like Sylvia."

"Good enough," Nicholas said.

They quickly agreed to play the hymns in the order in
which they had rehearsed them.

"But let's leave 'For All the Saints' to the very end of the
service," Joan said. "It's loud and if we don't let it drag, it can
be peppy, like the jazz black players used to play on the way
back from the cemetery. They can talk if they want to."

"Won't they be following the casket out?" Charlotte
asked.

"I don't know that there will be a casket."

"It's not about her body," Birdie said. "It's about Sylvia."

Joan hoped Reverend Eric Young, who had married her
and Fred, was up to holding a service for someone he'd never
met. It's not for Sylvia, she reminded herself. It's for her sister,
and for all the people who cared about her.

The small congregation was turning into a respectable
crowd. "I didn't know she had so many friends," Joan said.
She recognized several violinists from the orchestra and John
Hocking, of course, who had worked with Sylvia as well as
played music with her. Near the back she saw Jim Chandler
and Alex Campbell sitting together. She wouldn't know the
other Fulford employees, though she thought a woman on one
side might be the receptionist she'd met the other day. She'd

had even less contact with most of the people who had supported the tree sit. No, there was Skirv, sitting alone halfway down the aisle.

"I see a few people from work," Birdie said. "And you know the ones from the orchestra. But I don't know anyone else."

"There's my sister," Charlotte said. "I'm surprised she could face anyone else's funeral this week. She said she wanted to hear us play. She might ask us to do it for Herschel's service."

"Okay by me," Nicholas said. "Maybe he won't have as many thrill seekers."

Of course, Joan thought. That's why the church is so full. It explained the buzz among some of the people. She hoped the numbers would comfort Linda, now being ushered to the first pew with her husband and little girls. No casket, though. Only the two baskets of flowers suggested that this was a funeral.

She saw Fred enter with Sergeant Ketcham. They sat together near the center aisle in the back row. If other cops had come, they were blending in.

"Five till," Nicholas said. "Let's start."

As Birdie had predicted, the hymns shushed the buzz. The minister came in through the choir room door and sat down. The Handel went well, Joan thought, the double-dotted long notes as they should be and their intonation as good as she could hope for. Nicholas, of course, was exactly on pitch. If the others occasionally wobbled, maybe the congregation would put it down to emotion. When they finished, Joan and the two violinists rested their instruments in their laps, and Charlotte laid her bow on her stand.

Eric Young climbed into the pulpit and began the service. He kept it simple, as Joan had expected, sticking at first to familiar scripture readings, which might not have meant any-thing to Sylvia but would speak to her sister and her family. Finally he came to Sylvia.

"Not even Sylvia Purcell's friends knew her well. She was, everyone agrees, a private person. But we know some of what mattered to her. She loved music, which she played well, and her friends from the orchestra have brought some of that music to remind us of that love." He nodded in their direction. "With no children of her own, she loved her young nieces, who delighted in the letters they received regularly from Aunt Sylvia." He smiled down at Linda's girls. "She was committed to standing up for defenseless creatures, and in the end, she gave her life for that commitment.

"There's an Indian saying that may describe her approach to life: 'When you wake up ask yourself the question: What good can I do today? And think, when the sun goes down, It takes with it a piece of the life allotted to me.'

"As we celebrate Sylvia Purcell's all-too-brief life, let us ask ourselves what good we, too, can do today and every day." He closed the service with prayer and crossed the chancel in front of the quartet to shake hands with Linda and her family. Then he started down the center aisle to the narthex, behind the seats.

Nicholas raised his violin, and the quartet struck up "For All the Saints." It wasn't "When the Saints Go Marching In," which wasn't in the hymnal, but they took it briskly enough to give it almost the same effect. The people began to file out, speaking to one another, at first softly and then more naturally. Nicholas signaled the quartet to repeat the music until the church was almost empty.

While they were still playing, Linda Smith made her way up the chancel steps, leaving her daughters with their father.

"Thank you so very much," she said when they finished. "It meant a lot to me that you played. Could I contribute something to the orchestra?"

"We've set up a fund in memory of Sylvia," Joan told her. "You might want to designate your contribution for that fund."

"Perfect. I'll get my checkbook." She went back to her family, presumably to collect her purse.

Another woman had come up and was talking with Charlotte Hodden. They looked more than a little alike.

"This is my sister, Gail Vint," Charlotte said, and she introduced the other members of the quartet.

"It was beautiful," Gail said. "Charlotte thought you might be willing to play at my husband's funeral."

"If we can, we'll be happy to," Joan said.

"Of course I'd pay. How much do you charge?" She was being very stiff-upper-lip and businesslike.

Joan thought of what Charlotte had told them about Gail's financial straits. "We don't charge a fee, but of course the orchestra would welcome a donation when you're on your feet again. There's no hurry. If you never can give us a penny, that's all right."

Now Gail's eyes filled, and her words came tumbling out. "That's so kind of you. I don't even know when it will be yet. The funeral, I mean. We're still waiting for the coroner to release his body. It's so awful—Herschel doesn't usually work Sunday afternoon, but he went out to check on some reports of animals being killed in the woods. Mostly raccoons and squirrels and such, but wild turkeys and other birds, too, and one small doe—it's not even deer season. No shot or slugs or bullets, and for some reason they were just being left to rot. That wasn't his job, but he was so conscientious. He didn't

take the children, the way he usually would of a Sunday, because he was afraid whoever was going after animals might
not stop at little boys."

Instead, Joan thought, he hadn't stopped at Herschel.

25

I'll bet she saw him," Andrew said. "From where I sit, I can see way into the woods. Clear across that creek, even. I'll bet she saw him hit a bird."

Walking to work after lunch with Fred, Joan hadn't been able to resist calling him to report that someone was using animals out in the woods for target practice. She hated walking with a phone to her ear, but she didn't want to call from work.

"I suppose it's possible," she said.

"It's more than possible. Don't you remember? She hollered out something like that right before she fell."

"Andrew, I couldn't hear her; you could."

"Oh. Yeah. Well, trust me, she did."

"I believe you. You think this guy shot her because he heard her?"

"He wouldn't have heard her. It's hard enough to hear down to the bottom of the tree—you know that. But she was standing up. He could have seen her."

"And killed her so she wouldn't tell anyone she saw him hit a turkey?"

"I don't see how he could expect to kill her. It was a freak accident."

"Don't count on it, Andrew. He's killed a lot of animals out there. Even a deer. You keep down."

"Yes, ma'am."

He said it, but she didn't trust him to do it. By now he had to be stir-crazy on that tiny platform, and there were branches within reach. How could he resist climbing, for the exercise, if nothing else? She couldn't remember ever seeing Andrew that still for any length of time when he wasn't sick.

She'd told Fred what Gail Vint had said about the reason Herschel had gone to the woods, but he'd already known.

"The sheriff interviewed her on Sunday," he'd said outside the church. "He's been good about keeping us informed."

"And you don't think it's important?"

"It proves the man can aim. Gives us that much more reason to treat these deaths as homicides."

"Oh." She stood there, the sun in her eyes, a chilly wind blowing her hair, and the weight of her viola case pulling on her shoulder.

"You want me to run that by the house for you?"

"Yes, please." She slid the strap off her shoulder and handed the viola to him.

He slung it over his own shoulder as if it weighed nothing at all.

"Why not come with me," he said. "It's past noon."

Why not, indeed. And so they'd gone home together for a quick bowl of soup. Joan had changed out of the suit she'd chosen for the funeral into comfortable slacks and shirt. On the way back, she'd asked him to drop her at the police station, to give her a few minutes in the fresh air.

At the door of the center, after talking with Andrew, she resolved to put him and the dangers he faced out of her mind, at least until the end of the workday she'd already cut short. But the people who greeted her when she came in made that impossible.

"You went to that funeral?" Berta Hobbs asked. As dummy now, while her partner played out their hand of bridge, she was free to talk.

"Yes," Joan said.

"She played the music," Annie Jordan said. "They had a string quartet instead of an organ. I never heard of such a thing, but it was downright pretty. None of that deedle deedle deedle those groups play, but regular hymn tunes."

Joan suppressed a smile. "Thank you, Annie."

"I kinda wanted to sing along, but nobody else was doing it, so I figured it wasn't the thing to do. But I sang inside my head, you know?"

Joan let the smile out. "I hope you weren't the only one."

"I don't expect I was. Till you got to that slow piece, right before the preacher started talking. What was that, anyway?"

"It was from Handel's *Messiah*." When Annie looked blank, Joan added, "The one with the 'Hallelujah Chorus.'"

"I don't suppose you could play *that* for a funeral," Annie said.

"Or without the chorus," Joan said.

"I like when everyone stands up for it," Annie said. "I don't know why, but they do."

"The story is, the first time he heard it, the king of England was so impressed, he stood. So of course everyone else had to get up. And a lot of people still do."

"Well, I never."

"Was Sylvia's family there?" Berta asked.

"Oh, yes," Annie said. "Her sister and the sister's husband

226

and little girls. The preacher talked to them especially. And he said Sylvia gave her life for little animals and such and we all should live like that."

Close enough, Joan thought.

"I don't know about that," Berta said. "My days for climbing trees are long past."

Ora Galloway, her bridge partner, laughed.

"You don't think I ever did?" She bristled. "You should have seen me. I was a regular tomboy. I could beat my brother at basketball, too."

"Did the preacher talk about the man who killed her?" Ora asked. "I figure he's still on the loose out there. It's only a matter of time before he kills again. Ow!" He looked at Berta. "Keep your feet to yourself!"

She's looking out for my feelings, Joan thought.

"Just play the cards," Berta said.

"Well, good grief, all I said was—" But he stopped when she glared at him.

Joan went to her office, stashed her shoulder bag in a drawer, and sat down. Annie followed her in.

"You all right?"

"Thanks, Annie, I'm fine."

"That Ora shoots off his mouth too much."

"Don't worry about me. I'm tougher than I look."

"The music was beautiful. And so was the service."

"Her sister liked it."

"Well, that's what matters, isn't it? Everybody's always trying to figure out what the dead person would like, when it's the ones in the pews they ought to worry about."

Good for Annie. "Yes. But you know, I think maybe Sylvia would have liked it, too, even if she didn't go to church."

"You get any lunch?"

"Thanks, Annie. We went home. Anything happen around here?"

"I wouldn't know. I went to the service."

"Oh, that's right. Well, it's quiet now. I'd better return a few of these calls." There were no message slips waiting on her desk, but the blinker on her phone showed several voice messages.

Annie left her to it. The first couple of calls were requests for more information about programs announced in the newsletter, which must just be reaching people now. That was quick, Joan thought, as she noted the numbers to call.

Last was a call from Alex. Her words, asking for a return call, were straightforward, but Joan thought her voice sounded agitated. She hated to think what was coming.

Taking the work calls first, she signed up two new people for the exercise group. The first, a man, said he was only doing it because his wife wanted him to. "She thinks if I don't do something about this paunch, I'm gonna keel over. I held out until she quit cooking anything decent. So I'm giving in."

"I hope you enjoy it," Joan said, and made a mental note to ask the pretty young leader to pay him a little special attention.

The second was a woman with enough arthritis that she worried about being able to participate. "I don't want to get stiff, but I'm not supposed to do anything that hurts, and I've heard it has to hurt to do you any good."

Joan assured her that she could take it at her own pace, whatever the class was doing. "That no pain, no gain business doesn't mean joints."

The third and fourth calls were from orchestra members complaining about the new text to the Britten. Joan already knew what John Hocking thought, but the first chair violist gave her an earful when she returned the call. "Bad enough to listen to those jokes, but to have insults about us spouted at our own concert goes beyond bad. I don't know if it was the kid or the narrator who wrote them, and I don't care. You stand up for us, you hear?"

Then the first flutist exploded in her ear. "I know some people don't like a piccolo, but Heather was almost in tears. That's no way to treat her. I expected something better of you."

"I didn't—"

"It doesn't matter. What matters is that you fix it."

With that kind of emotion among the players, she dreaded calling Alex back. Maybe the new, softer Alex would be easier to take, or was that only in Jim's presence? They hadn't come up after the funeral, but of course the quartet had been talking to Linda Smith and Gail Vint. No reason for Alex to butt in.

"Alex? Joan."

"I need another favor." Calling it a favor was a step in the right direction, but otherwise it was the same old Alex. She just whacked you with what she wanted from you. "I've been getting complaints about the new narration."

Joan wasn't surprised. But what was Alex going to ask her to do about it? Shut up the complainers?

"And you want me to . . . ?"

"I want you to look over what I've done to it. See whether you think this version will offend anyone." Amazing. Maybe Alex really had changed. Maybe she really cared about the feelings of the players. "I couldn't wait at the church to talk to you, and besides, there were too many people up there, and I was with Jim."

"Yes."

"So I'm going to bring it over to you now."

"Alex, I'm at work. I was gone all morning. I can't spend the afternoon on orchestra business."

"Just a quick look—it won't take you a minute."

Uh-huh. "Why the big rush? You could bring it to me after work. I'll be home by six."

"But I want you to take it to Jim before he goes home."

Time to put her foot down. "Alex, I can't. If you bring it to me at home, I can look at it there."

"By that time he'll be home, too."

"So?"

"He lives way out in the boonies. Past where Sylvia was protesting. I don't want to drive you out there."

"I suppose I could drive myself." And see Andrew while I'm at it. Does Alex not know he's there now? Or is she blocking it? Why can't she drive out there? It could hardly be called throwing herself at him.

"That's settled, then. And Joan, there's no reason to tell him I'm the one who made the changes."

Oh, it's like that, is it? "I won't volunteer it."

"Not even if he asks."

"Not if I can help it." But I won't lie for you, Alex.

The rest of the afternoon went so quietly that she might as well have given in and read the thing at work. As it was, Alex got what she wanted without having to drive past the middle of town.

And I promised to drive all the way out there this evening.

It would make more sense, she knew, to call Alex back and ask her to take it to him in the morning, but she didn't want to go through another argument.

Look on the bright side, she told herself. At least I'll see Andrew. I'll go there first, before it's too dark to see him.

She thought she'd come to terms with her own wimpiness, but when she pulled out the center's checkbook and settled down to pay bills, she dug the ballpoint pen into the first check hard enough to tear a hole in ordinary paper.

26

*S*tanding on Joan's front doorstep, Alex thrust the familiar envelope at her. "I didn't have time to type them all clean, but I'm sure you'll be able to make them out."

Joan pulled out the pages and saw the changes inked above the lines in a cramped scrawl. "You're not asking me to give him clean copy?"

"Well . . ." Alex didn't meet her eyes.

"I couldn't if I wanted to. I don't even have a printer here." Hers had given up the ghost, and she hadn't yet replaced it. If she had to print something, she took a diskette to work. But that was more than she had any intention of telling Alex.

"If you remember, I wanted to take it to you at work."

"Honestly, Alex, I'm the orchestra's manager, not your private secretary. You can't expect me to do nonsense like this for you, much less at work."

"It's not for me. It's for the good of the orchestra. People were threatening to quit at the last minute."

Joan believed her. "I'll look at it, and I'll show it to Jim. But you or Jim will have to deal with the clean typing." Whoever did this version could just make the changes on it.

She took it back to the kitchen with her, where her teriyaki chicken was simmering in a wok. No self-respecting Japanese cook would acknowledge it, she thought, but after browning the chicken, she'd poured store-bought teriyaki sauce over the pieces, sliced some onions onto them, and covered them to finish cooking without her help. The rice, on the other hand, would boil over any minute if she didn't watch it. One of these days she was going to treat herself to an automatic rice cooker that would let her dump in the rice and water and forget about it. There—the rice was boiling. She turned the flame down, picked up the pages Alex had given her, and sat down at the kitchen table.

This time she gave the text a much more careful reading than when she'd seen it before passing it to Jim at Fulford Electronics. It was a far cry from Ogden Nash, but even with all the messing around Jim and Alex had done, she liked it better than the original, boring words. And Alex's edits helped, she had to admit. She'd come up with a line about their rich tone that should mollify the violas even while adding a little pizzazz to what had come with the Britten score. She hadn't done anything for the piccolo player, though. Joan thought about it and then tried her own version. "You have to ask yourself how such amazing sounds can possibly come from the piccolo, the smallest instrument in the orchestra." Was that really true? Maybe not. A triangle probably would beat it. "The smallest flute" would be better. And "music" would be better than "sounds." She penciled the change above the line that had reduced Heather Mott to tears and crossed it out. Then she crossed out her own "possibly." All right.

Could the oboes object to being told they "cut right through you"? Maybe, but they hadn't bothered to call about it yet. She considered something like "pierce you to your very soul" but rejected it as overblown, not in keeping with Tory's casual tone. Tory was right about what would speak to kids. Let it be for now. She could deal with the oboes later.

Where was Fred? It was time to eat, if she was going to see Andrew while it was still light outside. Tucking the pages back into their envelope, she stuck them into her jacket pocket. She quickly tossed a salad. Even as she was thinking she might have to start without him, Fred called.

"You mind if I come home late?"

"Of course not. It'll keep. And I have to go out."

"Oh?"

"I promised Alex I'd drop off a new version of the Britten text at Jim Chandler's."

"That's the next turnoff past Andrew's tree, isn't it? The woman who showed us the cave told us he lived down the road from her."

"Right. I thought I'd stop and say hi to Andrew on the way."

"Why doesn't she take it herself?" he asked. "I thought they were an item."

"Beats me. I've quit trying to understand Alex."

"Be careful out there. Those roads are treacherous in the dark."

She was touched by his concern. "I don't plan to stay late."

"Neither do I."

"Supper will wait for you."

Maybe, she thought, after she hung up, I should let the chicken keep simmering till I'm back. But memories of too many blackened suppers told her to turn it off. She put some chicken and rice in a couple of plastic bowls with tight lids and salad in another couple of bowls, slid the bowls into a plastic bag, wrote Fred a note, and left.

Andrew was glad to see her and gladder still when she sent a hot supper up in his basket. "Wow, Mom, this is great! How come?"

"I had to come out this way anyhow, and Fred wasn't going to be home in time for supper, so I thought why not?" She settled herself on the bed of leaves under his tree, leaning against it, and opened her two bowls. Rats. She'd forgotten utensils. Well, it wouldn't be the first time she'd eaten with her fingers.

On the ground beside her, the cell phone said something. She picked it up. "What? I had to put you down to pull off the lids."

"It's good, Mom."

"Thanks. You'll forgive me if I don't chat while I eat. I need one of those hands-free phone gizmos." Especially now, she thought, with chicken and rice on her fingers. But as long as she ate with her right hand and held the phone with her left, it wouldn't be too bad. If she used the slippery hand for the phone, she'd drop the thing. "I'm getting the hang of it now."

Even so, they ate silently.

"So how come tonight?" Andrew asked finally.

She told him about the text to the Britten.

"You'd think old Alex could come this far herself. But she always was weird, wasn't she?"

"I don't know how she is about men. This is the first time I ever saw her involved with one." She leaned back against the tree and licked her fingers.

"What's he like?"

"Alex thinks he's grand. He's good-looking, I'll give him that. A salesman. Knows how to turn on the charm."

"But? There was a but in your voice."

She looked up. He was lying on his belly, hanging over the

edge of the platform to look down at her. "I suppose there was. I don't really know him. But I heard him giving Birdie Eads a hard time when he didn't know I was there."

"What did she do wrong?"

"Nothing, far as I could tell. She works in the same place he does—where Sylvia did, too—and it sounded as if she was afraid he'd get her fired. Or make her job intolerable, so she'd quit."

"That's what you did."

She looked up again, surprised. They'd moved to Oliver after her boss had tried to assault her in the office. She'd known she couldn't stay after stopping him. How much had Andrew understood? She was sure she hadn't talked about it to him, but he must have seen how upset she was.

"You're right. But I was lucky. I had my parents' house in Oliver, and as it turns out, I had friends here who found me a job."

"So help her."

He made it sound so simple, but maybe there was something she could do to help Birdie, if it came to that. A new thought. Not that she had any ideas, but if she could find work for Bert, she ought to be able to think of something for Birdie, even if she couldn't hire her, too.

"I'd better go."

"Thanks for supper, Mom." He lowered the basket with the empty bowls in it.

"You're welcome." The damp breeze rustled the treetops and felt good on her face. "I hate to leave."

"There's not enough room up here for both of us."

"You're welcome to it. I like it fine down here." She took a few moments to walk around and look at her surroundings. Fiddlehead ferns were poking up from the forest floor beside her, and under the next tree mayapples were about to unfurl their umbrellas. Just a little farther into the woods, she could see a red trillium, a few white bloodroot blossoms, and lots of speckled dogtooth violet leaves. That spot of bright yellow couldn't be a dandelion, though, not way in here. No, she saw, when she went closer, it was a Celadine poppy, already. And nearby, there would soon be more—she could see the fuzzy buds. She walked back to the oak. The light had begun to fade, and Andrew's face was less clear than when she'd arrived. "I'd better drop this off while I still can see my way."

"See you, Mom."

"Bye." Dropping the phone in her pocket, she took a last look before turning her back on the woods.

And ran smack into Tom Walcher, the setting sun bright on his blazing hair. How had he sneaked up on her like that? Easy, she thought. I wasn't paying attention.

"You don't get it, do you?" He stood in her way, unmoving.

"Get what?" She was playing for time. Would he hurt her? She hadn't asked Fred whether he'd ruled Walcher out. He was such an obvious person, all except for that hair. Vint had laid into him, too.

"You're sneaking food to that guy up in the tree, aren't you?"

There was no way to hide the plastic bag she was carrying. Could she make him grab for it? Then she could give his prints to Fred.

"What's in the bag?"

"You wouldn't want it." She tried to bat her eyes at him flirtatiously, but it didn't come naturally. She hated to think how it looked to him.

However it looked, it didn't work. He kept his hands to himself; whether purposefully or not she couldn't tell. Now she was sorry she hadn't held the bag out to him. But he didn't give her time to think of anything else to try.

"Get out!" He leaned into her face. Short as he was compared to Andrew, she was shorter, and he loomed over her, the tendons in his neck taut and his nostrils flaring. "Get out now, and don't come back!"

"I was just leaving." Not proud of herself, she turned and all but ran.

When she started the car, a raucous twentieth-century symphony blared forth from the radio, a Russian, she was sure. Sounded like Shostakovich. Threaten me, will you? she thought, and turned the volume up higher than she herself could stand. Take that! But he hadn't threatened her, really. Not in so many words. It was his stance and the fierce look on his face that had scared her. And Andrew was far too high off the ground to come to her aid.

He would have been a witness, though, she thought. And Walcher knew someone was up there, even if he didn't know it was her son. He wouldn't have risked anything with another man watching, would he? Or would he have whipped out his handy-dandy Wrist-Rocket and taken care of him, too?

27

*O*nce out of Walcher's hearing, Joan turned the radio down and felt more than a little silly. How childish had that been? Never mind, she told herself. If that was the only way I had the guts to yell back at him, at least the music did it for me.

Too bad you couldn't call up exactly the response you want when you want it. Birdie needed something like that when Jim treated her like dirt. They made little pocket sirens for people to use against burglars—there ought to be a big market for a pocket gizmo that would let you push a button and have it come up with the right music to fight back with. *You done me wrong* would have to be a country song. *For you don't scare me,* good old Shostakovich, or maybe Charles Ives in one of his most raucous moments. And love songs for shy persons. All right, so it was silly. But she felt better.

She heard the radio switch to a Mozart violin concerto. Perfect, she thought, and turned it back up to a reasonable level, feeling it lift her spirits.

Now she'd turned onto what had to be Jim Chandler's road. Like the road to Andrew's tree, it was bumpy, and she slowed as much for the car's benefit as to let her watch for the right house. Set back on a long driveway was a little cinder block house painted green that didn't look like the kind of thing he'd live in. No, a thin woman stood on the skimpy front porch with a shaggy dog. Some kind of small collie. Joan had never been good on breeds of dogs. The one dog Andrew had loved in his childhood had been a mutt from the pound.

She wondered whether Andrew could see this far. He'd know her car. Could he watch her drive along?

She knew he was off to her right somewhere, but the tall trees were now on both sides of the winding road. On the left, though, more of the trees were scrubbier, shorter, closer together, with thinner trunks. She could see why the protesters had chosen the spot they had, besides, of course, the fact that the place they'd chosen was threatened by the apartment construction.

A little house trailer on her left, again, didn't look likely for Jim, nor did the sunbonnet goose in its garden plot. Then, up ahead, she saw what looked like a very old log cabin, the logs rough and weathered to a silvery gray. The road ended just beyond the cabin, which left no doubt about it. Unless she was on the wrong road altogether, this had to be Jim Chandler's. Joan pulled into the driveway and parked. The cabin had a walkway paved with limestone slabs, and a limestone chimney climbed up its side. On foot, she could see that the cabin was bigger than it had appeared at first. It was at least as big as her own house, with almost a full second story. A bright red porch swing hung from chains at one end of its wide porch, and the door had been painted the same shiny red. As she came closer, light flooded the front yard. Had he seen her? Unless maybe the light was activated by motion. Good against burglars, but it must startle the occasional deer that meandered through the yard.

She climbed the broad wooden steps. No doorbell, but she used the heavy iron knocker on the door.

She heard no response, but when she lifted the knocker a second time, the door opened and pulled it out of her hand. Jim Chandler's face lit up. "Joan, what a surprise! What brings you out here?" He was wearing blue jeans, a faded red flannel shirt, and work boots.

"I came to see my son, and Alex asked me to drop off the new version of the Britten text."

"I didn't know you had a son living out this way. Come in, won't you?" Standing back, he held the door open for her. It was low enough that she thought he probably had to stoop to go through it.

"It's a long story." She was glad to get a chance to see the inside of the cabin. Who would have expected this man to live in such a house?

A fire crackled in the big fieldstone fireplace, and more split logs waited in a limestone alcove beside it. The work clothes might be genuine, Joan thought, not put on for effect. Maybe Jim got those muscles cutting, splitting, and stacking logs, not working out in some gym. She looked at him with grudging respect. But she doubted that he'd woven the bright rag rugs scattered around the room or made the rustic wooden rocking chairs in front of the fireplace. The rest of the furniture was old, saggy, and comfortable looking. He might have built the plain shelves that housed books and various oddments, though, including baskets that looked more likely to have been woven in Indiana than in China. The front wall showed the logs, but the other three inside walls were rough white plaster. A painting of woods that could have been the ones in which Andrew was sitting hung over the fireplace.

"Jim, this is lovely."

"I'm glad you like it. Please, sit down." Gesturing to one of the rockers, he took the other.

She sat, enjoying the warmth of the fire. Now that the sun was nearly down, it was more than a little welcome. She felt almost guilty being so comfortable, with Andrew up there in the chill.

"How long have you lived here?" she asked. "And how did you find this place? It really is old, isn't it? I mean, it looks genuine." You're babbling, she thought. Stop it.

"It really is." His rockers sang against the wide pine floorboards as he rocked. "I heard it was for sale, and I bought it. Just like any other house. I knew I didn't want to live in the middle of town."

"Did you have to do much to it?"

He laughed. "Just about gutted the place. Didn't touch the outside, though, except to patch the chinking between the logs. There were holes you could see through. The floor is original, too, but I sanded it."

"You did it all yourself?"

"Some things, and some I hired done. I couldn't do wiring, for instance, or plumbing. And I couldn't afford to have everything done at once."

"How long did it take?"

"It feels like half my life. A couple of years, I guess. And there are still a few things I want to do. But I have all the modern conveniences except a furnace."

"Is this your only heat?"

"Yup. Unless you count splitting the wood. You know how they say it warms you twice, once when you split it and once when you burn it."

"Do you cut all your own wood, too?"

"No. I don't have enough land to keep up with the amount I burn. Or time enough to do it."

"I can imagine."

He walked over to the fireplace and laid another couple of logs on the fire. With a stone hearth as deep as his, she realized, he didn't need to bother with a screen. Any stray sparks would land safely on the stone.

"My next project will be a stove."

"How do you cook now?"

"Not for the kitchen—for here."

"Oh . . . but the fireplace is so beautiful."

"Sure, in April. But come January, I'd be glad not to lose so much heat up the chimney. It gets cold upstairs."

"Of course."

"I have to admit, though, that I'd miss it. It's probably why I've taken so long to get around to it."

"You couldn't put a stove upstairs, instead?"

"I've been thinking about that. Maybe a little coal stove."

Her own rockers sang. She could love a place like this, she thought, though she wouldn't want to face that road in winter. And when it came right down to it, all that wood burning would be hard work. Hard on her viola, too. It had to dry out the air. The poor thing would crack wide open.

"So, let's see what you have for me."

Startled, she reached into the shoulder bag she'd parked on the floor and passed him the envelope. "Alex and I have both been getting calls from players objecting to things they thought made them sound bad."

"Uh-huh."

She looked around the room while he read. A collection of hand-carved walking sticks leaned against the wall in one corner, and a Scoutmaster hat that looked like Smokey the Bear's sat on a shelf next to a row of mugs with dates on them—"1994 summer camp" beside "1995 Camporee." The baskets on his shelves held collections of attractive things that he or his Scouts must have picked up here and there, as Andrew had done—a cocoon on a stick, an abandoned wasp's nest, and a small bird's nest in one. In others were arrowheads, rocks, and shells. She couldn't see them clearly from her chair.

A generous basket was heaped with what looked like lost-and-found items—mittens, neckerchiefs, a compass with a cracked lens, a blue Cub Scout flashlight that looked like the one Andrew had cherished when he was seven. Plastic cord stood ready for lanyard making, and bits of red and green rope had to be for tying knots. Closer to her, a tattered Scouting manual and a pile of Boy Scout badges with name tags on them waited for boys to claim them. She wondered whether there was a badge that had to do with music. He'd said he was going to tell his Scouts they should come to the concert.

He looked up when he finished reading. "Touchy bunch, aren't they?"

That got her back up. "They know they're not perfect, but they do the best they can. They don't need to be insulted—not in their own concert."

"I see you violas couldn't take it. It figures." She recognized the tone he'd used on Birdie. One minute charming, the next nasty.

"It was our first chair who called Alex, and she's an excellent player."

"For a viola. You know what they say about violas—"

She cut him off. "I've heard all those jokes."

"What do you call it when two violas play the same note? A half step."

She glared at him.

"It's a joke."

"I think it's time for me to leave." She struggled to her feet, wishing there were a more graceful way to climb out of the rocker.

He jumped up. "I should have known. You women are all alike. First you're all flattery and then you take offense at the least little thing. It's all a tease—tease a man and then think you can just walk out on him."

Reaching behind her, she backed toward the door. "But I didn't—"

"Oh, yes, you did, and nobody makes a fool out of me." Something in his eyes scared her even more than his words.

"I wouldn't—"

" 'It's so lovely.' " He mimicked her voice. " 'You did it all yourself?' " He grabbed her. "I'll show you what I can do!"

"No, Jim." She tried to say it firmly, but she could hear her voice shake. And she couldn't pull away from his grip on her arm. "Jim, stop! You're hurting me!"

He laughed. "You want it. You know you do. I've been watching you. I could see it in your eyes ever since the first time you saw me. And now you've come to me."

Shaking her head, she fought the fingers that dug into her arm, but her strength was no match for his. "No, Jim. I—"

" 'No, Jim,' " he mocked her. Pressing her body against the log wall, he jammed his wet mouth onto hers. He fumbled with her shirt buttons while his teeth dug into her lips.

Her fingers, groping behind her for something to use as a weapon, felt only old mittens.

Then, as suddenly as he'd begun, he pushed her away. "Get out of here. Who'd want such a scrawny thing, anyway? God, you're nothing but a stick, like my mother."

Dazed, she grabbed the bag she had dropped and ran the last few steps to the door.

He followed her and stood in the doorway watching her stumble down the stairs and into the car. She kept expecting him to make some last crack, but he stood silent. When she backed out of the driveway, he was still standing there, but the look that had frightened her had disappeared from his eyes. Or was it only that she was no longer close enough to see it? The man in the doorway of the cabin seemed as charming as ever. As she drove off, she couldn't help looking back. He was waving.

Joan shuddered and wiped her mouth with her hand. She tried to tell herself she was blowing the whole thing out of proportion. After all, Alex was dating this man. All he'd done was grab her and kiss her.

No, she thought, remembering his eyes. And that crack about her wanting it. She could still feel the spots where his fingers had dug into her arms. They were going to bruise, she thought. He knew he was hurting me. He wanted to hurt me.

What would Fred say? Would he laugh at her, or would he tear Jim Chandler apart? She didn't want him to do either one. She wanted time to think.

28

When she came to the turnoff to Andrew's tree, she was tempted to stop again, but she held back. It wasn't fair to unload on him, especially not with him way up where he couldn't do a thing.

Then her cell phone rang. Nobody had that number but Andrew and Fred, though Fred never used it. She pulled over to a convenient wide spot in the road and stopped to pull the phone out of her pocket.

"Andrew?"

"You okay, Mom?"

"Sure." She tried to sound casual. "Why?"

"I was watching you with my binoculars."

"You what?"

"I can see a long way from up here. Not where you are now, but across a creek to that road you were on before. I saw you go into that cabin, and when you came out, you took off like someone was after you. You sure you're okay?"

She was flabbergasted. "Nobody's chasing me, Andrew." But she couldn't help looking back to confirm it.

"Then what happened?"

The shudder returned, and she gripped the steering wheel hard with her free hand. "I—I don't quite know." Her voice trembled in spite of her best effort to control it. "He came on to me."

"He scared you?" Andrew wasn't laughing at her, and he certainly couldn't tear anybody apart from up there. "The man who was standing there when you left?"

She nodded, knowing full well that he couldn't see her. "He grabbed me by the arm. Hard. I couldn't get away from him."

"But you did."

"No, he pushed me off. Told me I was too skinny. I wasn't good enough for him. If he hadn't, I don't know what would have happened."

"You're not going back there. Ever." This authoritative man was her child? But he was right.

"No, I'm not." Was that why Alex wouldn't go? Even though she dated him, was she afraid to be alone with him? So she sent me! Joan was suddenly angry.

"And Mom, don't take this wrong, but you're not skinny."

She was past taking it wrong. "Compared to Alex. Jim's the man I told you about who's dating her."

Andrew had met Alex. "Well, sure, compared to her."

Or compared to Birdie, she thought. If she was right, Jim Chandler and Birdie had been a couple first, and Birdie was still angry about the breakup.

But suppose she'd read Birdie's tension all wrong.

Andrew broke into her silence. "Mom? You all right?"

"Just thinking. Andrew, before Sylvia fell, you could hear her saying something. Where was she looking?"

"Into the woods, why?"

"That's what I remember, too. But couldn't she have been doing what you were doing today—looking past the woods?"

"I guess."

"Exactly what did she say?"

"I told you—something about birds. Or a bird."

She didn't want to put words into his mouth, but they weren't in court and she wasn't a cop. "Did she call it Birdie, as if she were talking to it?"

"That's right. How did you know? She yelled right into my ear, 'Birdie, no!' Then she fell."

"I've got to talk to her."

"Mom, she's dead."

"Not Sylvia. Her friend Birdie. Birdie Eads. See you later, Andrew." She flipped the phone closed.

Now, if only Birdie would be at home. Joan pulled up to the little house. Lights were on in the living room—a good sign.

Birdie answered her ring. "Joan! Are you okay?"

Joan automatically put a hand up to the hair straggling down the back of her neck. How bad must she look? "Can I come in?"

"Of course." But Birdie ushered her in as if she were at least ninety years old, and an old ninety, at that.

Bad, then, she thought. Sitting beside Birdie on her love seat, she didn't know how to begin. "Alex sent me out to Jim Chandler's tonight."

Birdie's hand rose to her mouth. "Oh, no!"

"You went out there the day Sylvia fell, didn't you?"

She hung her head. "Yes."

"After Sylvia tried to talk you out of it."

"Yes." Almost a whisper.

"Why? Why didn't she think you should go?"

"Because I'd told her."

"What had you told her, Birdie? What did he do to you?"

"You know, don't you?"

Not speaking, Joan took her hand.

Finally Birdie looked at her. "Did he rape you, too?" And the tears came.

Joan held her close until her sobs subsided. "You never told anyone but Sylvia?"

"I was too ashamed. And Sylvia made it sound so easy. She wanted me to report him to the police. Or our boss. But Jim said they'd fire me, not him."

"So you didn't."

"I couldn't, don't you see? Nobody would believe me. It would be my word against his—he never left a mark on me."

A rape kit at the hospital might prove it, Joan thought, feeling her own bruised arm. "Is he still—"

"No. He started seeing Alex, but I never thought he'd hurt her—or you."

"Just my arm. I'm not his type."

"Not fat, you mean, like me." The words were matter-of-fact, but her mouth trembled, and her eyes flashed. "He likes women with a little meat on them, he said. At first I was flattered. But then he wouldn't take no for an answer—and, oh, Joan, I'd never even been with a man."

You poor baby, Joan thought. "I'm so sorry. But Birdie, why did you go out there? Was that when he was still being charming?"

"No. He made me do all kinds of things and kept on—he just kept on hurting me. He was so strong. He threatened to tell them lies about me at work to get me fired. He knew that job was all I had."

And he browbeat you into thinking there were no other jobs for a woman like you. "So you went. In the middle of the day."

"Yes. On days when he supposedly worked at home, he'd

make some excuse for me to take him something or other from work, like his personal errand girl. But that day, I was early, and he wasn't home. I was so relieved, I just left whatever it was and went back to work. When your husband came to tell us about Sylvia, I was in the office and could give him my key to her apartment."

"That helped, I know," Joan said.

"It helped her sister. But nothing helped Sylvia."

The only person you trusted, Joan thought. I've got to help you find another job, away from him.

"Did he know you told Sylvia?"

"He laughed."

"Laughed?"

"He said she was a kook, and nobody would believe anything she said."

She'd have to tell Fred, Joan thought.

Ketcham caught Fred on the way back from Captain Altschuler's office. "Andrew for you on line one. Sounds upset."

Fred took it at his own desk. "What's up?"

"It's Mom."

He had to press the receiver against his ear to hear the faint voice. "Is she hurt?"

"I don't know."

"What do you mean, you don't know?" He caught himself bellowing but didn't care.

"You know she went out to deliver something to the man Alex is dating. Jim somebody. Brought me supper first."

"Yes, and?"

"When she came back—well, she didn't come all the way back here again. . . ."

"Andrew, get to the point. Is she hurt?"

"I don't know. I think maybe he attacked her."

"And she's still out there?" He was on his feet.

"No. I saw her get in the car, but she looked terrible. She drove off. So I called her cell."

Was there no way to speed him up? Fred forced himself to slow down, as he would with a witness to something he didn't care so much about. He loosened his hand from its death grip on the phone and waited.

Andrew went on, louder now, "She said he came on to her."

"That's all?" Joan was capable of dealing with a flirt.

"No. He grabbed her arm, and she couldn't pull away from him. Then all of a sudden he let her go—pushed her, even. Anyhow, that's what she said. But isn't it true that a lot of rape victims are too ashamed to tell? That's how she sounded, ashamed. And scared. I saw her almost fall down the steps when she came out of his cabin."

"Where is she now?"

"She didn't let me see her again. She said she was going to see a friend of Sylvia's. Oh, that's the other part. The woman's named Birdie, and that's what Sylvia said just before she fell: 'Birdie, no!' Mom thinks she meant that Birdie. But I don't know where she lives."

"I do. Thanks, Andrew." If she was with Birdie, she was safe for the moment, anyway.

"Fred? You think I should come down?" The voice shrank again, as if he'd pulled away or maybe couldn't make himself say it.

Fred held back the explosion he'd been resisting ever since Andrew first dropped his own bombshell on them. "Of course I think you should come down. You never should have gone up in the first place."

"I can see this guy's cabin from up here, you know. Let you know if he leaves."

"He's in there now?"

"Yeah. Hasn't come out since he watched Mom drive off. He stood there and waved at her, can you believe it?"

That was the sheriff's territory. Pursuing someone out there was one thing, but staking out his residence in the county would be entirely different. Andrew, inside the city limits, could do the job without overstepping any boundaries. If you overlooked his ongoing trespass on private property, that is.

"The last thing I want to do is keep you up in that damn tree," Fred said slowly. "But as long as you insist on staying up there, I want to know the minute you see him do anything. You have my cell phone number?"

"Yes." Andrew's voice combined seriousness and joy in that one word. "And Fred, I won't let you down."

He didn't use the siren on the short trip to Birdie's. But his fingers gripped the steering wheel as tightly as they'd gripped the phone, and he had to work to keep from flooring the gas pedal.

Relief flooded over him when he saw Joan's old car standing alone in front of the house. He took the porch steps two at a time and punched the doorbell.

"Lieutenant," Birdie said. "Come in."

He nodded and reached Joan in three steps. Then he couldn't speak. And he hesitated to take her in his arms.

"Fred, what are you doing here?" she said. Her hair was coming loose, but her shirt was buttoned and hardly rumpled, only a little more than usual for this time of day. Most of all, her manner was calm for a rape victim.

"Andrew called. He was worried after he talked to you."

She smiled. "As hard as I work at not hovering, now he's doing it?"

"Are you really all right? He didn't hurt you?"

"Come sit down. Birdie has something I think you need to hear."

He sat in the chair she pointed to, and she took Birdie's hand and led her to the love seat. Birdie's face was tear streaked.

"Tell him, Birdie," Joan urged softly. "Fred will understand."

Birdie shook her head and stared at her lap. "I can't."

"I won't let anything happen to you. It's different now. I'll back you up. People will have to believe you. I'll even find you another job, if you don't want to stay there."

"Really?" Birdie looked up at her. "You'd do that for me?"

"Of course I would. And I'm sure there are all kinds of people who'd be glad to have you working for them. We just have to find the right one. Someone who will treat you like a human being."

"What happened, Birdie?" Fred asked gently.

She raised her eyes to his. "Jim Chandler—the man you met at Fulford . . ."

"Yes."

"He raped me. More than once."

"At work?"

"At his cabin. Where Joan went today. That's how she knows what he'd do."

"When?"

"The last time was before he started going out with Alex—you know Alex?"

Fred nodded. That meant there was virtually no chance of finding any forensic evidence. Birdie would have bathed many times and almost certainly laundered her clothing since then. And any abrasions there might have been probably wouldn't show by now.

Birdie went on telling her story. At first she could hardly get the words out, but then they came faster and faster. Yes, she'd washed her clothes. No, she'd never gone to the hospital or filed a police report. But she had told a friend.

"What friend?" he asked.

"Sylvia Purcell. I made her promise not to tell anyone. She didn't like it, but she promised."

"Did you go out to the cabin the day Sylvia fell?" he asked.

Her eyes opened wide. "How did you know?"

"We have a witness who heard her call your name just before she fell." He avoided Joan's eyes, though maybe she'd already told Birdie what Andrew had said. "She could see his cabin from the tree, you know."

"I know." She was staring at her lap again. "She'd call me at work after I'd been out there and tell me I was a fool for keeping his secret."

"Did he know you'd told her?"

"Yes, but he didn't take her seriously, and he didn't think anyone else would, either. And now she can't tell."

"But you can. If we need you, would you be willing to testify?"

She nodded mutely.

29

On the short trip home, Joan wished they hadn't driven separately.

But she let Fred sit down on the sofa to take off his shoes before asking, "Have you excluded Jim Chandler from your list of possibles?"

"Not yet," he said. "Until today, the man seemed squeaky clean. A Scout leader. He was working at home the day Sylvia was hit—Andrew heard her call out to Birdie not to go there. And he was in Tell City the Sunday Vint hit the tree."

"That's what he told Alex, but I wonder. Birdie didn't tell you that he wasn't home the day Sylvia fell."

He straightened up with a shoe in one hand. "He wasn't?"

"When he didn't answer the door, she left whatever she was supposed to deliver and got away while she had the chance. So he might have been near Sylvia's tree. He's dangerous, Fred."

"Show me that arm." She held it out to him, and he pushed up her sleeve. Even though he held it gently, she couldn't help wincing. "It's going to bruise. Better ice it down."

"I will." Reclaiming her arm, she slid the sleeve back down. "Fred, he could have been near enough. That thing of

Andrew's shoots a hundred yards. But we thought she just fell. All our attention was on her—we weren't looking for anyone else. And the Petoskey stone proves somebody did kill her."

"I don't suppose you spotted a Wrist-Rocket in his house."

"No. But there was a lot of odd stuff in his lost-and-found. And I saw a basket of shells and likely looking rocks in with the Scout stuff. I hope he didn't notice that I was trying to see into it better. We've got to go back there before he gets rid of them."

"You're not going back." He said it flatly, and she could tell from his face that he wasn't kidding.

"You sound like Andrew. But I won't go, if you'll promise to."

The phone in his pocket rang, and he held it to his ear. "Yes? . . . When? . . . I'm on my way." He took her hand. "That was Andrew. Chandler just drove off."

Which way? she wondered, but of course from that end of the road, there was only one way, and Andrew wouldn't be able to see the car when it reached the main road—he hadn't been able to see hers when he called her.

Fred held on to her hands. "Promise you won't go to his house." His blue eyes stared into hers.

"All right, I promise."

He kissed her. "I'll be back as soon as I can."

"I'm all right, Fred. You do what you have to do."

He hadn't even eaten, she saw when she went into the kitchen. She put away his food and cleaned up the kitchen, but her mind was racing.

Of course, Jim Chandler could be going somewhere perfectly innocent. Maybe he was taking Alex out to dinner. If she didn't refuse his advances, Joan thought, that romance might continue in an ordinary way. Alex had no idea how

dangerous he could be. She was only being her ordinary obnoxious self when she sent me out there.

But he'd gone too far today, and he had to know that she
knew Birdie. And if he suspected her of having guessed why
Birdie was avoiding him, even though she had taken forever to
figure it out, he could figure Birdie would talk to her, probably soon. Would he try to stop her? Or, if it had been worth
killing Sylvia because Birdie had told her, would he now go
after Birdie or her?

Either way, she thought, we'll be safer together. I'd better
warn her. After drying her hands, she picked up the phone.
"Birdie, I'm coming back. Don't let anyone in until I get there,
all right?"

"Don't worry about me," Birdie said. "Your husband already sent an officer to stay with me tonight."

With you? she couldn't help thinking when she hung up.
What about me? No officer has shown up at my door. She
didn't usually lock the doors while she was at home and awake.
Not in Oliver. But tonight was different. She turned the dead
bolt on both the front and the back doors and checked the window latches on the first floor. All locked, good. She turned on
both the front and back porch lights and even pulled the living
room curtains shut, something she rarely did. But the dark outside made her feel too exposed with the lights on indoors.

From the corner, her viola and music stared reproachfully
at her, but she knew she'd never be able to concentrate enough
to practice. This kind of tension called for a good book. Not
a mystery, though. The last thing she needed was suspense.
She rummaged in the bookcase for her collection of Jane
Austen's early, unsold works. Just right, she thought, and
curled up on the big old sofa to let Lady Susan's machinations
take her mind off what worried her.

Even so, when the phone rang, she jumped.

"Mom?"

"Andrew?" But that wasn't Andrew. "Good heavens—Rebecca?"

"Has it been so long since I've called that you can't even tell me from Andrew?"

There was a time when a crack like that from Rebecca would have worried her. Her daughter had gone through a long prickly stage, when almost nothing Joan could say had rubbed her the right way. But tonight she sounded merely amused.

"Forgive me. It's been a strange day. A strange week, for that matter."

"He's all right, isn't he?"

"Far as I know. I took him supper."

"Took him—Mom, where is he? He's called a couple of times, but I thought he was at home. And why can't he come home for supper?"

Joan wanted to kick him. If he hadn't told his sister what he was doing, that was one thing. But to call her and omit a little detail like making the call from seventy feet up in a tree was something else. She was tempted to make him do it himself. How much would be too much to tell Rebecca, stuck in New York as she was? Her bank job didn't allow weekend trips home to visit her family.

"Mom?"

She'd been silent too long. "I'm sorry. Are you ready for a long story?"

"Shoot."

So Joan leaned back into the sofa and told her, beginning with her own impatience at poor Sylvia when she announced that the tree sit protest took precedence over the orchestra concert.

"Andrew was supporting Sylvia's protest, and when she fell out of the tree, he took her place."

"She fell? And he's up in a tree? So how did he call me?"

"Cell phone. It's the only way the rest of us can talk to him."

"Where is this tree, anyhow? And why can't you just go there?"

"Just inside Oliver. Andrew can see outside the town from his platform up there. But he's technically in town, which means that Fred is involved in anything that happens there. We can go there, of course, but without the phones we'd all have to scream. Most of the time the connection's pretty good, and we can swap batteries and recharge them for him. The people who were supporting Sylvia help him, too." Rebecca was going to think she knew who those people were, but Rebecca didn't need to know everything.

"How high is he, anyway?"

"About seventy feet."

"That's a seven-story building! How did his friend survive a fall like that?"

Joan hesitated, but she couldn't lie to Rebecca. "She didn't. She was still alive when the ambulance came, but she died in the hospital."

"You know all that because of the orchestra or Fred or what?"

"I was there. With Andrew. We saw her fall."

"Oh, Mom! I'm so sorry. And now Andrew's up there."

"Yes."

"You must be scared stiff."

"Yes." You don't know the half of it.

"I'm going to call him right now and tell him he ought to come down. He doesn't have the right to worry you like that! Or me!"

Joan laughed. Rebecca, coming to her defense? It was wonderful. Also unlikely to do any good. But she gave her daughter Andrew's cell phone number and enjoyed imagining the resulting fireworks.

She had hardly opened the book again when the phone startled her again. She grabbed it. But this time, it was Fred's brother, Walt, asking for him.

"He's out, Walt. Is something wrong there? Your parents?"

"They're okay. Mom asks for him all the time, but of course she's totally forgotten you."

"That's all right. I didn't expect her to remember about me." Helga Lundquist, whom Joan had met for the first time back before Christmas, was in the early stages of dementia, probably Alzheimer's. Joan hoped the family would get her properly worked up and diagnosed soon but was keeping her nose out of their affairs for now, at least. They were doing a good job of helping Fred's parents manage living in the house where he had grown up. Already, though, Helga had begun wandering, and neighbors in their little village sometimes had to help her find her way home. Joan wished they were closer. From Oliver to Bishop Hill, Illinois, was too long a drive for a weekend jaunt.

"I'll tell him you called. I don't know what time he'll be home, though."

"No problem. Tomorrow's soon enough. If it gets to be late, tell him I'd rather he waited till morning." Whatever was on Walt's mind wasn't something he offered to share with Joan.

She promised. "Give your family our love. We still expect Kierstin to visit sometime." Walt's daughter, a high school senior, had entranced Andrew during their visit and had invited herself to visit them. "I take it she's not serious about looking at Oliver College."

"No, she's accepted at Illinois. There's no way I could afford a private school, and she knows it. But if you wouldn't mind, she'd get a kick out of coming to see you. One of us would help her with the driving, of course, but we'd have to go straight back. Between the restaurant and the folks, there's not a lot of spare time."

"We'd be delighted." Once Andrew's safely out of the tree, that is. "When is her semester over?"

"Not for another month. Graduation's in late May."

"That ought to work. Good to hear your voice, Walt. I'll be sure to tell Fred you called."

The phone was finally silent then, and she caught herself nodding off. Not tonight, she thought. Not till I know what's going on. She went to the kitchen and brewed a pot of coffee before settling back down with Lady Susan.

If you'd had Lady Susan for a mother, Rebecca, she thought as she read, you'd have had a right to bite her head off the way you used to do mine.

This time when the phone rang, she reached for it almost absentmindedly.

"Mom?" This didn't sound like Andrew, either, but it wasn't Rebecca. It was more muffled.

"Andrew?"

"Mom, is Fred there? I can't rouse him on his cell."

"No, he went back to work after you talked to him before."

He said something unintelligible.

"I can't hear you."

"I'm inside my sleeping bag." That was clearer.

"Is it that cold now?"

"No, but I think someone's been shooting at me."

"Shooting!" Her feet hit the floor. "Bullets?"

"I don't think so. There's no bang, but I hear things whizzing by my head, and I think one landed on the platform. So I'm as flat as I can get, inside the sleeping bag. Rebecca just called and told me I should get the heck out of here, but I'm safer this way."

"Andrew, you call 911, and I'll work on finding Fred. I'll find someone, anyway. Can you see who it is?"

"Maybe Walcher?"

"You saw him?"

"No, it's too dark. But I heard one of his bulldozers arrive down there about half an hour ago."

"You haven't been hit?"

"Not yet. But I'm well padded, and I'm flat. I'm not budging till someone tells me it's safe. I remember Sylvia."

So did Joan. She called Fred's number but got no answer. Then she tried his cell phone. It invited her to leave him a voice mail. She hung up on the recorded voice and tried the number Fred had given her for when his desk phone didn't answer.

"Ketcham," a familiar voice answered. Thank God.

"Sergeant, this is Joan Spencer. I've been trying to reach Fred."

"I thought he went home." She could hear him wondering whether he should have lied for his lieutenant.

"He did, but he got a call and left again. Didn't he check in with you?"

"Not yet. He knows I'm here, though."

"I can't find him. But Andrew just called. He says someone's shooting at him. He had the good sense to crawl inside his sleeping bag, head and all, and lie flat on the platform. I told him to call 911, but I need to find Fred. I don't understand why he's not answering his cell phone."

"He must've let the battery run down again. We'll get someone out there right away."

"I'm coming, too." She hadn't known it until it was out of her mouth.

"No. If you got caught in a gunfight—"

"It's not a gunfight."

"You said—"

"Andrew said there's no bang, just whizzing past his head. Or there was, until he got inside the sleeping bag. I don't know how much he can hear now. But it sure sounds like the man with the slingshot."

"Give me Andrew's number."

She did.

"And leave his line free."

"I will." Not that it's a line. But I can't stay home. Not if someone's out there shooting at my son. "And Sergeant, he says he heard a bulldozer drive up."

"Thanks. You sit tight. We'll handle it from here."

30

Fred would skin her alive if he knew what she was planning, but there was no way Joan could sit tight, as Ketcham had put it. She pulled on a black turtleneck and pants and dark sneakers and socks. The socks were probably navy, but all that mattered was not to show up in the dark. Cover your skin, she thought, and rummaged in the living room coat closet for the ski cap in shades of blue, none too light, that Annie Jordan had made her for Christmas. If she pulled it all the way down, only her eyes would show. It had slid off the shelf, but she found it mixed in with the boots on the floor. Her navy gloves would hide her hands.

I'm not going to his house, she told herself. And I'm not going to butt in. But I have to know what's going on. That bulldozer . . . I don't know whether Fred ever checked Walchcr. There's so much I don't know.

She soon was bouncing along the rutted road, not even trying to dodge the ruts. But before she reached the clearing, she pulled off to the side and killed the lights and the motor. Even the tiny flashlight in her pocket would give her away. She'd risk turning an ankle, instead. It seemed to take forever for her eyes to adapt to the darkness, but when the black sky sprouted more stars than she remembered ever having seen, she thought she must be ready. Almost as an afterthought, she reached into the wayback for her walking stick. It would give her a fighting chance at staying upright. She turned off the dome light before she opened and softly closed the car door.

No sign of the police. Where were they, anyway? She shouldn't have been able to beat them out there.

When she came to the clearing, she saw the bulldozer standing smack in the middle, silent and bulky.

The moon gave a little light. A little more would be friendly, she thought, but of course it would give her away, too. A few feet inside the woods, she skirted the clearing and made her way toward the oak tree. No point in making her silhouette an easy target.

So where was this shooter? She wished she could ask Andrew whether he was still hearing anything up there, but she didn't need Ketcham to tell her not to call now.

The man who had shot Sylvia hadn't been in the clearing that day, she knew. If he had, she and Andrew couldn't have missed him. But now—could someone be taking shots at Andrew from the other side of the bulldozer? She edged her way around the clearing toward it.

She'd put the knitted hat on, but when she pulled it down to hide her face, it obstructed her vision so badly that she slid it back up. Just as well. It would have muffled her hearing, too. She strained for any faint sound that might have been a stone hitting a tree or landing on dried leaves, even while she tried to keep her own careful steps as quiet as possible.

Just ahead, an owl hooted. Then a far-off owl answered. Finally, when she thought she was within the range of a Wrist-Rocket from Andrew's tree, she eased herself into a sitting position under a tree. Whatever happened, she'd be here for him.

At first, she sat coiled to jump up, as if she could somehow interfere. Gradually, though, suspense turned to peace. She leaned back against the tree trunk and tried to identify constellations. Even broken up by branches, the Big Dipper was easy, and she was reasonably sure she spotted Orion's Belt, but after that, her pitiful command of the night sky let her down. She wished she knew more.

Then she heard a *thwack* into the trunk of the tree beside hers. A few moments later, a sharp pain in her head on the side closer to Andrew made her yelp.

"Hey!" she yelled into the darkness. No point in staying silent if he'd already spotted her. She pulled the knitted cap down over her ears and face to give her a little protection, if nothing else, and scooted around to the other side of the tree—farther away, if the shooter was off to her left, and safer. Dark-adapted or not, her eyes gave her no clue. She wished the tree trunk were thicker.

In her pocket, her cell phone startled her by ringing. She tapped it to stop the sound and then held it to her ear.

"Mom? Was that you? Where are you?" Andrew asked.

"Down here," she whispered.

"Are you okay?"

"Yes, but he got me with a stone." She lay flat and patted the ground around her with her free hand, feeling for that stone or the one she'd heard first.

"I can't see you."

"Good."

"Where are the cops?"

"That's what I want to know."

"I'll call them again."

"Good." She pulled off a glove, closed the connection, and slid the phone back into her pocket. Flat on the ground felt good. And if the shooter was aiming at a silhouette, as he must be, it would show him almost none.

Sudden light blinded her. Involuntarily, her eyes squinched shut. "Turn that light off!"

"You again! What the hell are you doing out here at this hour?"

She still couldn't see him, but the voice was unmistakable. "Mr. Walcher?" He was the one? The bulldozer should have prepared her, but in spite of having made the case to Fred, she found it hard to believe.

"You better believe it, lady. And you better get your butt out of here before something happens to you."

But the light moved away from her eyes. Gradually, she was able to focus on the man standing above her.

"You've got two minutes to get off this property!"

He was all bluster, she thought. He couldn't have been shooting at them. Nothing in his hand but a flashlight, for one thing, and no bulges in his pockets. Still, she wasn't sure. Should she take a chance?

"I—I can't."

"What do you mean, you can't? You hurt, or what?"

While she hesitated, he jerked and swatted at his arm. "What the—!"

Now she knew. "You know that guy up there in the tree?" she said.

"Not to speak to. More like to yell at."

Not to shoot at, either. "He's my son. The one you met. And someone's trying to shoot him down."

"Look, lady, I been out here most of an hour. Nobody's shooting anybody."

"Not with a gun. With a slingshot and a stone, the way he shot down Sylvia Purcell. That's what hit your arm."

He clapped his hand to it. "How'd you—?"

"And my head." She turned her head to show him, though there was no way he could see anything through the knitted cap. "See? He must not have been close enough to hurt us badly. But that doesn't mean he can't. One man from the DNR said he brought down a young deer."

"Omigod. But who—?"

"I'm pretty sure I know. And if we can find the stones that hit us, they'll prove it's the same guy. Shine your light down here and help me hunt. But be careful not to touch them."

"Right, like they're gonna find fingerprints on rocks." But he aimed the light at the ground.

Almost immediately, she spotted two smooth stones on top of the leaf litter. One was shiny white, a lake pebble. The other was unmistakably a Petoskey. "There!" she told him.

"Those little things?" Keeping his hands to himself, he bent down.

The phone in her pocket rang again. She dug it out.

"Mom, they're on their way. What's going on down there? What's that light?"

"It's Mr. Walcher."

"He's the one?"

"No, he just got hit, too. And we've found some of the stones. Have you reached Fred?"

"No, but I think Sergeant Ketcham did."

"I hope so."

"Mom, you shouldn't be there."

"Neither should you, but we can't leave now."

When she pocketed the phone, Walcher said, "Your kid?"

"Yes. Please turn off that light! Or aim it away from us.

Maybe you can spot him—the shooter, not Andrew. And mess with his night vision."

He moved away from her and aimed the light in the direction from which they'd both been shot. Joan flattened herself again and crawled a few feet in the opposite direction, leaving her stick to mark the location of the two stones.

Then the light went out, and she couldn't see him anymore. But she no longer believed keeping still would protect her, and she no longer cared about the stars. Come on, Fred, she thought, and kept crawling. When she reached a tree big enough to hide behind, she risked slowly sitting up.

The quiet settled on her again, but without the peace she'd felt before. Even so, her breathing gradually slowed, and her heart stopped the loud pounding she felt anyone could hear. She no longer was sure of her directions, though the clearing was visible through the tree trunks. The bulldozer seemed to have turned, but of course it hadn't. Using it as a landmark, she reoriented herself. She could hear the wind in the trees and occasional rustling in the leaves. Raccoons, maybe? Or Walcher, moving around.

Suddenly a strong arm grabbed her around her chest, pinning her arms and jerking her to her feet. Strong fingers digging into her face kept her from opening her mouth to scream.

"Don't move, and don't make a sound," an urgent whisper said into her ear. He was squeezing so hard she could barely breathe.

She shook her head and tried to twist around to see him, but the man's hands stopped her. Instead, he pulled her ski cap off her face and hair. "You!" he said.

This time, enough of his voice came through the whisper that she knew him. In pulling off her cap, he'd released her face enough to let her suck in a little air.

"Can't . . . breathe," she managed to get out. The pressure on her chest eased, but only a little. "Thanks," she got out, trying to sound humble.

"You won't scream?"

She shook her head, but she was encouraged. He knew they weren't alone, or he wouldn't be worried about being heard.

When her cell phone sounded softly in her pocket, the arm tightened around her. Knowing it was impossible, she made no attempt to reach it. Let it be Andrew, she prayed. He knows I'm down here. Not answering is almost as good as screaming. And he can tell Ketcham.

Now what? Whatever else he had in mind, he couldn't shoot at anyone while his arms were holding on to her. And he wasn't harming her. If she didn't call him by name, he might think she didn't recognize him and would be safe to release.

"Can I go now?" she asked softly, as if this sort of thing happened to her all the time.

The pressure increased again. Mistake.

"What do you want me to do?" she asked.

Rather than answer in words, he began dragging her deeper into the woods. Giving him very little help, she stumbled along in his wake.

Was he going to take her all the way to his cabin? Even though Andrew had been able to see that far through the woods, it would be a long way to drag someone, especially up and down the hills she had seen in the daylight. She couldn't let him carry her off in silence. She'd have to risk angering him by screaming if it came to that.

Not yet, though. Now they were circling the clearing, faster than she would have thought possible. When she could, she kept her eyes on the bulldozer, her one clear landmark. She wondered where Walcher had gone. No sign of that unlikely ally. Couldn't he hear them?

They had to be almost opposite Andrew. Now that the arm across her chest was reaching under her left arm to drag her, she could move her right arm a little. Could she do it without being noticed? She inched her bare right hand over to the pocket and slid it in. He didn't react. Inside the pocket, her fingers found the cell phone. She couldn't look, but it was already turned on. Andrew was first in the alphabetical list of numbers in her phone's memory. She felt for the flat screen and touched the button underneath it to select Andrew and then the one beside it to place the call. After giving him time to pick up, she dragged her toe until she felt something it could catch on.

"Oh!" she cried, and fell to the ground as convincingly as she could. She hoped Andrew could hear her through the fabric of her pants.

Jim Chandler jerked her to her feet. "I said shut up!" In the heat of the moment, it was almost his natural voice.

"I'm sorry. I can't go so fast." She said it as loudly as she dared. Come on, Andrew, she thought. We're down here, and moving. You might be able to see us, even if it is dark. Tell them!

She couldn't hear his response, if there was one, in her pocket. Good. Neither could Jim. But Andrew couldn't call the police unless she broke the connection, or could he with cell phones? In case he couldn't, she touched the button to break it and hoped he'd know what to do.

Now she let her whole body sag. Let Jim haul her dead-weight. He'd find out she wasn't as skinny as he thought.

"Shut up and move it!" he whispered.

Staying as limp as she dared, she worked to snag dry twigs with her feet, make noise any way she could that wouldn't tempt him to stop her breathing permanently. Here we are! she cried out silently.

He managed her without apparent strain until they came to a steep hill. That slowed him down, and he began breathing harder.

Suddenly he yelped and dropped her. This time her fall wasn't faked.

"Run, Mom, run!"

Andrew? Down here? She scrambled to her feet and ran, stumbling down the hill in the dark, toward his voice.

Behind her, Jim was swearing and crashing through the underbrush. She'd never outrun him, she knew. But then she heard shouts.

"Stop, or I'll shoot!"

"James Chandler, you're under arrest!"

She turned. Powerful flashlights lit the scene. Men with *OPD* on the backs of their jackets were forcing a squirming figure facedown on the ground. Tom Walcher stood off to one side, watching.

And, from opposite directions, Fred and Andrew were running toward her.

31

$\mathcal{F}$red sent her home while he supervised Jim Chandler's transportation and booking. "I'll deal with you later," he said. He sounded tough, but the strength and warmth of his embrace left no doubt about his intentions.

While she drove the now-familiar road, Andrew told her that he had indeed heard her cry out when she faked a fall and that he'd heard Chandler shutting her up. "That really worked, Mom."

"But how did you get down so fast?"

"I slid down the rope." He inspected his hands. "Couple of rope burns, looks like, but they're not bad."

"How did you know he dropped me?"

"I made him do it. I had my Wrist-Rocket up in the tree. And I took along a few smooth rocks in case I ever needed to defend myself. When I knew you were in trouble, I slid down and shot one of my rocks at him."

"How could you aim in the dark?"

"Moonlight. I've been out there awhile, Mom. You get used to seeing with a lot less light than at home."

It was true. She'd seen much more than she'd expected.

"And I was close to him by the time I let fly. Hit him pretty hard. That's why he dropped you. I was ready to shoot again, but I didn't need to. Fred and the rest of them reached him before he could get you."

"You knew they were coming?"

"Sure. Ketcham made sure someone gave Fred a fresh battery, so he and I were talking. But I already knew they were coming through the woods from Chandler's cabin."

"I wish you'd told me. I kept expecting them to come this way." She gestured out the window.

"Fred didn't want him to escape into the woods. And he didn't want to spook him. They had this road blocked, just in case, and they found his car parked halfway down his own road. So they followed him in."

When they arrived home and Andrew shed his clothes for a hot shower, Joan had time alone to think. Jim Chandler wouldn't have expected to find her in the woods. In fact, when he peeled the ski cap off her face, he sounded surprised to find her under it. He wasn't interested in her body; she already knew that. She'd only been a nuisance to get out of his way.

So why had he been over there to begin with, much less at night?

He was shooting at Andrew, not me, she thought. I told him I went out there to visit my son, and he figured it out. He knew if Sylvia could see his house, Andrew could, too. I would have been next. He wasn't worried about Birdie—he was sure he could control her. But if he could terrorize Andrew into giving up, he could do what he wanted out there. Maybe that's all he was trying to do with Sylvia. Only he killed her, instead.

And Vint could have been the same kind of freaky accident. Vint got in his way while he was out there shooting animals. Or saw too much—probably the slingshot. So he shot at him, too. It was Vint's dumb luck to hit that tree when he tried to leave.

No, Jim had to know Sylvia would fall, standing on the edge of the platform the way she was. And he had to know Vint would crash. By then, the mayor had told the world they thought she'd been murdered, and Jim had to know that meant they had some idea how. He couldn't let anybody tell about seeing him use the Wrist-Rocket. He would have gone back after Andrew.

And he would have come after me if he hadn't found me in the woods. As it was, he would have squeezed the breath out of me and left me for dead near Andrew's tree, not his cabin, before he melted back home.

Shivering through the warm black sweater, she remembered how his eyes had frightened her, how shaken she'd felt even after he'd rejected her and pushed her away. She hadn't been wrong to feel that way, she knew now. From one moment to another, the man switched from charming, to nasty, to dangerous, if he felt crossed in any way. He'd sneered at Birdie before turning his nastiness on the violas. And he'd made Birdie believe he thought Sylvia was a joke—when he really felt threatened enough to knock her out of a tree.

Even knowing he was under arrest, Joan checked the doors. Then she shed the clothes that reminded her of him by their very touch on her skin, pulled on her softest, warmest nightgown and a fleecy robe, reheated a cup of the coffee Fred hadn't drunk, and curled up on the sofa to wait.

Andrew wandered through the living room in nothing but a bath towel knotted around his hips. Water sparkled on his dark curls, which smelled of shampoo.

"Okay if I eat some more of that chicken?"

"Sure, if you leave enough for Fred." They'd probably

sent out for something at the station, but she hated for him to come home to an empty kitchen.

Andrew stuck it in the microwave and went upstairs. Life was back to normal, she thought.

By the time Fred rolled in, they were sitting together, Andrew in jeans and shirt, eating chicken out of a bowl on his lap, and Joan drinking the last of the coffee.

"Got any more of that?" He bent and kissed her.

"I'll make it." Andrew bounded into the kitchen. "You have no idea how good it feels just to get up and walk around."

They laughed.

"You still like Starry Night?" Andrew stuck his head into the living room and held up a small bag of the coffee beans. "There's more supper, too, if you want it."

Fred nodded, and Andrew ground the beans and zapped a bowl of teriyaki chicken and rice. While the coffee was brewing, he brought the bowl and chopsticks into the living room. "So tell us all about it."

Fred untangled himself from Joan and took the food. "There's not a lot to tell." He lit into the chicken. "Mmm! This is good."

"Fred!" Joan said.

"We had him red-handed, of course, but he still tried to talk us out of it. Said we had the wrong man. All sweet reason—didn't sound anything like the foulmouthed guy we arrested."

Uh-huh, Joan thought. He turns it off and on. "Did you find my stick?"

"Sure, and the two stones. He had no idea where they came from, of course, and he'd managed to toss the slingshot away, but one of our men found it, and they all had his prints on them."

"And?"

"He's our man, without a doubt. His prints match, and they match the ones we already had for Ward Utterback."

"Huh?" Andrew said.

"When we told him that, he demanded his lawyer, and he hasn't said a word since."

"Who's this other guy?" Andrew said.

"Good question," Fred told him between bites. "Chandler was arrested in Michigan years ago under that name."

"What'd he do?"

"We don't know what he's done in the past fifteen years, though you can bet we'll investigate. Back then he was accused of assaulting a woman. Those charges were dismissed."

"They better not be this time."

"This time, thanks to your mom, we're going to nail him for Sylvia's murder."

"Because Mom went out there tonight?"

"No, that was a damn fool thing to do. I should have sent an officer to the house to keep you safe there."

"That's how you caught him," Joan pointed out in her own defense.

"We would have caught him anyhow, once we knew he was out there shooting at Andrew. We had the Tell City police talk to his mother, by the way. She says she hasn't seen him for months, but she wasn't surprised that he'd lie about it. Says he's pulled stunts like that ever since he was a boy, and she'll say so in court if we need her to. I already had a search warrant for his house. We didn't need you to get yourself half-killed."

"Only Andrew?"

"I was fine, Mom. Lying down in my sleeping bag. There was no way he could hurt me."

"No? You used your Wrist-Rocket to get up there, didn't you?"

"Sure."

"He had one, too, and muscles you wouldn't believe."

"Which you were protecting me from?"

"Well . . ." She knew better. "I didn't expect him to see me."

Andrew rolled his eyes at Fred. Just like old times, with the two of them ganging up on her.

"All right for me to tell Birdie?" she asked.

"She knows. Ketcham called off her police protection. But she's going to need all the support you can give her. We'll need her to testify, and that's never easy in a rape case."

"She has to go through that? Wouldn't it be hard to prove now? Isn't it enough to go after him for murder?"

"Motive."

"Oh."

"We'll need your testimony as well."

"Of course." She'd redeem herself on the witness stand. But she had a new worry. "That won't be anytime soon, will it?"

"Don't worry."

"Easy for you to say. We still have a concert to play. Alex will be impossible when she hears, and I need a new narrator!"